ALSO BY RITA MACE WALSTON

*Paper & Ink, Flesh & Blood*

*PRAISE FOR*

# The Forager Chefs Club

"*The Forager's Chefs Club* has everything I love in a novel: complex characters, beautifully described settings, a ton of heart and empathy, and incredible food. Curl up with this one by the fire and enjoy."

—J. Ryan Stradal, *New York Times* bestselling author of *Kitchens of the Great Midwest* and national bestsellers *Saturday Night at the Late-Night Supper Club* and *The Lager Queen of Minnesota*

"What a treat—it's not often that foragers get to see our pastime realistically depicted in a work of fiction. I had to stay up late in my hammock reading by moonlight just to find out how the threads of all five forager chefs were tied together in the end."

—Samuel Thayer, foraging expert and author of *Sam Thayer's Field Guide to Edible Wild Plants*, winner of the 2023 National Outdoor Book Award, *Incredible Wild Edibles: 36 Plants That Will Change Your Life*, and *Nature's Garden: A Guide to Identifying, Harvesting, and Preparing Edible Wild Plants*

"Michigan native Walston, an avid gardener/forager now living on a small homestead in rural northern Virginia, showcases the bounty of her home state and develops an array of interesting contestants within this novel's effective competition construct, which has the excitement and feel of high-stakes reality TV. Readers will relish the abundant descriptions of food and drink. A flavorful mélange of intriguing characters and *Top Chef*-style reality TV."

—*Kirkus Reviews*

"Rita Mace Walston's *The Forager Chefs Club* is a love letter to foraging and cooking, full of mouthwatering descriptions, cooking tips, and even a few recipes. Walston highlights the world of competitive cooking with a deft eye, chronicling the ups and downs of the competitors. This heartfelt story will keep you reading."

—Ellen Birkett Morris, author of *Beware the Tall Grass: A Novel* and *Lost Girls: Short Stories*

"This novel has it all: suspense, wisdom, humor, intelligence, and so much great food! The competitors are all wonderfully distinct and memorable, and the sparkling prose delivers surprise after surprise. This is a book you won't be able to put down, creating complex tones of anticipation and dread, awe and recognition. A wonderful read."

—Fred Leebron, author of *The News Said It Was, Out West, Six Figures*, and *In the Middle of All This*, coeditor of *Postmodern American Fiction: A Norton Anthology*, and coauthor of *Creating Fiction: A Writer's Companion*

"The crisp prose and well-drawn characters make *The Forager Chefs Club* a captivating book to the very end. The compelling story follows five chefs through a unique culinary experience in rural Michigan where the bounty of the earth provides creative possibilities for their meals and their personal growth. It's easy to get lost in the story and the meals in this delightful read."

—Beth Dotson Brown, author of *Rooted in Sunrise*

"Author Rita Mace Walston's immediate standout feature as an author is her ability to craft complex, multidimensional characters whose personal struggles and ambitions are deeply engaging to watch as different attitudes and approaches clash. The unique concept of environmentally balanced cooking and foraging brings the culinary world to life in a competitive and exciting way, making the novel a literal feast for the imagination. Walston's skillful weaving of plot twists and character interactions keeps the story dynamic and unpredictable as the contest and the interpersonal drama heat up, keeping readers hanging on for the next unexpected change of pace. *The Forager Chefs Club* is a superb work of drama and suspense that's sure to please both the imagination and appetite."

—*Readers' Favorite* Review

*The Forager Chefs Club*
by Rita Mace Walston

© Copyright 2024 Rita Mace Walston

979-8-88824-469-2

All rights reserved. No part of this publication may be reproduced, stored in a retrieval system, or transmitted in any form or by any means—electronic, mechanical, photocopy, recording, or any other—except for brief quotations in printed reviews, without the prior written permission of the author.

This is a work of fiction. All the characters in this book are fictitious, and any resemblance to actual persons, living or dead, is purely coincidental. The names, incidents, dialogue, and opinions expressed are products of the author's imagination and are not to be construed as real.

Published by

3705 Shore Drive
Virginia Beach, VA 23455
800-435-4811
www.koehlerbooks.com

# The Forager Chefs Club

RITA MACE WALSTON

VIRGINIA BEACH
CAPE CHARLES

*To my mom, who instilled in me a love of gardening and growing food and to my husband, Tim, who built for me my absolute dream of a greenhouse.*

# JANUARY

# INTRODUCTION

Dane Randall hung up the landline and wondered if it would come down to what mattered to him versus what mattered to the Club's Founders Circle. Those two had mostly aligned over the past twenty-five years.

Mostly.

He unzipped his Italian leather portfolio and flipped through the contents of five manila folders. From the inbox on the corner of his desk where Elena had yet to deposit today's mail, he picked up five square envelopes. He stroked a thumb over one, noting the thick texture of the paper, the swooping calligraphy of the name written in blue ink. The invitations must be delivered by hand. And directly to the competitors. The Founders Circle had been adamant about that.

His office at the Forager Chefs Club wasn't large but well appointed, with an antique table that served as his desk, a built-in bookcase, and a small fireplace with a fieldstone hearth and surround. He locked the desk drawer where he kept the framed photo he never set out. He tucked the five envelopes into the portfolio, zipped it shut, and took his heavy winter coat and fedora from the wrought iron stand in the corner. He had a lot of miles to travel in the next week.

He thought again about the photo in the locked drawer.

Would she be there? If she were, would she remember him?

# Celeste

Celeste turned another page of *The Saucier's Apprentice*, sighed, and closed the book. Sokolov made creating classic French sauces sound so easy.

Time-intensive, and, okay, maybe not *easy*, but not unachievable. Follow the steps, and *voilà!* a sublime béchamel or velouté or espagnole sauce that would elevate a dish from good to eye-roll amazing. She watched a lot of YouTube videos whenever she was somewhere with decent Wi-Fi, but her attempts to replicate what they did had been only moderately successful. And moderately just wasn't good enough. After three years in the kitchen of the Grand Hotel, she was still relegated to mundane tasks. It shouldn't matter that she was only twenty-one and hadn't gone to cooking school. She was determined to change how Chef and the others in the kitchen saw her when the hotel opened for the season.

Her heart had pounded when she'd found *The Saucier's Apprentice* shelved like some commonplace volume in the thrift shop this afternoon. It was out of print. The library didn't have it anymore—*likely pilfered*, Celeste thought bitterly. The thrift shop had priced it at three dollars. Finding it reminded her of when people discover valuable paintings at garage sales.

Celeste ran her fingers over the faded book jacket before carefully tucking it into her backpack. Books beat YouTube videos every time.

She still had a few months before the hotel and its restaurant opened again in May. Plenty of time to practice—to perfect. This book could make it all possible.

She glanced at the large clock on the wall of the St. Ignace air terminal above where Ray stood behind a counter, ever vigilant in ensuring that no one went through the doors to the tarmac without a valid ticket. She pulled out her cell phone. No text messages.

Celeste was counting how much money she had left from her trip into town when a salt-and-pepper-haired man in a well-tailored coat entered the terminal. Carrying a small suitcase and with a leather portfolio tucked under one arm, he walked to the far counter where Evelyn sold tickets. Following a brief exchange, Celeste saw Evelyn smile and hand the man a ticket and a schedule. He thanked her, then walked across the room and took a seat three down from Celeste's. He looked at his watch.

Celeste looked at her phone and then through the terminal's windows. Shadows were getting a bit long. No one crossed the ice bridge after dark, if they could help it. There was still time before sunset, but she'd hoped to have a text message by now.

She looked at the man three seats over.

"You know the fudge shops aren't open now, right?" Her voice sounded loud in the small terminal. She heard Ray snort from behind the counter where he was filling out paperwork.

"What's a seven-letter word for worth more than its weight in gold?" Ray asked out loud. Ray frequently asked for help with his paperwork from whoever happened to be in the terminal at the time.

"Truffle," Celeste called to him, then turned her attention back to the man. His coat was camel-colored and looked expensive. He wore a fedora. Fancy attire for a winter trip to Mackinac Island. "No, seriously," she said when he didn't answer, "pretty much everything on the island shuts down in the winter." She slid the backpack with its precious book from her lap to the chair beside her. "I come over every few weeks or so to get stuff for my mom."

"Nope, that doesn't fit. It's gotta have an n," said Ray.

"Why does it have to have an n? It's gotta be truffle. Check your other word. The one that has an n. I'll bet you've got that one wrong."

"Thank you, but no, I'm not going for the fudge," said the man.

"The clue for the other one is a container for a letter. That's envelope. So worth more than its weight in gold has to have a last letter of n," said Ray.

"Then why are you going? Do you have family there?" asked Celeste.

"Leave the man alone, Celly. He's a paying customer," said Ray, bent over his paperwork. "Which is more than I can say for some people waiting on a plane ride." Ray was in his forties and a little pudgy around the middle, but he still had a full head of hair, which would get him more dates, Celeste had told him, if he'd use the shampoo her mom had made for him. Dandruff, she had confided in a low tone, was *not* sexy.

"Maybe it's not envelope. Maybe it's mailbox. And I'm not waiting on a plane ride. I'm waiting on Maddox. I saw him in town earlier, and I texted him for a ride back on the ice bridge." While not sanctioned as a travel route by the state of Michigan, the frozen straits provided a winter highway between the island and St. Ignace for snowmobiles and intrepid cross-country skiers. "And I'm not bothering him," she added. "I'm being sociable. You don't think I'm bothering you, do you?" She leaned over and held out her hand. "I'm Celly."

"Mailbox doesn't have enough letters."

"Nice to meet you, Celly. I'm Randall. No, you're not bothering me at all. In fact, you might be able to help me. You live on the island?"

"My whole life. Year-round." That came out with a little bit of pride. On a typical summer day, as many as fifteen thousand visitors would come to Mackinac Island, mostly by ferry. But there were fewer than five hundred people who lived there all year. "My mom moved there when she dropped out of college. I was born there. She's always been kind of a free spirit, into the New Age stuff and all. Which is fine. I mean, who's to say for sure who or what's running the universe, right? I'm just not into dancing around a bonfire naked on the summer solstice and that sort of thing, that's all."

She heard another snort from the direction of the paperwork.

"I see," said Randall. "Well, I'm looking for someone."

"Aren't we all," muttered Ray, loud enough to be heard. "Right now, Celly is looking for someone to give her a ride back to the island."

"There aren't a lot of someones on the island this time of year," she said. "Why do you need to find them?"

"I need to deliver something."

"I could take it for you. I know pretty much everybody."

"Thank you, but I need to hand-deliver this."

It sounded to Celeste like a scripted line for a hit man. But Randall, despite his fancy coat and hat, didn't look like a hit man. At least not the ones she'd seen when she talked Ben into turning something on other than hockey down at the bar. She and her mom didn't have a television.

"What is it?" she asked.

Randall didn't reply and looked past her out the window. Celeste turned her head. Icarus McKay's plane was coming in for a landing. She glanced down at her phone. Maddox hadn't responded to her text message.

"Like I said, I know pretty much everybody. But I don't want to get anybody in trouble." Celeste stood up. "Good luck finding somebody on that island if you're bringing trouble."

Randall looked up at her. The noise of the landing plane was louder.

"I'm delivering an invitation."

"Like to a party?"

"Not exactly. Let's call it an invitation to an opportunity. A very exclusive opportunity. And I'm paid to be sure that the invitee, and only the invitee, receives it."

The plane was taxiing to a stop. Randall stood up.

"Okay," said Celeste. "I believe you. Who are you looking for? Like I said, I know pretty much everybody. I can save you some time.

I could even introduce you, maybe."

The man considered her. She wondered how he saw her. She was bundled up against the cold, but she'd pulled off her hat and gloves and unzipped her jacket in the warmth of the air terminal. She wondered if her hair was standing on end. It had been well past her shoulders a month before, and she'd still been deciding if dreadlocks had been a good idea—they made her scalp itch and were kind of lumpy when she tried to sleep. The decision of yea or nay was made easier when her mother told her that the only Christmas gift she wanted was for Celeste to get rid of them. "It's just not the right look for you, sweetie," she'd said.

Which was quite a statement coming from her mother.

Celeste had positioned several mirrors, gotten out the scissors they used to cut strips of dyed wool to make the silk-and-felt scarves and hats her mother sold to summer tourists, and cut it herself. Short. Really short. Not shaved—it was winter in northern Michigan, after all—but she suspected it was sticking up in red whorls and spikes from pulling her hat off.

"I'm looking for Celeste Harp," said Randall.

"Well," said Celeste. "I can save you a trip to the island."

Celeste saw Icarus walk into the terminal, and her breath caught. She always imagined him a modern-day version of the Greek legend—lean and beautiful with a slightly tragic air—except this Icarus was Irish and a very careful pilot.

"Hello, Raymond," he said as he walked to the counter. "Hi, Celeste."

Icarus never used nicknames and didn't allow anyone to make one of his. Celeste could understand that. The options for Icarus weren't particularly good.

Celeste turned back to the man, but he was now pulling a folder out of his leather portfolio. He opened the folder, looked at a page, and then looked up at her. He tucked the folder back into the portfolio and took out a thick, creamy envelope before zipping the leather closed. Her name was written on the front in calligraphy.

"You're right. It appears you have saved me a trip. Nice to meet you, Celeste," Randall said, handing her the envelope.

He turned to go.

"Um," said Celeste, putting a hand on his arm. "Since you don't need that plane ticket anymore . . ." Thirty-five dollars was thirty-five dollars, after all.

He paused, reached into the pocket of his coat, and gave her his ticket. Walking out of the terminal toward the parking lot, he tapped two fingers on the center of Ray's paperwork as he passed the counter.

"Saffron," he said. And then he was gone.

# Christian

The benefit of an old, colicky furnace was that it made you grateful. Grateful that it worked at all. Grateful for the warm, hand-pieced quilts his grandmother had made in the years after she came from postwar Germany to America as a bride. Grateful that the house was small, so the heat the furnace put out wasn't asked to spread too thin. And a cool house meant an even cooler basement—perfect for the needs of a root cellar. These were his mother's words in his head—and true—but Christian kicked the furnace anyway as he passed. The clank of his shoe against the metal panel wasn't satisfying.

After turning the potatoes and cabbages, he selected several kohlrabies. The carrots were a bit hoary but would still be good for his soup. As always, he would make sure his mother heard the staccato of his knife against the scarred wooden cutting board as he prepared their meal. She ate more when the ingredients came from their garden and his foraging.

He'd expanded the backyard vegetable and herb garden after his father left three years ago, channeling his anger into physical labor that made him too exhausted at the end of the day to do anything but tumble into bed. He'd expanded it again last spring when the house next door was abandoned, using bolt cutters to snip and snap the chain-link fence that divided the two yards. He'd moved back to Flint a month later, leaving culinary school—and Rachel—behind.

*You can't hold me to plans when people abandon vows.*
*What about our vows?*
*We didn't make vows.*
*We made promises.*
*That's not the same.*
*Isn't it?*
*My dad left, Rachel. And my mom is dying. She doesn't have anyone else.*

The bank put a for-sale sign in the front yard of the abandoned house next door, but no prospective buyers ever came. In time, he knew, the small house—built, like their own, during the optimism and prosperity of the automotive industry following World War II—would fall into decay like so many around them. At least he could keep the druggies out of this one. He had a well-cultivated reputation that deterred the regulars. And for those unfamiliar with his reputation, a shotgun. The *cha-chuk* sound was so satisfying. As for the handful of times he'd put a hole in a wall or ceiling of one of the abandoned houses on their street? Well, maybe seeing those scars would give future unwelcomes pause, and they'd go elsewhere. If anyone from the bank ever complained, he'd tell them they should thank him. And then go to hell.

*Gratitude*, he reminded himself while climbing the stairs to the kitchen.

It was supposed to help him focus on the positive, on the things he could affect. It was a tool to keep the anger at bay. The ever-present, destructive anger that most people didn't see coming—until it was there.

He was a better cook than a baker, but he hoped the fragrance of bread in the oven would pique his mom's appetite.

The heat of the oven warmed the kitchen. The snow he could see through the window over the chipped enamel sink made the room feel cozy. Christian set two places at the kitchen table. On a whim, he crafted the cloth napkins he'd stolen from the upstate New York culinary school into the likeness of snowy swans. Rachel had shown him how to do it his second week there, laughing at his clumsy first attempts. It had all been new, and everything had seemed to shine with potential. Even when the routine had set in, her shine—her hair, her eyes, her laughter—never faded. *Where was she now?* He put the thought aside to stir the soup.

He'd left the empty water bottles on the counter so his mother would see he'd not used Flint tap water. He tasted the soup, considered, and added another generous dose of his special seasoning: thyme, summer savory, Thai basil, marjoram, and caraway.

He caught the fragrance of her presence and turned. She smelled of lemon verbena and medicine. The lemon verbena was the scent she'd favored as long as he could remember. He bartered with a woman at the farmers' market to make sure his mother always had lemon verbena soap and shampoo.

He worked, argued, and fought to make sure she had her medicine.

He hoped it was the simmering soup, but he suspected it was the scent of baking bread that had drawn her out of her bedroom.

"It smells wonderful," she said. She looked at the napkin swan as he set it down and smiled.

She seemed to grow ever more translucent. It was like holding an onion up to the light as you peeled away the layers, one, then another, the light becoming brighter even as the onion disappeared, layer by layer.

She was beautiful.

She held out an envelope. Christian stiffened his shoulders at another bill, another threat to their fragile hold on this place. But it wasn't the typical long, thin business envelope with its impersonal window exposing name and address. It was square, ivory-colored, and thick, with *Christian Gallo* written with flourish in blue ink.

"A man came to the front door while you were in the basement," she said. "I know you said never to answer, but he kept knocking, so I peeked through the window. He looked so nice." She faltered. "I thought I recognized him . . ."

"It's okay, Mom," said Christian. "Come sit. Have some soup."

He put a hand on her elbow and another on the small of her back to guide her to a chair at the kitchen table. She didn't wave him off, which she would have four months prior. She was being stripped of her strength by cancer and this city. This city that had been, itself, stripped of its strength. Both had been so strong once.

"And did you know him?" asked Christian as he seated her and then took the bread out of the oven. He tapped the crust. Not bad. Maybe he could be a baker after all.

"I thought I did, through the window. I should clean those windows. But then when I opened the door . . ." She faltered again.

Christian set the bread on the table. "Don't worry about the windows, Mom." The man at the door hadn't been his father. The spreading tumor was encroaching on her memories but from the horizon of the distant past. She'd have recognized her husband. "What did he say?"

She brightened and stroked a long finger over the writing on the envelope. "He said it was for you. That he wasn't supposed to give it to me, but he trusted me and knew I would make sure you received it. He said it was an opportunity." She laughed, which seemed to take all her breath. She coughed.

He gave her time.

He'd give her more if he could.

She held the envelope out to Christian.

He turned to the stove and brought the pot of soup to the table.

She leaned forward and tilted her head to draw his gaze to her. Her hand remained steady as she held the envelope out to him. "Son, it's been some time since opportunity came to Flint. Couldn't you at least consider it?"

It was likely a scam. Or some sort of court or bank notice in fancy wrapping. Regardless, she wouldn't be denied. And he couldn't deny her whatever she wanted. He was all she had left.

He took the envelope from her hand.

# Eden

Eden's roux was a deep golden slurry in multiple large pots, and yeast was working its magic in the bread dough by the time the sun crested the building across the alley and sent pale winter rays through the iron lattice protecting the mission kitchen's windows. She browned the carrots and onions, then the venison—a donation from a local Hunters for the Hungry group. Into the pots went rich, homemade beef stock, juniper berries, and generous dollops of her grandma's currant jelly.

Mid-morning, she sang to the dough as she punched it down, a tune she'd learned at Grandma's elbow to encourage the yeast to rise again. She browned the mushrooms in butter and olive oil and set them aside to add later.

By mid-afternoon, the aroma of venison stew mingled with that of baking bread, giving the commercial kitchen a homey feel.

Eden rummaged through the large chest freezer, making notes in a small spiral notebook. Supplies from last year's harvest were getting low, and she'd have to stretch what was left with canned and other donated goods. There were only two gallon bags of sweet corn, another two of okra, and three of green beans left from what she and Grandma had prepared back in Idlewild in the fall. She'd spent a few days with her grandparents earlier in the week, driving back to Detroit the day before with Grandpa in the passenger seat and a cooler filled with gallon bags of chopped vegetables and two boxes of home-canned goods in the bed of her pickup truck.

The Lift Your Voice Mission in Detroit, led by her father, had an ever-growing following for its Thursday evening Sing His Praise dinners. There was a rotating calendar of music provided by Detroit's local singing groups and aspiring jazz soloists, trios, and quartets, accompanied by wholesome food served at the table by volunteers. Eden's food was good, but she knew it was also the music that brought them, providing sustenance of a different sort.

The dinners had real plates, cutlery, glasses, and cups—gifts from an organization trying to reduce landfill waste. Eden didn't mind the extra work of washing up. It was about dignity. It was nicer to receive food on a ceramic plate rather than a paper or plastic one—nicer to serve it too. Women smiled when served, children were better behaved, and men nodded their thanks and sometimes seemed almost reverent when a volunteer placed before them a real plate with a fine dinner on it, as though recalling a particular restaurant or a family dinner in a time now vanished.

And she was never left to wash up alone. It was almost the best part of the evening, the relaxed laughter and conversation among the volunteers who stayed to wash, dry, and stack the plates and bowls, shelve the glasses and coffee cups, and organize the cutlery into the proper drawers.

They still used paper napkins, though. As soon as she could get a benefactor to provide a reliable clothes washer and dryer, Eden was determined to drum up cloth napkins. Maybe even some tablecloths to go over the mismatch of school cafeteria tables in the dining hall.

Eden checked her watch. They would be opening the doors and seating people now. She heard the music start—a jazz trio. Eden smiled. Grandpa was here tonight, and his son knew how much he loved jazz. Before the evening was over, she knew her grandfather would be telling stories about the town of Idlewild's heyday, when everyone who was anyone in the Black community—B.B. King,

Aretha Franklin, Cab Calloway, and Louis Armstrong, among many others—performed there.

Stacy poked her head in the kitchen, and Eden nodded. It was time for the servers. Eden could hear her father giving the blessing in the dining room, his deep voice carrying to all corners.

"I think we've got a benefactor in the house tonight," Stacy said as they worked in a well-rehearsed dance to fill serving trays that volunteers carried to hungry people. "Either that, or he's one of those social savior wannabes working on his PhD."

Eden laughed. "Okay, place your bet. Which is it?"

Stacy pursed her lips and lifted a finger into the air. She walked to the swinging doors and poked her head out, the sound of the music spilling in louder to the kitchen. She let the doors swing shut again. "Benefactor," she said. "That coat he came in here wearin' is just too pretty for somebody who doesn't have money. He better keep an eye on that thing, or he may find it gone. I'm sure I ain't the only one who's noticed."

Eden was washing down the counters when her father came into the kitchen.

"There's a man in the dining hall who would like to speak with you," he said.

"The benefactor?"

"What makes you think he's a benefactor?"

"Stacy saw him and thinks he has the look of one."

"Well, if he is, I don't know why he wouldn't want to speak with the pastor of this mission, but apparently, he does not. He wants to talk to you."

Eden folded up the towel and set it aside.

"Do you want to talk to him? You don't have to, you know."

"Sure, I'll talk to him."

"Speaking of talking . . . I have something I'd like to discuss with you. Maybe we could chat over coffee in the morning?"

She kissed him on the cheek as she walked out the door. "Of course. That sounds great, Dad."

The man was White, a little taller than her father or grandpa, with closely cropped salt-and-pepper hair. He was standing to one side, his hands in the pockets of the camel-colored coat Stacy had admired, watching the children spin and dance to the music on the faded and scuffed linoleum floor. He laughed when one little boy—Elijah—jumped in the air and executed a half-spin mid-spring to land with knees bent, clapping his hands. The four-year-old looked pleased with the calls of approval around him. Eden was glad his mama had felt at ease enough to leave the women's shelter and walk the five blocks to the mission to allow her young son this freedom. It was moments like this that made the work and the miles worth it. Eden shifted her focus to the man. Stacy was right; he didn't look like he needed Sing His Praise Thursday to get a meal, but he also didn't have the look of those who occasionally visited, passionate in their desire to make a difference, sure that they had a new way of approaching poverty, violence, and the other social ills that plagued Detroit and elsewhere that would change it all—just as soon as their thesis was published and hailed for the groundbreaking study that it was.

That left benefactor. They came from time to time, unexpected yet often timely, like when the roof of the Lift Your Voice Mission had quickly gone from could-use-replacing to buckets in hallways and rooms to catch the fat, steady drips from two solid weeks of rain. A woman had come to see her father that time and left a check that paid for a new roof. They never saw her again.

That's how it so often happened. Benefactors seemed to be people who felt they had to atone for something or had a sudden realization that their wealth didn't fix everything—or maybe anything. They were looking to fill a void or balance the scales. Typically, it was her father who talked to them, sometimes Grandpa when he came out from Idlewild. There would be conversation and prayer, sometimes tears, and then the benefactor would give Dad or Grandpa a check. There would be a handshake, sometimes a hug. Dad would invite the benefactor to come back to see the good work done with the contribution. But they never came back. They were different from regular donors—the people and businesses that kept the mission afloat. Benefactors were God's instruments, Dad said, ensuring their modern-day five loaves and two fishes would be enough—and sometimes more than enough—to meet the needs of those who came for sustenance and help. He continued to pray for the benefactors—weeks and months after they'd gone—that they found whatever peace or atonement they sought.

Walking across the hall to the visitor who had asked for her by name, stopping to smile and exchange a word with the regulars who reached out to her, Eden didn't think he fit the benefactor profile. He was too at ease as he watched the jazz trio and the children dancing between the tables.

He turned to watch her last few steps. His eyes were a piercing blue.

"You are Eden Ross," the visitor said. "Your venison stew was sublime. I can't remember ever tasting better. Thank you." He drew his hand out of his coat pocket and held out an envelope to her. "This is for you."

So a benefactor after all.

"Thank you," said Eden, taking the envelope. The paper felt thick, like the envelopes used for wedding invitations. Her name was written on the front in an elegant script. "My father is the pastor. I'm sure he'd like to thank you as well."

"I must be going," he said. "Thank you again for the meal."

He paused as he passed Stacy at the doorway, said a few words, reached into his pocket again, and handed her something. And then he was gone.

Stacy approached Eden. She held up two fifty-dollar bills. "He asked me to give one of these to the jazz trio and the other wherever it was needed most." She looked at the envelope Eden held. "What's that?"

Eden paused. "I'm not sure," she said. She tucked the envelope into her apron pocket and returned to the kitchen to ensure that the cleanup was finished properly and to consider the events of the evening.

# Daniel

Daniel counted some bills and handed them to his expectant son. Ethan had already pulled his mittens off with his teeth. He slid the money from one hand to the other as he counted, his soundless lips moving as he concentrated.

Daniel laughed. "It's all there, buddy. I promise you."

The boy blushed. "I know. I just like to count it myself too."

"Smart move. Good habit." Daniel tucked the bulk of the cash in his shirt pocket, put the pickup truck in gear, and headed down the driveway he'd just plowed.

The main roads were in good shape, scraped down to the blacktop. They gleamed where beams of late-afternoon sun dodged the snow-weighted pine limbs on either side and struck the pavement, stronger in the short stretches framed by deciduous trees, bare branches offering little hindrance.

Daniel liked winter. You knew pretty much everyone you met in town. You could get a seat at the diner's counter without someone's elbow right next to yours. Street parking was plentiful, even for his truck. And winter was a time of eating what you had harvested and stored in the warmer months, hunting and gleaning what you could from the land after the first hard frost. Daniel liked that.

And winter was not July.

Daniel glanced at his son. Winter was good for Ethan too.

Everyone wore long sleeves; his son looked like any other six-year-old boy. No questions, no comments. Daniel made sure his son had plenty of sweaters. Ethan even had an expensive Skye Island sweater that one of the Royal Trolls had gifted back at the September dinner. Daniel had felt his anger rise but then tamped it down and thanked him for it. The man meant well and had genuine affection for his son. It was an honest gift, and Thistle told him it would be wrong not to accept it.

He always listened when she spoke in his head. He was afraid if he ever ignored that voice—even once—she might stop talking to him.

On top of all else that had happened, that would be too much to bear.

There were dark patches on the road where the sun didn't reach between the trees. They would be slick after dark. And while Daniel had plowed their own narrow, winding lane from the house to the county road, the wind had picked up and likely would undo some of his work before they got back. He glanced at his watch. They had a couple of hours to run errands before full dark.

"Bank, then mercantile, then home," he said to Ethan.

The boy turned his attention away from the tree trunks whisking by. "Hot dogs?"

"Hot dogs! Do you know what kind of crap they put in those things?"

"They serve them sometimes for lunch at school. They're pretty good."

Daniel gave him a sideways glance.

"I forget my lunch sometimes!"

"'Sometimes' as in when you know there are hot dogs on the school lunch menu? I've got a dry-aged steak with our names on it and the makings of a poivre sauce, and you want hot dogs." Daniel came to a four-way stop and waved another car on before turning left. "Okay, we'll look at the ingredients on the package. If there's anything you can't pronounce, it's a no-go. Agreed? Maybe I'll share my steak with Biscuit."

It started snowing heavy, fat flakes again, and Daniel stomped his boots clean of snow and directed Ethan to do the same before pushing open the door of Escanaba Mercantile. It was crowded for a Friday. Then again, the weather had kept most people indoors for the better part of the past week. He handed Ethan their list and went to wait his turn at the counter.

The mercantile had been a department store once. It had stood empty for a few years; then Stan Siskel and his wife Marty bought the place. That was almost fifteen years ago. There were still the old mannequins here and there, but now they sported camouflage, overalls, and hunting vests of bright orange and pink. The housewares section was much as it had been for decades, featuring canning jars and tools, glass measuring cups, pressure cookers, slow cookers, and Lodge cast iron. More recent was a small selection of Le Creuset enameled cast iron that Marty insisted they stock after watching the movie *Julie & Julia* and ordering a copy of *Mastering the Art of French Cooking* from the transcendental bookstore down the street because she refused to order anything from Amazon. Daniel had been there when Stan had pointed out to his wife that the transcendental bookstore had likely ordered her copy from Amazon—it wasn't something they carried—but Marty had just sniffed and said he didn't understand. She was buying her book from their local bookstore. Period.

Thistle had always liked Stan's wife. Thistle had brought some of her home-dried tea made from herbs and flowers she'd foraged herself when Marty had had that persistent cough. Thistle's tea had helped, Marty had told him, putting her hand on his arm at the funeral.

The section of the store that had once been devoted to "yarn goods"—sheets, towels, and the like—was now dedicated to those who fished Bay de Noc. It took up about a third of the store. Fishing was big in this part of the Upper Peninsula.

If you were a year-round resident of Escanaba, the mercantile was a staple destination, and you were practically family. If you were a seasonal regular, Stan prepared ahead of time but could order a quick drop shipment of whatever was not in stock. If you were a tourist, the staff knew to strap on their patience. Tourist season was key to carrying everyone through the rest of the year.

Winter was not tourist season.

"There was somebody here asking about you," said Stan. "Came in just after noon and has been roaming in the store, off and on, ever since. Brett saw him sitting at a window table at the diner a while ago."

"What kind of somebody?"

"Not one of your clients, though he looked like he has the kind of money to be one. When's the next dinner, by the way?"

"Yesterday. So he's not one of the Royal Trolls?"

"You know, it wouldn't kill you to invite me one of these times. I get along good with some of those guys."

"He didn't say what he wants?"

The bell over the door rang, and Stan looked over Daniel's shoulder. "You can ask him yourself," he said quietly.

The man was tall and wore a fedora and a camel-colored coat that looked more suited to Michigan Avenue than Escanaba. Daniel turned his back on the stranger and pointed to the shelf behind Stan that held neatly stacked boxes of shotgun shells.

Ethan came up beside him with an empty plastic shopping basket, the list Daniel had given him, and a packaged fishing lure. "Hello, Mr. Siskel," he said to Stan. "Dad, they have the Red Grape Shiver Minnow. Can we get it? I saw Mr. Skolarus, and he said we could use his ice fishing shanty if we want."

"Red Grape Shiver Minnow?"

"Newest thing," Stan said. "Said to draw walleyes like nothing else. Tell you what," Stan said to Ethan. "You go grab another of those, so you have one for you and one for your dad. Presents from me. Who knows? If you get lucky with your catch, maybe your dad will invite me to dinner." He winked at the boy and looked up sidelong at the father.

Ethan dashed away when Daniel nodded.

"Daniel Metsja?" said a male voice behind him.

Daniel looked over his shoulder at the tall man standing a yard or so behind him. It was no one he knew. He directed his gaze back to Stan and pointed again at the shelf.

Stan turned to pull the usual four boxes of shells.

"I apologize for interrupting you this way, but when I went by your property this morning, it was inaccessible."

"Depends on what you're driving, I guess."

"Yes, well, when I landed, Enterprise said all the snowmobiles were taken."

The visitor lowered his gaze to Ethan as the boy came back, two fishing lures and the plastic shopping basket, still empty, in his hands. "And this must be Ethan."

The man smiled at Ethan. His demeanor didn't change; he was polite, reserved.

Alarm bells went off in Daniel's head.

"Ethan, go get in the truck," he said.

They'd been in the store a matter of minutes. There would be residual heat in the truck. And he wouldn't be long behind. Then again, who was this man who knew his son's name? And where he lived? Was this the next custody gambit by his in-laws? Who else might be outside?

"No, wait," Daniel said, putting a hand on his son's shoulder.

"Ethan," Stan said. "Could you go to the back storeroom for me? Mr. Elias is there. Tell him I need another box of the light bulbs Mrs. Gaffke likes for that antique chandelier she has in her dining room. He knows which ones I mean. It might take him a little time to find them, but maybe you could help him."

"Good idea," said Daniel. He loosened his hold on Ethan's shoulder. "I'll come fetch you if we need to go before you and Elias find the light bulbs." He nodded his thanks to Stan as Ethan ducked under the scarred wooden counter flap between a showcase of fishing reels and another of utility and pocketknives and scampered back to the usually off-limits storeroom.

Daniel turned to face the visitor, who had taken a step back.

The man held up an envelope in one hand.

"This is the reason I came to Escanaba. To hand-deliver this to you."

"And why would I want that?"

"It's an invitation. I've come a long way to give it to you. To you, personally."

"Then you've wasted a trip. My social calendar is full," said Daniel. He scooped up the boxes of shells and the two fishing lures. "Put these on my tab, Stan."

Daniel walked out of the mercantile, the bell jangling loudly over the door. Striding to the back of the building, he pounded on the metal loading dock door. After a minute, it opened to an older, wiry man holding the door handle with one hand and a crowbar with the other. Daniel nodded to him. The man nodded back, handed Daniel the crowbar, and disappeared back into the building. Daniel put his foot out to keep the heavy door from swinging shut and looked around to ensure the stranger hadn't followed him.

Ethan appeared at the door, his warden behind him.

Daniel smiled. "There you are. Time to go. Were you a help to Elias?"

"Definitely was," said Elias. He put a hand on Ethan's shoulder. "Would have taken me a lot longer to find those light bulbs without him. Found them just as you knocked."

"Thanks, Mr. Elias," said Ethan. The boy held a hammer. At Daniel's glance, Ethan flushed. "Mr. Elias said I could have it."

"Never too early to start collecting the tools of life. Can't get much done without a good hammer," said Elias.

"Truer words never spoken," said Daniel. "Thanks, Elias. Time to go, Son."

Daniel kept an eye on the rearview mirror on the way home. There wasn't much traffic once they turned onto the county road that led home, and no vehicle was near when they turned for the last quarter-mile he'd plowed that afternoon to what Thistle had called Heaven's Glade. The flakes were falling thick and fast when they pulled up to the side of the log house. The tires were barely still before Ethan jumped out of the truck, landing solidly on both feet. The boy slammed the truck door behind him, lifted his head, and shouted to the sky, raising his new hammer high. Daniel heard Biscuit's deep bark inside the house soar from threatening to a frantic welcome. Daniel bit back a reprimand not to shut the door so hard. He felt himself relax.

Fat flakes gathered on Daniel's sleeves as he collected the shotgun shells, fishing lures, and six German frankfurters wrapped in white butcher paper. He looked at the front door of the house. It was thick, solid, and slightly open. He heard Ethan laughing with the dog that had welcomed him home. The dog they'd rescued together, he and Thistle, found thin and scared on the side of the road long after all the seasonal Trolls had retreated below the bridge.

The dog hadn't allowed them to come close at first, but Thistle had been patient. She'd spoken softly, her tone nearly a lullaby, sitting on the grass just off the edge of the road shoulder, a mere few feet from the dense tree line where the woods went on for miles, and anything (or anyone) could appear or disappear. Daniel's assigned role had been traffic cop, signaling the sporadic cars and trucks to make room for the intervention underway. He'd kept one eye on the dog and that tree line. He'd never told Thistle, but he'd brought his gun out from under the front seat and tucked it in his waistband, just in case the large, skinny object of his wife's attention wasn't in the mood to be rescued or was some sort of diversion. Eventually, the starving dog had accepted a buttered biscuit, and then another from Thistle's hand, made by her that morning and left over from their picnic lunch. And the dog had gotten his name and a home.

Daniel could almost hear—it was there, just at the edge—her laugh, her delight at the dog's joy at their son's return home. Daniel stood still, willing the laugh to come clear, until Ethan, taught well, shut the cabin door, and Daniel was left standing outside in the windy shush of evergreen trees and fat flakes of falling snow. Her laugh was gone, but she was still here. He just had to be still. He closed his eyes and turned his face up to let the snowflakes fall on him, feeling each as a sudden spot of cold.

His whole face was numb, and his eyelashes felt heavy when he became aware of the smell of smoke. His heart leaped. He rubbed his face with one hand and sniffed deeply. It was fine. Ethan had lit the fire that was stacked and ready in the fireplace. No doubt doing it in the manner Daniel had taught him. *Good boy,* he thought. He didn't want their son to be afraid of fire. Thistle wouldn't want that either. Daniel took a deep breath and lifted his face one more time to feel the falling snow. He whispered to his wife. They were still raising their son together.

The radio weather guessers said another six to nine inches were on the way. Daniel decided he wouldn't answer the phone for the next couple of days. They had what they needed. They could be self-sufficient until the spring thaw and well after if it came to that. He'd give an explanation later to his plowing customers. They'd accept it, or they wouldn't.

The stranger had said his home had been inaccessible that morning. Daniel had plowed since, but Thistle was sending this snow to make it inaccessible again.

# Blaise

Blaise raised the small spoon to his mouth and tasted. Good. Better than good.

But still not quite right. Not the same complexity of flavor as when Bradley had made it the week before. When he *and* Bradley made it, Blaise corrected himself.

Ingredients and proportions weren't enough. As Blaise had told his brother on more than one occasion, you also needed to know the correct techniques to create an elevated dining experience.

Blaise had paid his dues to learn those techniques. Grueling hours, abrasive and belittling chefs, months of lowly tasks at culinary school, and then yet more months of lowly pay in various kitchens; it had taken him years to get where he was now. It rankled. He'd be thirty in a couple of years; he should have wider renown at this point in his career, a few appearances on some of the better Food Network shows under his belt—something beyond just regional acclaim. He'd made the decision not to go to New York or LA. Maybe that had been a mistake. Maybe he should invest in a publicist.

He put a few juniper berries in his palm, considered them, and then put them back in the small prep dish. He pulled his phone out of his pocket and then put it back. No point. Bradley wouldn't answer. He never answered his phone. And texting would leave proof. Proof that he'd had to ask. Bradley likely wouldn't answer a text either. He did sometimes, but it was never a sure thing.

Blaise plucked a tasting spoon out of a stoneware crock that had held more than a dozen at the start of dinner prep. He selected a plump caper berry from another dish, sliced it thin, and added half of the slices to the sauce. A splash of tawny port went in next. After several minutes of careful stirring, Blaise tasted again. It was very, very close. He could almost convince himself that it was perfect, but he never permitted himself lies or even near-truths in the kitchen. There were other rooms for that. He poured the sauce into a chinois for its final strain.

The roasted beef was rested and ready to slice. The root vegetables were tender yet retained the correct snap. Their blend of colors complemented the rich hue of the sauce. Blaise prepared sixteen plates with precise, artistic brushstrokes of sauce, arranged the sliced meat and the vegetables to his liking, then added a few more dots of sauce from a squeeze bottle in an asymmetrical pattern. The sauce wasn't the same as the other one—the one he and Bradley had concocted with the demi-glace base he'd taken three days to prepare from scratch—but it was delicious. Blaise knew it would satisfy his very-particular client, providing to her and her guests art for the eye, the nose, the palate.

He signaled the three servers he'd hired for this private dinner, instructing them as to the exact orientation of how the plate should be placed before each guest to ensure his design achieved maximum, identical effect. It was time for the main course.

Lyra Markham was almost as well known for the monthly dinners she hosted in her home in Grand Rapids' wealthy and historic Heritage Hill neighborhood as she was for her high-profile divorce three years before. The notoriety of the divorce came from revelations in court of Gregory Markham's social media habits. The renown of the dinners stemmed from the eclectic guests one could anticipate meeting as well as the experimental, yet somehow satisfyingly familiar, dishes prepared by the up-and-coming chefs Lyra lured to her expansive kitchen.

This was the third time in a little over a year that Blaise had gotten the call. He had accepted immediately, of course. You didn't play coy with Lyra. You never knew who her dinner guests might be, and this business was built on relationships. Hard work and talent counted, yes. But the lifeblood of a career was relationships. Word was that two well-known artists, an architect, and a recent Golden Globe winner owed their careers to Lyra Markham. Pure speculation, of course, but there were too many stories for them *all* to be fabricated.

The guest list varied greatly from month to month. On Blaise's second stint, Lyra's dinner guests had been a dozen homeless men. The entire house had been buzzing that day as she'd provided showers, haircuts, shaves, and a fresh change of clothes for each guest. The dinner conversation, from what Blaise gathered, had been lively and full of stories. Tales of battles and wars, fortunes won and lost, and loves fought for, won, and then lost. Blaise hadn't been sure what the reception to his menu would be, but all the plates had come back scraped clean—except for one. The server explained that one guest had declared that he hadn't liked liver as a kid and wasn't going to eat it now, no matter what fancy rhyming name they gave it.

You couldn't please everyone. And foie gras didn't really rhyme, anyway, so you had to consider the source.

A newspaper story and social media posts on various outlets had lauded Lyra Markham. There were photos of her posing and laughing with some of her post-transformation guests. Three had gotten job offers within days. Blaise had been mentioned as the evening's chef, so though there hadn't been a quote or photo of him or his dishes, he'd decided to count it as a win.

Remembering that dinner, how appreciative those guests were, how *revived* they'd seemed, sitting down to a good meal in fresh clothes after a shower and a shave, Blaise had decided to offer his services at the local soup kitchens. He could do it once a week—okay, realistically, maybe once a month. He could rotate between them—there were plenty of deserving shelters. He imagined getting write-ups like the ones with Lyra's photo prominently displayed. He didn't tell

Bradley about his idea—he'd do this on his own. Homeless people weren't looking for eclectic flair in their dining experience. Blaise had been truly energized. But then he got busy, and after a few weeks, the idea faded to the background, pushed back by other good ideas.

Standing in Lyra's kitchen again, Blaise remembered the mood of that second dinner and the publicity that had followed it. It was winter now. He really should offer to make dinner at one of the soup kitchens in the next few weeks. He'd just have to carve out some time to pick which one. And then craft a menu. And figure out how to pay for the ingredients—he doubted the shelters had much of a budget. Maybe he could leverage the experience and menus into a cookbook or something. He'd been tossing around some strong ideas.

As was his custom, Blaise visited the dining room about ten minutes into the main course. He wore his toque because diners liked it—identifying him as a true chef. His white jacket was embroidered with his company name, épicerie de blaise. He liked the French flare. He'd had it embroidered in cursive, all lowercase, after a graphic designer he'd met for drinks said it would be more pleasing to the eye. The relationship hadn't gone beyond drinks, and he'd been debating ever since his decision to follow her advice.

"Bravo!" greeted an exuberant guest, her cheeks flushed with the effects of the Châteauneuf-du-Pape he'd selected as the main course pairing. Several guests added applause, one hand delicately patted against the palm of the other. Blaise tilted his head in acknowledgment, his hands demurely clasped behind his back. He made his way around the table, making small talk with the guests, noting jewelry, watches, demeanor, and table alliances to gauge who might be worth further cultivation.

Blaise saw Lyra place her hand on the well-tailored arm of a man to her right. She looked up and around the table. Finding Blaise's eyes, she motioned him over with the barest crook of a finger.

"Blaise," Lyra said in her silky voice when he arrived at her side, "I want to introduce you to Mr. Randall. I'm delighted to say he's even more charming in person than over the phone. He insisted on being introduced to you." She leaned toward her guest, and Blaise knew Randall had an enviable view of cleavage pampered and enhanced by the best spas and plastic surgeons a substantial divorce settlement could provide. "Please assure me your motive tonight is not to steal my favorite chef from me," she murmured loud enough for Blaise to hear. That salved his pride. Randall could be important, and Blaise was here as much for connections as for Lyra's generous fee, but it still grated to stand, summoned like waitstaff, while Lyra cooed and purred over the man. Favorite chef, though. She'd said favorite chef. He wondered if she meant it. Women so often lied.

Randall placed his hand over Lyra's where it rested on his arm. "No thievery. And you've given me an evening I'll not soon forget," he said.

"Well, the evening isn't over yet. I'll have to think about what I could possibly do so that it *never* leaves your memory." She delivered a bright smile to the room, breaking the spell she'd woven while seemingly dismissing Blaise. "Everyone, I do hope you'll join me for a digestif and dessert in the parlor. I've arranged for the most marvelous sculptor to provide us with a private viewing of his work. And, yes, Gwen," Lyra added in a mock whisper to a woman seated at the far end of the table, "he did agree to donate one piece for the charity ball." On cue and with a ripple of laughter, her guests rose from the table. "I do hope you brought your checkbooks," Lyra continued. "There is a silent auction for the metalwork piece I think really is the best of the collection. Whoever buys it must promise to invite me to see it *en place*. I told *Vanity Fair* I couldn't bear to let it leave my home otherwise. Proceeds go to Habitat for Humanity!"

Along the far wall, someone from the bartending team slid apart vintage stained-glass panels framed in chestnut wood to reveal a high-ceilinged parlor. Lyra's guests dutifully filed through, chatting in groups of two or three. Blaise could see multiple pedestals adorned with sculptures of metal and glass, flickering flames from floor-standing candelabras, and two servers providing a selection of the dessert "tastes" Blaise had orchestrated. The women gravitated to the dessert and art, the men to the right side of the room out of view where Blaise knew a bar had been set up. It was well known that Lyra maintained an exceptional selection of bourbon and scotch whiskeys.

It didn't take long before there were only three people left in the dining room.

"You never disappoint. Thank you," Lyra said to Blaise. She touched Randall's arm again. "Don't keep me waiting too long." She walked through the doors and to the right. She didn't look back, and she didn't rush. Blaise was reminded of the Marilyn Monroe scene in *Niagara*, reputed to be the longest walk in cinema history—one hundred and sixteen feet of film with no words, just Marilyn walking away from the camera. Regrettably, the distance from Lyra's dining room to the parlor wasn't nearly that long.

Blaise turned his gaze to Randall, who, apparently, Lyra had only met in person tonight. Yet, somehow the man had earned a coveted seat at her dining table.

Randall had asked Lyra for an introduction to him.

"This job has its challenges," said Randall, looking at the space that had framed Lyra's exit, "but most decidedly its perqs, as well."

Randall was a bit taller than average, probably in his fifties, with creases at the corners of his eyes that spoke of time spent outdoors. He didn't appear particularly wealthy but seemed comfortable, judging by the fit and fabric of his gray suit and expertly knotted tie. He had held his own with the crowd at this table, and, given the guest list, that spoke volumes. He could be an up-and-comer, but his age made it unlikely. He could be fabulously wealthy and "slumming"—that would have certainly piqued Lyra's interest—but Blaise doubted it. Press? The next Anthony Bourdain?

Lyra thought Randall was here to meet her—and perhaps explore a further relationship. Blaise suspected the man's purpose was to meet *him*.

It was an extremely interesting thought.

"A marvelous dinner, truly," said Randall. "I have something for you." He reached into his suit jacket, pulled out an envelope, and offered it to Blaise.

Blaise took it. All this show, this lead-up, for a tip? He changed his mind as his hand touched the envelope. It was thick, substantial. This wasn't some hotel stationery envelope you grabbed on your way to a dinner.

Randall's sardonic smile told Blaise he'd been sloppy; the man had read the range of emotions on his face—anticipation, disappointment, realization.

"I expect we'll meet again," said Randall. He nodded, then left the room, tracing Lyra's steps.

# Eden

Eden touched the paper. It was thick and the color of her favorite daffodils in her grandma's garden. They looked the palest yellow when you first saw them, but when you leaned in, held one cupped in your hands, the veins in the petals were revealed, and you saw the true color, not the one displayed to those who only glanced. It was the color of thick cream—not the kind you got in the store, but the luscious, yellow cream that came from Mrs. Abrams's dairy farm on the outskirts of Idlewild.

Mrs. Abrams would skim the milk from her cows, then pour that gorgeous cream into the wooden churn her grandfather had made. It had been repaired and parts replaced over the years, but Mrs. Abrams insisted there were land memories in that churn, and she refused to use any other, even when her son, grown and successful at a law firm in Chicago, bought her a fancy electric model. Mrs. Abrams's churn looked like a small barrel with a metal crank on the end. Up until she graduated from high school and got accepted to culinary trade school, Eden would visit once a week to turn that crank and, as a reward, take home fresh butter wrapped in a clean, waxed cloth. She'd slather a good portion on bread and then hold it up to the light to see the sunshine on that beautiful color before sinking her teeth into the butter she helped churn on the bread she helped her grandma bake. That butter always tasted better than any other. Mrs. Abrams said it was because of where her cows grazed. Her pasture bordered the Huron-Manistee National Forest. When a fence "broke"—a frequent occurrence—her cows would wander among the trees and glades. Mrs. Abrams confided to Eden that what the cows foraged there—shade-loving plants, leaves, and tender pine branches that didn't grow in pastures—was what made the difference. Eden didn't doubt her. The milk and cream from Mrs. Abrams's cows had a richness and depth she'd never tasted anywhere else.

Eden ran her fingers along the paper again. It wasn't just the color that reminded her of Grandma's daffodils. The invitation felt alive. Alive with promise. Alive with opportunity.

Her grandpa would say this invitation could be her pendulum—the pendulum swinging to the point where she should hop on and then gauge when to hop off.

The tall clock with its swinging pendulum stood in the hallway in Idlewild, and before she could reach it on her own, Grandpa had lifted her up and let her insert and turn the special key used to wind it once a week, always just before they left for church. He'd built it with his father in the years when music and the local economy flourished in the Michigan community known as "Black Eden."

Back from church, with Grandma finishing up the preparation of what would be their best meal of the week, Grandpa had often taken her on his knee, pulled her in close, and pointed to the clock.

"See that pendulum?" he'd say. "It swing back and forth, back and forth. That's like life. Now, some people, they sit back and watch, just sit and sit and watch and watch that pendulum of life swing back and forth, back and forth. And after a while, they ponder and complain why nothin' ever happen in they lives. And then there are others. These others, they jump up on that pendulum of life. And they hang on and hang on and swing back and forth, back and forth. And they holler out to everybody watchin' how nothin' good ever happen but then somethin' bad also happen. Over and over again. Back and forth and back and forth. But you know who's happiest?" And then he'd turn his head to look at Eden, and she'd look up at him, no matter how many times she'd heard the story, and ask who. "I'll tell you who," he'd say and hug her tight. "Those are happiest who grab onto that pendulum and jump up on it, just at the right time, and then have the good God-given sense to let go when the pendulum swing up high to the good side and jump off. And wherever they land, they make a life. And they make a good life. Because with all the bad come good. You just gotta have the courage to jump on that pendulum at the right time and then the good sense to know when to jump off so as you land on both feet." Then he'd touch her nose with the tip of his finger. "Or, if you like me, you kinda land on one foot, but I got excellent balance, so while I kinda wobbled on one foot, I reached out with my strong hand and grabbed ahold of your grandma's, and that steadied me sure. Right there in the good place. Been there ever since."

Eden pulled out her cell phone and called the number on the back of the invitation.

# FEBRUARY

# Celeste

Celeste had never ridden in such a fancy car. She ran her hand along the smooth, pristine leather of the seat, then looked up to make sure the driver hadn't seen her in the rearview mirror. She wanted to give an impression of confidence, not of a newbie experiencing her first ride in a luxury car. The driver was a Hispanic man of middle height with dark hair that was gray at the temples and a nose that looked like it had been broken more than once. He wore a charcoal suit, a deep-red tie, and a heavy, well-made overcoat. He'd looked like he could be dressed for a funeral—except maybe for the color of the tie—standing there in the small terminal of the Manistee County Airport when Celeste had entered, Icarus at her side, to see him holding an iPad with her name prominently displayed in bright white pixels on a black background.

Icarus had spoken to the man quietly and asked to see identification. Apparently, Aunt Tilda had given the pilot explicit instructions regarding the delivery of her niece. Celeste had focused on not being nervous. Icarus must have seen it in her eyes. Unexpectedly, he hugged her.

She'd closed her eyes and returned the hug. She sometimes fantasized about a moment like this—on her quiet walks foraging in the woods or alone in her bed some nights, when she'd hear murmured conversation and throaty laughter between her mom and whatever man was staying with them that summer—before the incident six years prior that had stopped any more overnight guests.

"You're gonna do great," Icarus said. "Go make us all proud."

Now, in the car, she took a deep breath and calmed herself by recalling Icarus's masculine scent, the security of his arms around her, his breath against her hair, his voice in her ear. She was twenty-one years old and could probably count on both hands the number of times she'd been in a car. They weren't allowed on Mackinac Island, where her usual modes of transportation were bicycles, horses, and her own two feet. Even UPS delivered via horse-drawn carriage. As kids, they had tried to hop unseen onto the back of the long, flat wagon to see how far down the street they could hitch a ride before being discovered and shooed away. It usually wasn't far. That wagon made a lot of stops. After high school, she'd applied for a job to drive one, but then Aunt Tilda had called in a favor and got her the job in the kitchen at the Grand Hotel.

Whoever the Forager Chefs Club was, they'd paid Icarus to fly her from Mackinac Island to the small county airport in Manistee on the northwest side of the Lower Peninsula. It wasn't unusual for him to fly people around Michigan. His hops between the island and St. Ignace were like a taxi service, he'd told her once. It paid the bills, but he'd have long ago nosedived into the straits if that were all the flying he did. He hadn't said much on this trip, the constant, loud buzz of the prop making conversation difficult. Celeste wondered what the travel agent had told him. If Icarus had known ahead of time that she was his passenger—the girl who hung around the air terminal bumming rides over the straits after the ice shut down the ferries for the season every winter.

Forty minutes later, the car turned from the two-lane paved road onto a plowed, snow-packed strip that wound its way between tall pines and bare deciduous trees. Celeste leaned forward to put her elbows over the front passenger seat but, at the slight turn of the driver's head, instead pressed her cheek against the cold side window.

Her breath repeatedly fogged the glass, so she searched along the sleek door for the button that would lower it. She found it just as the car came to a smooth halt. The soft whir of the motor lowering the window seemed loud without the crunch of tires on packed snow. The driver looked over his shoulder at her. She raised the window again, both listening to the whir until the window was firmly closed. He got out of the car and went around to the back. Celeste didn't wait to see if he was coming to open her door the way he had at the airport. She scrambled out of the car, careful not to leave her backpack behind.

The driver took her suitcase out of the trunk and carried it to the front porch of the building, ignoring its wheels. He nodded politely, then got in his car and left. Celeste didn't watch the car as it retraced its route between the trees. She was looking at the building.

Her mother would love it instantly, she knew. Would love its mismatched angles, the patchwork of materials. The main section with a wide, covered porch was made of hand-hewn, squared logs, shrunken with time until, in places, the off-white chinking material was nearly as wide as the original brown-gray timbers. The pitch of the roof over the porch and a row of dormer windows hinted at a loft. Bookending this original section were fieldstone additions, each rising a full two stories. There were also two wings anchored to the fieldstone on either side that jutted forward, creating a wide, shallow courtyard. These had clearly been added much later than the fieldstone expansions and likely not at the same time. One was covered in smooth, painted stucco, and the other with wooden plank siding. Both were painted a pleasing herb green that complemented the forest setting, even now in winter. This was a building that had been established long ago. Established, loved, and expanded multiple times. Perhaps fought for, defended. Perhaps abandoned, then reclaimed and loved again. It spoke to Celeste of generations living and growing and dying and then new generations doing it all over again. Just looking at it, she could imagine that inside were misaligned hallways, short flights of steps leading to full staircases, unexpected alcoves, secluded spaces under the eaves, and a maze of dirt-floor cellars. There would be rooms for gathering and others in which to be alone and still. Rooms kept warm by fireplaces and stoves, and those kept cool by the absence of these. Looking with a practiced eye at mounds of earth clearly put to rest for the season, Celeste imagined the courtyard in which she stood alive with a garden when spring came.

She glanced behind her. The car was gone. The wind was lighter than what she was used to coming off the straits. Pine branches stirred, dark green against a sullen blue, late-afternoon sky. Snow was thick under the trees and pocked where clumps must have dropped from laden branches in the sunshine of the day now coming to its end. It was quiet, just the murmur of the trees conversing in the breeze.

If her mother were here, she would laugh and tug Celeste by the hand through the courtyard and up the wide wooden steps to the porch. Celeste pulled out her cell phone and took several pictures. She'd send them later. She looked at her suitcase on the porch, sitting expectantly like a well-trained dog. She'd bought the suitcase at the St. Ignace Hope thrift store. Only ten bucks, and it had wheels and a handle so you could easily pull it. It was a magenta color that she didn't really like, and the previous owner had doodled a pirate in blue ink on one corner, but the only other option cost fifteen dollars. Five bucks was five bucks. She'd never owned a suitcase before. Had never needed one.

She thought of the invitation tucked in the backpack hanging off her shoulder. She remembered the feel of the thick paper when she'd carefully pried the wax seal loose and opened the envelope. She'd waited until she was on the plane and felt its wheels leave the earth, Icarus taking her back to the island, courtesy of the ticket the man in the camel-colored coat had given her. Randall, he'd said his name was. He'd known that the seven-letter word for "worth more than its weight in gold" was saffron. The paper, with its black ink, had felt so substantial. *A select opportunity.* Fifty thousand dollars. That didn't seem real. What on earth would someone do with so much money anyway?

She wasn't here for the money.

With one foot on the bottom step that led to her puppy-dog-pirate suitcase, Celeste noticed a carved sign in what she imagined might be a bed of iris in the spring.

*The Forager Chefs Club*
*Members & Invited Guests Only*

The sign was weathered with a symbol long ago burned into the wood above the words. It was the same symbol that had been on the wax seal. It looked like ragged radiant beams of a star with the letters FCC vertically inscribed down the middle. Celeste raised her chin and exhaled, her breath a visible puff in the cold air. She walked up the steps, took hold of her thrift store suitcase, and shrugged her backpack more firmly on her shoulder. She crossed the expanse of the porch and pulled on the braided wrought iron handle of the heavy front door. She didn't know if she qualified as either a member or a guest, but she had proof she was expected.

# Blaise

Blaise stepped out of the car that brought him to the Forager Chefs Club like he was stepping onto a stage. There could be cameras anywhere, everywhere. The building threw him off a bit—he'd expected something more elegant rather than what looked like it had been designed by an architect with a penchant for Dr. Seuss, but producers could be eclectic. He envisioned Lyra Markham chatting about it over cocktails—how she was approached to find talent for a new reality show. Audiences, whether at a table or elsewhere, always hungered for something new, different, fresh.

The reception area was satisfyingly grand, in a rustic sort of way. Through an archway framed by hewn logs, Blaise could see a large fieldstone fireplace already ablaze, several deep, cushioned chairs, and one sofa positioned to take maximum advantage of the heat and ambiance. The woman who checked him in and led him to his sleeping room introduced herself as Elena. She wore a knit sweater the color of peach sorbet with pearl buttons up the front. It would have been less distracting had one additional button been fastened, but Blaise didn't mind. He had disciplined himself to appreciate such diversions and then move beyond them. He exercised this discipline as the woman led him through a maze of corridors to his room, her hips swinging in her tight, wool skirt. It was the color of a creamy caper and olive sauce he'd once concocted. The sauce had been delicious. When she handed him his room key—an actual, heavy, old-fashioned key with a brass tag engraved with the room name—he smiled at her. He debated making a remark about the color of her skirt and the tastiness of the sauce it sparked in his memory but decided against it. Better to get more intel on what was going on before giving the cameras too much fodder. She smiled back and reminded him in a cool, professional voice that he was expected in the common room at five o'clock. *Oh, yeah,* thought Blaise. She sounded like a television ad for Hilton, but there was a Bond girl edge to her. He didn't ruin the moment by looking around for the cameras, but he did let his gaze linger on her departure before inserting the long key into the elegant iron lock. Let those behind the cameras make of that what they would.

# Christian

Cell service here sucked, which didn't really surprise Christian, given it had been twenty minutes between the last signs of civilization and pulling up in front of what the driver had said was their destination. His mother had said she'd be fine, that she had everything she needed for the few days he'd be gone, but he'd spent the money to get one of those month-by-month phones, and now it looked like it was pretty much useless.

Christian finally found what he'd been told was the common room, arriving a few minutes after five o'clock because he'd been wandering around the building with its odd hallways and unexpected turns, holding his phone in the air, trying to find a wayward signal. Instead, he had gotten lost. He was glad there hadn't been anyone to see him other than a taxidermied raccoon atop a bookshelf holding what looked to be a chicken head. Who stuffed a raccoon for display? Let alone a chicken head?

Elena, who had shown him to his room when he arrived, greeted him with a silver tray of drinks. He selected a glass of red wine.

An attractive Black woman who looked to be in her late twenties sat at one end of a leather sofa facing a large fieldstone fireplace. She looked up from her conversation with a younger woman with pale skin and short, wavy red hair who sat at the opposite end. The Black woman took a sip from her wineglass. She didn't smile. The younger woman followed her gaze, saw Christian, and did the same but with a smile and an expectant look in her eyes. In a leather chair adjacent to the couch, a lanky, dark-haired man sat at ease, his left leg crossed over his right knee, a cut-crystal glass of brown liquid, neat, in his hand. Standing with his back to the crackling fire was a tall man with salt-and-pepper hair. He wore a button-down shirt open at the neck and a sports coat with leather patches at the elbows. One hand was in the pocket of his jeans, and the other held a glass similar to the lanky man's.

"Welcome to the Forager Chefs Club, Christian," said the man in front of the fireplace. He indicated an empty chair. "Join us."

# The Competitors

"He's serious? Every ingredient has to be from Michigan?" Blaise looked at his glass. He should have gotten a refill before letting himself be ushered with the others into the kitchen.

"Not everything," said Celeste. "We get to pick one group exception, and then each person can have up to three exceptions for their competition meal. It's brilliant, really."

She opened a cupboard containing colanders and sieves. She pulled one out. No, not a sieve, a chinois. When the chef corrected her back at the Grand Hotel kitchen, she endured snickers and sidelong glances from the rest of the kitchen staff.

"Brilliant, says Pollyanna," Blaise said. "Where'd you go to culinary school?"

"I know what our group exception has to be," said Christian.

Everyone looked at him because it was the first time he'd spoken.

"It's pretty clear why they're giving us one mutual exception," he continued. "There's something we all use in cooking that can't be sourced in Michigan." He opened a lower cabinet and pulled out a cast-iron skillet, hefting it as if judging its usefulness by weight. He turned it over and looked at the stamp. "And it's not French brandy or red snapper caught on a full tide or whatever other bullshit you think you learned at the CIA in New York." This he directed over his shoulder at Blaise. He put the skillet back and straightened. "Unless you think heading over to the local department of transportation is the best place to get salt, that's what our group exception has to be."

"Salt," said Eden. She opened and closed a few more cabinets, but as Randall told them, they were bare of anything consumable. They were here to get acquainted with the cooking tools the Forager Chefs Club would provide. "We've got a lot of water in and around Michigan, but it's all fresh, so no sea salt."

"Exactly," said Christian. "There's a huge salt mine under Detroit, but it's industrial grade. It has a blue cast to it—that's how you know it's Detroit salt—but I don't want to use it in my cooking."

"We'll all need salt. It's a good choice," said Celeste.

"How do you know it's blue?" asked Blaise.

"I drive a truck in the winter."

"You drive a truck," said Blaise. "Wow. You drive a salt truck. Man, they'll let anybody into this competition, won't they?"

"Okay," said Eden. She hadn't quite made up her mind, but she was very close to deciding that Blaise was an asshole. "Salt it is. We've got ten minutes left in this kitchen before we have to give Fred and Ginger our answer. If you two are done flirting, I'd like to spend that time scoping out the rest of this kitchen."

"I thought his name was Randall," said Celeste.

"I mean," said Eden, "that Randall and Elena are like a well-rehearsed act. This whole competition thing is a stage, and we're the performers."

*She's twigged on it too*, thought Blaise. A stage, indeed. He bit back a retort and focused on looking in control for the cameras. There were a lot of places in a kitchen to hide cameras. "So. Salt," he said. "Since I don't want Christian to get fired from his Department of Transportation job for sneaking salt from his truck to the kitchen, I'm good with us choosing that as the group exception."

"Salt," agreed Celeste. She wished she knew who Fred and Ginger were, but she didn't want to ask any more questions. The other three were so confident, so sure of themselves. They were older and more experienced in the kitchen than she was. Except maybe Christian, who apparently drove a salt truck.

They all seemed oblivious to the absolute *wonder* of this place. The walls breathed it—in and out, in and out. Didn't they feel it? She had sensed it when the car dropped her off in front of the building. It became stronger when she crossed the threshold and was welcomed by Elena, who had waved away her offer of the cream-colored invitation from her backpack as proof she belonged and instead had led her through a warren of hallways and half-staircases to a room out of a dream. She had felt it when, after Elena left, she'd placed one hand—the other still holding the heavy key to the room that made it hers, if only for a little while—against an interior wall and had taken a moment to be silent.

Silent. Present. Patient.

The roof sheltered this place, those under it. The heavy, exposed wooden beams were strong limbs above her, their grain sinew and tendon. She breathed. Deeply. In and out, in and out, as her mother had taught her. She hadn't closed her eyes. She looked around. *Felt* the place. Remembered the hallway and staircases she'd walked. The two hidden alcoves she'd already glimpsed, the many rooms she hadn't yet entered—it was like foraging. You had to notice details, be respectful. Take note of the time of day and its light, the seep of air and sound down hallways and from under doors, the season of the year and its rhythm. All of it—all of it!—carried to the taste at the table.

Her three companions—competitors, she corrected herself—seemed oblivious. Were focused instead on the rules of the competition that Randall outlined. In the common room, the three of them skimmed with practiced eyes the legal documents Randall handed to them. Now, given their fifteen-minute access to the kitchen, they were thrusting open cabinet doors, cataloging, and assessing. Celeste took pictures of the huge stone, smoke-blackened hearth framing a fireplace that was nearly as tall as she was and three feet deep, with a cast-iron grate for grilling and a long, wrought-iron arm with a bulbous witch's cauldron suspended at its end. Of the windows where light would stream in come morning, filtered by trees that swayed in a wind that had picked up since she'd arrived, perhaps following her from the island. Of the butcher-block set in the middle of the room, its substantial legs rooted to the floor, its surface scoured clean and oiled but still bearing the scars of decades of knife work. As she touched it, she imagined she heard the staccato of a knife against it, chopping vegetables and herbs. A ghost of sound, of fragrance. She placed her hand against its surface. The wood felt warmer than the air.

There would be time later, when the others weren't here, to introduce herself properly to this kitchen so, when she cooked for the competition, it would welcome her.

"As you know from the rules we covered earlier, you'll each create a dining experience for five distinguished guests," said Randall once they were all back in the common room, drinks replenished. "This is a *terroir* competition—a focus on a specific region. You have up to three personal exceptions and the group exception, which you have determined is salt. Local farms, small-scale producers, mills, your own foraging—these are your sources. Your five diners are your judges. I strongly advise you to adhere to the spirit as well as the letter of the rules.

"Dinners will be one per month, beginning in April and concluding in October. That's seven months for five competitors." He held up a hand to stave off the obvious question. "There is a potential fifth competitor who could not join us this evening."

"Why only potentially? And shouldn't he be disqualified for not showing up tonight?" asked Eden.

"How do you know it's a he?" said Blaise.

"Because, in this industry, only a guy would pass up an opportunity like this."

"Attendance tonight was not mandatory."

"How do we know what month we have for our dinner?" asked Celeste.

"Ah, and there is the question that really matters. Since you will be gathering and foraging from a confined geography, the time of year matters a great deal. And so, the assignment of months will be random."

He looked to Elena, who stepped away to reveal seven identical boxes on a sideboard table.

"Eden," said Randall. "Would you please select a box?"

"Why does she get to go first?" asked Blaise.

"Since you are all selecting a month, we decided the order of selection would be by the month of your birth. Eden was born in January."

"You and your Forager Chefs Club sure do know a lot about us," said Eden.

The boxes looked like the type that held fancy scented candles. Each was green with a cream-colored lid and tied with green and cream baker's twine. The lid was embossed with the same emblem as the sign at the front of the building.

Eden looked at the row of boxes for a moment. Her pendulum. She selected the box to the left of the middle. It was light. She took it to the couch and held it on her lap.

Celeste was next, then Blaise, and finally Christian.

"You may open your boxes when you wish," said Randall. "Elena has made a note of which box you selected, so we know which month you are assigned."

*Of course, she has,* thought Christian. There had been four boxes when he'd made his choice. His wasn't last. Close, but he was from Flint. He was used to being at or near the bottom.

"The list will be posted here in the common room tomorrow," said Elena.

No one seemed inclined to open their box, though Celeste had pulled the twine loose on hers. She'd stopped when she saw she was the only one.

"A couple more things before we enjoy some dinner." Randall held up his fingers to enumerate his points. "You are each a welcome guest of the Forager Chefs Club. Your sleeping room is yours for this calendar year. This will give you the opportunity to explore the property, its resources, and the surrounding area." He held up another finger. "Very important—this is covered in the legal document you received—while you may explore the property, you may not forage it in any month that is assigned to another competitor. Whatever is available on the property that month is for the exclusive use of the competing chef. As Elena said, we will post the list tomorrow. For the moment"—he extended a hand in invitation—"please join us for an evening repast."

# Celeste

Celeste sat on her bed with the unrolled parchment in her lap. She stared at it in disbelief.

April.

The word was centered in large, elegant script. There was a lot of blank space on the thick paper around that single word, making it the undeniable center of attention. A wide, colorful, intricate border framed the empty space around it. Unrolled, it looked like a monastery piece, as though a monk of old had spent months carefully crafting that single word and the elaborate border by hand, perched on a high stool, hunkered over a tall, wooden desk, inks at hand, pen dipping and scribing to create this colorful, detailed, devastating message in spring greens, yellows, and browns. It was a beautiful piece of art.

Which didn't do anything to take the lump out of Celeste's throat.

April.

She'd had second choice. There had been six boxes left after Eden chose hers. Celeste had hoped for September; she would have been very happy with August. Even June would have been nice—lots of wild berries by mid-June.

Instead, she'd chosen the box that held April.

March was known historically as the "hungry month"—the time of year when stores laid down to last through the winter were nearly depleted and spring had barely arrived. But April wasn't much better in the northern reaches of Michigan. There was so much bounty on her island for those who knew where to look, but much of it would just be rousing from its winter sleep in April. She lived the farthest north of any of them in that room, and she'd managed to assign herself the earliest month.

She saw a damp splotch appear. She brushed it away, rolled up the thick paper, and put it back in the box. She closed the lid and retied the twine. She sat on the bed a while longer, listening to the wind outside that she imagined had followed her. Maybe it had followed her to call her home again.

Celeste looked at the sheaf of papers next to the box. She had three days to decide. She picked up her cell phone. Still no bars. She fell back against the pillows and looked up at the ceiling. The Grand Hotel and its kitchen were closed for the season. She could stay here as long as she liked, rent free, the Club's kitchen and its acreage at her disposal.

But what was the point?

She listened to the wind. The beams and walls no longer seemed to want to reveal their essence and history to her. Or maybe she was blocking them out, her mother would say. So be it. She really didn't want to hear what they had to reveal right now. Or what Aunt Tilda would say. Aunt Tilda wasn't here. Hadn't met Eden and Blaise and Christian.

After a while, Celeste picked up the house phone on the bedside table. It rang without her pressing any of the buttons. She recognized Elena's voice.

"Elena, would it be possible for me to get a ride home tomorrow morning?"

# Daniel

Daniel sat at the counter of the diner and held the trifold pamphlet in his hands while his coffee got cold. The paper was glossy and the colors bright. Inside, expertly written copy extolled the technologically advanced techniques, the caring environment, the world-class staff, the specialization in the unique needs of pediatric burn patients.

Stretching exercises would continue to help, Dr. Whitney said, but as Ethan grew, the scarred tissue wouldn't be able to keep up. He needed grafts, and soon. The best place would be the Children's Hospital Pediatric Burn Center in Detroit, David Whitney told him, one hand on his shoulder as he handed him the pamphlet. He knew Daniel didn't have medical insurance.

It had been Ethan's regular checkup, but David had lifted his gaze to meet Daniel's eyes as soon as Ethan took off his shirt. The doctor joked with the boy as he instructed him to breathe in and out, pressing his stethoscope here and there and tapping his chest and back with strong fingertips. They'd spoken later, out of Ethan's hearing, as the six-year-old fished through a bucket of stickers to select his reward. It wasn't Daniel's imagination. Ethan was dropping his right shoulder a bit. The scar tissue ran up his rib cage from his hip and partway down the inside of his right arm. It was thick and looked like lava flow, though not nearly as red as it had been. It was red and wet at first, had crusted as the skin sought to heal. Ethan was three when it happened.

Daniel pressed his fist against his mouth, tapping it against his chin.

He reached for his coffee cup and then made a face and set it down. Loretta must have noticed because she whisked the cup away and, in less than a minute, brought a new one, steam rising. He nodded his thanks and lifted the cup to his lips. Someone sat down beside him at the counter.

"You don't give up easy, do you?" Daniel said.

"I notice the snow piles have grown."

"Spring should be here by Mother's Day. The ladies insist, and I guess the *Farmer's Almanac* just doesn't want to let them down. Until then," Daniel said to the man he'd last seen at the mercantile the month before, "I hope you're wearing a thick sweater under that fancy coat."

The man reached for the cup of coffee Loretta set down in front of him.

"You know why I'm here," he said, tipping half-and-half from a small metal pitcher into the coffee but ignoring the nearby sugar packets.

"And you know what I told you last time."

"It's an invitation that you can accept or decline. My job is to ensure you receive it." The man reached into the pocket of his camel-colored coat and brought out the thick, cream-colored envelope Daniel recognized from their meeting at the mercantile.

"Déjà vu all over again," said Daniel.

The man didn't reply. He just held out the envelope with a steady hand, his elbow on the counter.

"Tell me how you knew my son's name back at the mercantile."

The man took a sip from his cup. "I was given the information I would need to find you to hand-deliver this to make sure it went to the right person without asking for identification, which would be in poor form, given that this is an exclusive invitation for a significant opportunity. And it *is* significant, Mr. Metsja."

The man looked at the pamphlet, and Daniel quashed the urge to move it out of sight.

"I'll make you a deal," Daniel said conversationally. He caught Loretta's eye as she came by carrying a full pot. She stopped. "I'll accept this envelope, and you stay right here while I open it. Loretta will freshen up your cup." She smiled and topped off Daniel's. "If what's inside is any sort of court order or summons or custody document, I get to punch your face."

The coffee splashed onto the saucer as Loretta suddenly withdrew the pot and took a step back. She tilted her head and looked at the newcomer.

"Agreed," said the man amiably. With two fingers, he pushed his cup a few inches toward the waitress.

Daniel took the envelope. He didn't recognize the handwriting on the front, his full name written in elegant swoops and whorls. He turned it over and glanced at the wax seal but wasn't familiar with the emblem. Was it the masons? His great-uncle had been a mason. He didn't think they sent out written invitations to join their order. He broke the wax in half and drew out the thick card. After a moment, he looked up. "You can go ahead and pour, Loretta. I don't need to hit him."

She breathed a mock sigh of relief and poured.

# Celeste

Celeste hadn't gone far before she decided walking home from the Mackinac Island Airport had been a bad idea. It wasn't the walking part; it was the dragging part. The tiny wheels on her doodled-pirate suitcase didn't work very well on packed snow. Still, it was only a mile or so home. She looked at the angle of the sun. She'd make it before dark.

She'd left the Forager Chefs Club later than she wanted. She didn't begrudge Icarus the fare—he had to make a living, after all—but it was unexpected to learn from Elena that the pilot had already been commissioned first thing in the morning to deliver Randall to wherever he was going before he could then come back to pick up Celeste. Celeste had wondered out loud if Randall's trip had something to do with the potential fifth competitor, but Elena hadn't responded. She'd just smiled and invited Celeste to get some breakfast. The dried cherry muffins were especially good, Elena had confided.

They *were* especially good. After her first couple of bites, Celeste had let a morsel rest on her tongue, savoring it, trying to discern the separate flavors. There was something there—it wasn't cinnamon or nutmeg—that gave the muffin a complexity of flavor beyond the dried cherries. Cardamom maybe? She'd cut the muffin in half, wrapped the unbitten portion in a napkin, and tucked it in her pocket. Her mother might know.

The stack of napkins on the table bore the same emblem that was embedded in the wax seal of her invitation and burned into the wooden sign at the front of the building. She now knew what the vertical letters FCC meant. But what she had thought were radiant beams of a star were a fishing rod crossed by a rifle. On either side were a foraging trowel and a long knife.

The tools of the Forager Chefs Club.

Celeste's reverie as she made one foot march in front of the other while dragging her now-soaked suitcase through the snow was interrupted by the sound of a snowmobile. She moved to the side of the road and held out a thumb, even though the sound was coming from the wrong direction—toward rather than from the airport.

The snowmobile stopped beside her. The rider took off a helmet that revealed a shoulder-length torrent of wavy brunette hair. The rider lowered a bright red scarf that covered all her face but her eyes. Hazel eyes that Celeste had known all her life.

"Celly, what in the hell are you doing out here?" asked Aunt Tilda.

It took some doing, but before long, Celeste was seated behind Aunt Tilda. The canvas suitcase bumped and dragged behind the snowmobile, tethered by a rope. Celeste looked back now and then to make sure it was still there. Snowmobiles weren't built for carrying two passengers plus luggage. They took it slow and still made it to Aunt Tilda's in far less time than it would have taken Celeste to walk home.

Aunt Tilda already had a fire going in the fireplace, burned down to mostly embers. She added a couple of logs and poked at them. She instructed Celeste to empty her suitcase on the floor and set the luggage in front of the fire to dry.

"I'll call your mom to let her know you're here. I don't want her to worry. We'll go over there in just a bit. I gotta thaw."

"She doesn't know I'm coming home today."

Aunt Tilda snorted. "Sure, she doesn't. And I just happened to be going out for a snowmobile ride toward the airport. I'll be right back."

Celeste did as instructed, moving the suitcase to one side to give herself room in front of the fire to dry herself out. In a few minutes, Aunt Tilda came back, carrying two glasses and an uncorked bottle of red wine. She sat down on the floor beside Celeste.

"Gotta thaw," she repeated, pouring wine into the two glasses. She extended one toward Celeste and then pulled it back. "You're twenty-one, right?"

Celeste took the glass. Aunt Tilda had been asking her that rhetorical question since she was fifteen years old.

Tilda wasn't really her aunt—at least not by blood. But Tilda Weems had always been part of Celeste's life. Except for her mom, there was no one Celeste trusted more. So the woman with the wild brunette hair—who had a knack for calming storms and creating them, who seemed to come and go as she pleased yet was always there for Celeste and her mom—was "Aunt" Tilda.

"I'm really glad you bought this house," said Celeste. "It's nice having you here more than just a few weeks a year."

"Especially when you find yourself trekking from the airport, dragging a suitcase in the snow."

"Especially then."

They clinked glasses.

"Nearly twenty years toiling for the esteemed firm of Walsh, Whitman, and Lloyd has earned me a bit of latitude. Another five, and I should be able to give up the commute to Grand Rapids entirely. Less if I get another divorce case like the one I had three years ago." Tilda settled back on one elbow and stretched her feet toward the fire. She was wearing two different socks. "Tell me what happened at the Forager Chefs Club. We didn't expect you back so soon."

Tilda knew the gist of the competition—she'd been at the airport to see Celeste off—so Celeste picked up the story where it mattered. She'd made up her mind the night before that she wouldn't be a contestant. Drawing the month of April—out of six boxes, she still couldn't believe that was the one she'd chosen—was fate's way of protecting her from making a fool of herself. Who was she to compete against the people she'd met? Eden—so self-assured. Running her own commercial kitchen and building her personal brand while doing so much good in an underserved section of Detroit. Blaise, lofty Blaise, who created gorgeous dinners for gorgeous people who paid him grand sums to do it. Christian, who, though he apparently drove a salt truck in the winter, had been to culinary school in New York, even if he hadn't graduated. And the unknown fifth—who knew what credentials this fifth contestant might bring to the table? She knew how to forage and loved to cook, but she was under-trained. She worked and learned in the restaurant of a grand hotel—*the* Grand Hotel—but she wouldn't even have that if Aunt Tilda hadn't called in a favor to get her the job.

Celeste realized she had tears and a little bit of snot running down her face. She wiped her face with the edge of her thermal undershirt and held out her empty glass.

Tilda raised herself from her elbow and filled it.

"You don't give yourself enough credit," Tilda said. "What about that winter solstice dinner you made? That was amazing. Everyone is still raving. I told friends in Grand Rapids about it. While Eden and Christian and . . . what's the other guy's name?"

"Blaise."

"Blaise. While they were all extolling their accomplishments, did you mention that dinner?"

"No. I thought about it, but no."

"But you *are* thinking about letting what other people think do your deciding for you." Tilda got up and poked at the fire, adding another log. "Do you know," she said, "that if everyone but your mother had had their way, you wouldn't exist?"

Celeste paused mid-gulp at this non sequitur.

Tilda sat down again and picked up her glass.

"I've known your mom for a long, long time."

"Since second grade."

"Since second grade. I've been married. I'm not now. There are two people in the world I don't think I can do without. My husband wasn't one of them, which is a big part of why we divorced. Your mom *is* one—and you are the other. I need you to know that. I need you to believe it to the core of your being."

"I love you too, Aunt Tilda." Celeste wondered what the hell this had to do with her abandoning the Forager Chefs Club competition.

"Okay," said Tilda. She took a long drink from her glass, looked at Celeste, paused, looked at the fire, and took another. "Okay," she said again.

Celeste bit her lip. Two "okays" and nearly half a glass of wine—*What the hell?*

"In college, your mom and I got into some weird shit," she said. "Not drugs," Tilda added, holding up an index finger.

"I know," said Celeste. "New Age, Wicca."

"Let me tell you that Wicca has some weird shit. Your mom still likes the New Age stuff, but thank God we both abandoned Wicca's weirdness. I'm told not all Wicca is like that, but still. Don't ever get involved. Promise me."

"I promise," Celeste said when it became clear it wasn't rhetorical. "No Wicca weirdness."

What did this have to do with quitting the competition? Why wasn't Aunt Tilda telling her she'd made the right decision to leave? Screw them all and go your own way?

Tilda took a deep breath and another pull from her glass.

"God, what am I doing," she said under her breath. She drained her glass and then filled it again from the bottle on the floor.

"You were conceived on the summer solstice," said Tilda. "I know you know some of this. Just let me finish, and then you can ask questions, and I'll answer if I can. That was a wild, wild night. It wasn't our first wild, wild night. But it was the only time your mom or I turned up pregnant. I don't know what went wrong, but that was completely unexpected. There was no way of knowing who the father was.

"When your mom found out she was pregnant with you, everyone in whom she confided told her she should get an abortion. Everyone. I was one of them. I was probably the loudest voice."

Tilda paused. The only sound in the room was the crackle of the fire.

Celeste knew she had been conceived during a summer solstice, but there'd never been any details, and she'd always imagined it as some romantic, Shakespearean *Midsummer Night's Dream*, star-crossed lovers interlude. This was different. She set down her glass and turned from Aunt Tilda to look at the flames.

"You have to understand, Celly. We were both still in college. We were young and dumb, as they say now. Neither of us had any money, and being a single mom in those days just wasn't done. It didn't make sense for your mom to throw away . . . to go through with something that would change her life so drastically."

Tilda lifted her glass to her lips to give herself a moment of respite. Celeste continued to watch the flames.

"Our families had vacationed on Mackinac Island for years. I talked your mom into coming up for Labor Day weekend. I figured that, with just the two of us, I could make her see . . ." Tilda's voice drifted off. "Do you know what she told me?" Tilda said, her voice strong again. She turned to face Celeste, who kept staring at the flames.

"Celly, your mom said she wanted to tell me a story. And she told me the story of Persephone and Demeter. Do you know that Greek myth? How Persephone was the beloved daughter of Demeter, and everyone who ever met her loved her. Hades, the god of the underworld, desired her and kidnapped her. There's a lot more, but the upshot is that while Persephone was in the underworld, Demeter, the goddess of agriculture and fertility, mourned, and for the first time, the earth experienced winter. It got bad, and the gods negotiated with Hades that Persephone could return for eight months each year. When Persephone returned, Demeter rejoiced, and the earth bloomed again in the form of spring.

"Your mom reminded me that you had been conceived on the summer solstice, which meant you would be born right around the spring equinox. Could I imagine how Demeter would have felt had Persephone not returned? How, then, she asked me, could she bear the coming of the next spring, if it came knowing she'd put to death her own daughter? And that's when I knew she'd made up her mind, and nothing was going to change it. She was convinced from the get-go you would be a girl. And wouldn't you know it? You were born on March twenty-first, the spring equinox—when the planet is poised in perfect balance and our hemisphere shifts from the slumber of winter to the bounty of summer."

Celeste continued to stare into the fire. A log shifted, throwing sparks. A few fell on the suitcase. The sparks went dark, leaving faint smudges of ash on the magenta canvas.

"You didn't want me to be born," Celeste said, her voice barely over a whisper. She'd heard the rest; she'd process it later. But right now, she focused on the fact that the person second-most dear to her in the world had advocated that she never exist. Tilda leaned toward her, and Celeste subtly shifted her body away.

"You are a gift in so many ways," said Tilda. "And one of your gifts has been in showing me that I was wrong. So very wrong. And I've worked, in my own way, to help others to see how precious every life is. Your mother helped me to understand that. And she gave me the two most wonderful gifts of my life. The first is that she forgave me, and the second is that she let me be a part of yours."

Celeste felt drained from the past thirty-six hours. She imagined that afternoon at the St. Ignace Airport when she'd met Randall. If only Maddox had answered her text, given her a goddamn ride on the back of his snowmobile over the straits. . . . She heard Tilda shift and stand up.

"I've wanted to tell you for a while; maybe I chose the wrong time," she said. "But here's the gist of why I told you now. In essence, your mother said you were her spring. That without you, there would be no spring. She didn't let what other people thought make her decision. Maybe it *was* fate that made you choose April as your month for this competition—when, as you say, there were six choices on the table. Fate, in a good way. You are the spring, Celly. And I am convinced that you can make a competition-worthy spring-foraged dinner."

Tilda held out her hand.

"C'mon. Let's go to your mom's. Grab what you absolutely need and leave the rest with your suitcase to dry a bit longer. And you're going to have to drive the snowmobile. I've had too much wine."

Celeste looked up into the hazel eyes she'd known all her life. She took a breath and then reached out and took her aunt's hand. The woman's grip was strong as she helped Celeste to her feet.

Of course, she had to tell the whole story all over again. It took longer because Celeste also described the building in detail, wanting her mother to see it through her words as well as the photos she'd taken with her phone. When she got to the part about the box, she pulled the rolled-up parchment out from the inside of her shirt.

Her mother listened intently and unrolled the parchment on the worn, painted tabletop. She smoothed it out with her hands and set a candlestick and three lake rocks to hold down the corners. She continued to listen intently, but Celeste saw her tracing her long, purple-stained index finger along the decorative border of the parchment.

"Nonsense," she said when Celeste finished her story. "Of course, you're going to compete."

"Mom," Celeste started.

"I do believe this parchment is a type of treasure map," her mom interrupted. "Did you notice?"

That caught Celeste's attention. "A treasure map?"

"Tilda, would you grab me the magnifying disk? I think I left it by the bookshelf."

"Oh, that narrows it down," said Tilda, getting up.

"By the herbals."

"Not helping, Brenda."

"The herbals on dyeing."

"Right."

Celeste stood to look over her mother's shoulder. At first glance, the design appeared to be random, but Celeste now saw that the intricate border depicted small, detailed scenes.

"How many acres did you say this Forager Chefs Club has?"

"I don't remember, but it's a lot."

"Thirty-four," said Tilda. She placed the large glass disk on top of the parchment, then sat down and pulled the sheaf of papers outlining the contest contract out of her shirt. "If I get a paper cut on my boob, it's your fault," she said to Celeste.

"Wear a bra, and you won't get a paper cut on your boob," said Celeste.

"Old habits die hard."

"Is there a reason the two of you need to use your shirts as document holders?"

"It's a little wet out there for my bicycle basket," answered Tilda. "Anyway, I want to spend some time with this contract before you sign it, if that's okay, Celly." She ran a finger down the first page. "Damn, where is it? I saw it at the house. Ah, here it is. They don't list the specific address for the Club, but they do say that it's situated on thirty-four acres. Wow. It's near Bear Lake. Some nice fishing there."

"How do you know?" asked Celeste's mother. "You don't fish."

"Don't I, now?" preened Tilda. "There's fishing, and then there's fishing."

Celeste's mother rolled her eyes.

"Icarus landed at Manistee County Airport, and a car took me from there," said Celeste, interrupting the familiar repartee. "They said we could forage whatever we wanted on the property but that no one could forage during someone else's month."

"Thirty-four acres. That's a lot of territory to explore," murmured Brenda. "Isn't it nice of them to provide you with clues?"

Celeste leaned in to look through her mom's magnifying disk. She felt a thread of excitement. "Are those honeybee boxes, do you think?" she asked, pointing.

Her mother leaned in. "I think you're right."

"But how would I know where on thirty-four acres someone is tending bees?"

"That's why it's a treasure map, dear heart. You'll have to spend some time with this, pick out which of these drawings represent landmarks, memorize what looks important, and then go back and memorize what doesn't look important, just in case it turns out to be."

"I wonder who drew it."

"Now, wouldn't that be a good person to identify and get to know? How much time before your dinner are you allowed to stay at the Club and explore the grounds?"

"As much as she wants," said Tilda, leafing through the pages. "She could go tomorrow. She can stay there all year if she wants to."

"Why would I stay all year? My dinner is the last Saturday in April. After that, it's out of my hands. April," she repeated. "There's hardly anything to forage in April—no berries, no nuts, no fruit, the list goes on."

"Who says you have to forage your ingredients in April?" said Tilda. "Nothing in this paperwork does—it's a *terroir* competition. So, you tap everything you've already foraged and stored. That winter solstice dinner you cooked was amazing. I *know* you didn't find those ingredients on the island in December."

Celeste thumped down into her seat and covered her head with her hands, her forehead against the table. She felt her mother put a hand on top of hers. It should have been comforting. It just felt heavy.

"I put everything I had into that winter solstice dinner," Celeste said, her voice muffled against the table, her breath hot as it exhaled and pushed against her face.

"Right!" said Tilda. "So, you put everything you have into this competition dinner—heart, mind, soul."

Celly lifted her head. "No, Aunt Tilda, you don't get it. I put everything I had foraged and stored all year into that dinner. It was important to all of you, so I didn't hold anything back. There's pretty much nothing left. Mom and I have been mostly living off store-bought groceries since New Year's." Celeste felt the tears come again. Foraged hazelnuts, acorn flour that had taken days to prepare, preserved raspberries and blackberries, garlic and onion bulbs stored in the communal root cellar, dehydrated mushrooms, dried apples and pears, pickled wild asparagus—all of it and more had gone into the dinner for her mom, Tilda, and their friends.

Tilda sat down slowly. "Everything?"

"That's why I didn't want April. I needed time to replenish."

"Then we'll enlist help to replenish," said Brenda with authority. "No one forages the way you do, Celeste, but there are a number of people we know who can contribute. You've a birthday coming up. I think it's time for a pantry-themed birthday party."

"Nothing that doesn't come from Michigan," interjected Tilda, flipping through the pages of the contest agreement. "She gets up to three exceptions—we want her to be able to choose those judiciously."

"I don't want to use any exceptions. Except our group exception. We had one that we all agreed on."

"And that is?"

"Salt. Michigan doesn't have sea salt."

Tilda looked thoughtful. "Smart," she said. "That was smart."

"A *terroir* dinner. I've never heard of it, but what a lovely word," said her mother. She stroked Celeste's head, drawing her hand down the side of her face to cup her chin.

*Her eyes are the color of the straits*, Celeste thought. *I can always return home, no matter how far away I may be, if I can just remember the color of my mother's eyes.*

She shook her head free, leaving the cradle of her mother's hand.

"It can't all come from someone else," she said. "I have to forage in *April* for the most important dinner of my life."

"Let's not be overly dramatic," said her mother. "You forage in April every year. It's spring. The return of life. Everything sprouting anew. Spring greens, mushrooms, ramps—the list goes on and on."

"Brenda, you're making me hungry," said Tilda. "By the way, Celly, Joe Hennessey is still ticked off you won't tell him where you find those morel mushrooms you collect every spring."

At her mother's words, an idea burgeoned in Celeste's mind. "It's a secret," she murmured. She stood up and went to a bookshelf. She had to bring up her idea in a way that wouldn't make her mom suspect Tilda had told her the story of her birth. That was a conversation she didn't want to continue tonight.

Tilda stood up. "I'm calling for pizza."

"You can't drive to get pizza. And you're spending the night here, in case you hadn't already figured that out," said Brenda.

"The pub delivers."

"Not after dark in February, they don't."

"They will for me. I'm renowned as an excellent tipper."

By the time Tilda ordered pizza and secured the promise of delivery, Celeste had found the book she sought. She grabbed a couple more at random from the shelves. Her mom and Aunt Tilda poured over the pages of the contest agreement, wine glasses in hand, and Celeste curled up in her favorite overstuffed chair. Her idea had already blossomed in her head, but she wanted enough time to pass for her mom to think she was researching spring themes before saying anything. She read the Persephone story, flipped a few pages, and read more. She turned back to the myth that would be the basis of her dinner, looking at the watercolor illustration in the book, letting her mind wander through memories of past springs. Walks in woods and fields and along stream beds, climbing scant paths and trails from the rocky shore of the straits to the heights of the island, basket looped on her arm, sharp knife that sometimes doubled as a digging tool in her hand. After a while, she closed the book of Greek mythology. It took a few moments, but Tilda noticed, and her voice trailed away. Her mom looked up and smiled.

That smile had warmed and calmed her and let her know all her life that she was loved. And now she knew it to be one of strength too. Her mother had smiled in the face of all the people who thought they knew what she should do with her life, with the burgeoning new life in her belly. She had smiled at all of them and done it her way.

Surely, some of that strength had passed down to her daughter. Strength enough to take on this challenge. To do it her way.

"There were six boxes available when it was my turn," said Celeste. "Six out of seven. And still, the box that drew me, that I chose, was the first month of the competition—April. I chose spring. I want a theme that will set me apart." She saw Tilda look a little wary, as if she knew what was coming. "I do want that pantry party, Mom—I'm going to need it—but there *is* a lot in the woods and in the fields, even in April, and the Club is south of here, so that could help. Like you said, it's the return of spring, the beginning of the foraging season.

"My dinner is going to be called *Persephone's Return*."

Her mom looked startled, but it could have been because, just then, there was a loud knock on the door. The pizza had arrived.

# Blaise

The others had left within a couple of days. Celeste hadn't given a reason; she was just gone by noon. Probably scared off. She was clearly very young and out of her league. Christian had left just after lunch. Blaise had overheard him explain to Elena that he didn't want to leave his mom for too long. A salt truck driver *and* a mama's boy—how that guy got invited to this competition was a mystery. Eden had spent most of the day in the kitchen cataloging kitchen cookware and tools before heading to Detroit. She divided her time between Idlewild and her dad's Detroit mission shelter, where she ran the food outreach and cooked once a week. When Blaise heard that, he immediately abandoned his nascent plans to do the same. He might be on the other side of the state, but he still wouldn't want anyone to think he was a copycat.

He'd spent the first day going over the contest agreement in detail. He probably should consult a lawyer, but lawyers were expensive.

The competition month assignments were posted. Celeste had drawn April, Eden had June, Christian had August, and he had September. May, July, and October were still up for grabs if the mystery fifth contestant ever made an appearance.

Blaise was satisfied with September. He would have preferred August since September got busy for him with his clientele back from far-flung vacations. Other than that wrinkle, he had drawn the best month of all—harvest month—and purely by luck.

"You're still here. Excellent. I was hoping we'd get a chance to talk privately."

Randall walked into the common room and to the sideboard, where he poured himself a glass from one of the crystal decanters.

"Still here," affirmed Blaise. "I thought I might take the Club up on the offer to spend some time to get to know the grounds and what else is around—farmers, other suppliers—but I do have an ask."

"You want to know if you can bring Bradley here."

Blaise took a sip from his glass to hide his annoyance. He no longer thought the competition was a reality show—something would have tipped it off in the fine print of the agreement, and he'd combed it for any hint—but that didn't mean this whole contest wasn't a show. Whoever had put this together clearly knew a lot about him.

"If you know I have a twin brother, then you know he has autism. Our parents are out of state and out of the picture. He depends on me."

"And do you depend on him?"

Blaise paused, bringing his glass to his lips. He set it down on the side table.

"We're brothers. We depend on one another, just as any family depends on one another." *Except for parents who divorce, abandon any reminder of their life together, and instead remarry and start new families in different states*, he thought bitterly. "Are you insinuating that because my brother has autism, I shouldn't depend on him?"

"Do you depend on him to be able to cook at the level that has earned you the regional renown you've gained so quickly and at such a relatively young age, as well as a spot in this competition? Renown that you have not shared with your brother? The culinary community is tight-knit, as you know, and prone to gossip. There are stories of the dishes the two of you created at the restaurant before you went solo—his creative use of ingredients combined with your structure and discipline. You have the technical skills that bring your brother's innovation and imagination to the plate." Randall relaxed in his chair and crossed one leg over the other. "Those are the whispers of the strategic role your brother plays in your culinary success. In the public eye, the two of you are not, say, Jean and Pierre Troisgros. You are building your reputation as a solo chef. Which is fine, of course—if it is authentic."

"I have no idea who you've been talking to."

"Very true. You don't."

Blaise picked up his glass. Should he appear offended or puzzled?

"Blaise," said Randall, "you don't have to answer the question. But know this: the *terroir* contest invitation was extended to you. Not to you and your brother. You have publicized yourself as a solo chef, and it is as a solo chef that you must compete." He held up a hand. "That said, we understand it will be difficult for you to devote the necessary time and concentration if you are distracted due to concern for your brother's well-being. So, yes, you can bring him to the Club. We will provide him a room."

*Neither*, Blaise decided. "Thank you," he said.

"But I must reinforce what I said the other evening. This is a subjective competition. It will matter to the judges how much attention is paid not only to the letter of the rules but to the spirit. Skirting them will not benefit you."

Randall stood up. "I'm behind on some paperwork. I never thought I'd make two trips to the Upper Peninsula within six weeks—and in the winter, no less."

"Will our fifth contestant be joining us?"

"Good deduction. Yes, I believe he will. Not sure if you'll meet him before our final gathering in December, but there is a fifth contestant."

"So Eden was right. It's a he. Which month did he draw?"

"October."

Randall paused in the doorway.

"Make sure Bradley knows all the rules about foraging on the Club acreage. If he's here under your aegis, it's your responsibility to ensure that he doesn't forage during another competitor's month and that he follows all the other rules outlined in the contract—both the letter and the spirit."

"Of course," said Blaise.

# Daniel

They'd moved to a table at the diner and talked a while longer. There had been some formalities, the man Daniel now knew as Randall providing him the gist of what he called a *terroir* competition and the agreement that he could take all the time he needed to review before signing.

It was a lot of money. Daniel thought of the brochure he'd tucked into the pocket of his Carhartt jacket, the procedures and therapies Dr. Whitney had said would give Ethan the best chance of growing up with full flexibility on his right side. They weren't cheap.

Randall had explained about the boxes.

"There are three left. I don't think we need a ceremony. How about I tell you the three months that are left, and you tell me which one you want?"

"Not July."

"Okay. How about I tell you the two months that are left, and you tell me which one you want?"

Daniel had chosen October. He'd have to let the Royal Trolls know there wouldn't be a dinner for them that month. They'd understand, or they wouldn't. Unless they wanted to pay him fifty thousand dollars to make them dinner in October.

"Can I ask you something?" Randall said when they shook hands in the parking lot a while later.

"Sure." *Just not about July.*

"Who are the Royal Trolls?"

"I'm commissioned by a group of guys with a lot of money to cook a meal for them once a month or so at their hunting lodge," Daniel said. "They're the Royal Trolls."

"Okay, I knew about the dinners." Randall had rolled his eyes at Daniel's sharp look. "You've been invited to a high-stakes cooking competition. There's gotta be some background for that to happen, right?"

"Okay. Right." Daniel had climbed into his truck.

"But why do you call them Royal Trolls?"

Daniel had shut the door, started the engine, and rolled down the window.

"Royal because they have a shitload of money and sometimes act like they own the world. Trolls because they're from the Lower Peninsula." He'd put his truck into gear. "They live under the bridge."

Daniel put a couple more logs on the fire and watched the flames, sipping an orphan barrel bourbon one of the Royal Trolls had given him in November. It was a cold night with a clear sky, a sliver of moon riding high. He'd tucked Ethan into bed, Biscuit stretched out beside him, and then stood on the porch watching the moon until it broke free of the bare branches that sought to hold it still.

Nothing held still. Ever. It all kept moving forward.

Not July, he'd told Randall. Everyone who knew him steered clear of him in July. He typically took Ethan on an extended camping trip. It was too hard to be at the cabin.

He hadn't been to Thistle's bee yard since it all happened.

She'd been so excited about that year's honey harvest. There was enough from the cappings to make any number of things: candles, lip balm, moisturizer. He laughed at her excitement and delighted in her enthusiasm. Thistle had been a beekeeper for three years, and this was the first year she would have not only honey but enough wax for her grand plans.

He knew she'd written to her mother about it. It had been a sore point between him and his wife. She always hoped they would finally accept her choices. He wanted her to accept that her parents were rigid and unyielding.

They had given her an ultimatum.

And she'd made her choice.

A part of him had trembled every now and then—though not in a way anyone could ever be allowed to see—at the thought that she might rethink that choice.

The official marriage had been at the courthouse just a mile or so from where she'd gone to high school. Her parents had declined to attend. The clerk had had to reprint the form when Thistle realized she'd signed with the name she'd adopted for herself years ago and not the one on her birth certificate. Two of her college roommates had been the witnesses. They laughed and cried in equal measure, made Daniel promise to make Thistle happy, and promised her they would visit them in Escanaba soon. Daniel had known it was an empty promise. He suspected Thistle knew it too, the way she had hugged each of them hard before she'd climbed into his pickup truck for the trip north, a few plastic storage boxes in the back all she chose to bring with her from the posh life she was leaving behind.

The ceremony that counted was on their way from Grosse Pointe to Escanaba. They'd pitched their tent in a small glade Daniel found along the Au Sable River. Thistle had lit candles while Daniel pulled the cork from a bottle of champagne he'd liberated from her parents' cellar and chilled in the river. They'd spoken vows to one another in that glade and sealed them with sweet lovemaking under the beneficent gaze of the moon, serenaded by the sounds of the river and its denizens.

Ethan had been born nine months later.

With just her presence, Thistle had transformed his utilitarian log cabin on twenty acres in the woods just outside Escanaba into a home. They didn't need much. He hunted and foraged; she gardened and preserved. They bartered for most of the other things they needed, money from Daniel's snow plowing and handyman services filling in the gaps.

It wasn't the life her parents had envisioned for her, but it was the life she'd chosen when she chose him.

Beeswax is very flammable, they'd told him later.

That July had been hot. For a stretch of days, the temperatures hit the mideighties, unusual this far north in Michigan. As he made his way along the winding lane of packed dirt and gravel to their home, he thought they should sleep on blankets and pillows spread on the floor of the screened back porch to catch the errant breezes, lulled to sleep by Thistle's low lullaby to Ethan, accompanied by the song of frogs and cicadas, protected from frustrated mosquitos by the screens and from any larger predators by Biscuit and the gun Daniel kept within arm's reach. Bumping down the rutted lane, Daniel smiled, knowing Thistle would suggest they head to the creek after supper for a late evening swim to cool off.

He stopped the truck in its usual spot off to one side of the cabin. Shut off the engine. Opened the door of the truck.

Heard the high-pitched scream of his son. Biscuit's frantic barking.

His son's scream tasted of salt—the weird, errant thought flitted through his brain as he ran toward the sound, aware he'd bitten his tongue or maybe his lip. As he rounded the corner of the cabin at a dead run, the flames engulfing the doorway and one side of his wife's wooden bee shed were yellow and orange and somehow smelled sweet—likely a figment of imagination and memory, some strange synapse related to knowing the scent of the honey and beeswax that was an accelerant for the fire.

He saw Thistle. She was yards away from the blaze, trying to carry Ethan to the house without touching his right side or her left. He ran toward her. She fell and turned at his hoarse cry as he dropped to his knees before her.

Biscuit was barking and whining, trying to lick Thistle's face and Ethan's head.

"Biscuit, go!" shouted Daniel, shoving him.

The big dog cringed, stepped back, tail down. He waited, whined, uncertain.

"I got the fire out," Thistle said, even as it crackled behind them. Most of her hair was singed away. One side of her face seemed peeled, red, raw. She was nearly naked, her sundress—the one he'd bought for her over her protestations on a trip to town—hanging limply to one side, the fabric on the left mostly gone, edges adhering to wet flesh, the curve of her breast. "I got the fire out," she said again. She looked at Ethan, cradled in her arms, as he continued to cry. "Oh, baby," Thistle said in a breathless coo, "it's not your fault. I should have been more watchful. Daddy's here now. Daddy will help." She looked at Daniel, her eyes frantic. Her breathing was shallow, like she couldn't catch her breath after carrying the toddler as far as she had. "It's not his fault. I should have been watching. He didn't mean to tip it over." Thistle reached out her hand and placed it on Daniel's knee. "I love you so much, Daniel. Promise me . . ." She gasped suddenly and squeezed her eyes shut.

"Anything," Daniel rasped. He pulled out his cell phone. No bars. They never had bars. No landline. Why would they ever need to connect with the outside world from this, their haven? What could they ever possibly need that they couldn't get for themselves?

Right now, an ambulance.

His truck. He needed to get them to his truck. He stood, lifting Thistle and Ethan in his arms as he did, trying desperately not to touch the open, burned flesh. It was impossible. Ethan's cries pitched higher as Thistle screamed. Daniel gritted his teeth and strode to the truck, its driver's side door still hanging open. He shouted Biscuit away when the dog moved to jump in.

One of Ethan's baby blankets lay in the back seat of the crew cab. He tucked it around his wife and child in the front passenger seat. Ethan continued to wail, but Thistle had her eyes closed, her lips slightly pursed as she seemed to practice the same sort of breathing cadence he remembered from Ethan's birth. He got behind the wheel and put the truck in gear.

Thistle opened her eyes and gave a ghost of a smile. "How fast can this truck go?"

Fast.

The back end of the pickup jolted when it hit a small sapling as Daniel fishtailed from their property onto the black hardtop of the county road. What was the quickest way to St. Francis Hospital? He'd been there the week before, dropping off Frank for his shift after lunch at the diner. But he didn't want to drive through town. The hospital was on Route 41. It was a left turn at the light coming up.

Ahead of him, the light turned red.

"Run it, Daniel, run it." Thistle's voice trembled, but her tone was adamant, a command.

Daniel laid on the horn and prayed.

He swerved in the intersection to miss a small hatchback, tires screeching as he made the turn, feeling those on the right leave the asphalt for a moment, holding his breath and praying harder. Thistle jostled against the center console and screamed as her left side met the hard plastic. Her scream, Daniel's horn, and the blaring response from other drivers were a cacophony of sound that silenced Ethan. Coming out of the turn and once again pressing down hard on the gas pedal, Daniel spared a glance to his right. The three-year-old's eyes were closed. So were Thistle's. She was breathing, but the silence from his son, wrapped in the blanket and his mother's arms, scared him.

He left more tire rubber on the road as he turned into the hospital's emergency room entrance. Horn blaring, he came to a stop and sprang from the truck, running to the passenger side while shouting for help. He heard voices as he lifted Thistle, Ethan on her lap and draped with the baby blanket. He turned to find Frank at his elbow.

Frank's eyes went wide.

"Daniel! What happened?"

"A fire. At our house," Daniel said curtly, pushing past him into the hospital, where two people in scrubs rushed a gurney toward him.

"A fire? Is it out?"

Daniel ignored him.

"Daniel! Is the fire out?"

# MARCH

# Celeste

Celeste's birthday "pack-the-pantry" party was a success, though a bit overwhelming. She and her mother didn't always fit in, but the half-dozen women who had attended the winter solstice dinner party answered Brenda's invitation. They gave her gifts that were the work of hands and hearts. Their chatter and laughter went on through the late afternoon and into the evening as a sharp March wind blew away the clouds that had brought morning rain.

Celeste now had a good supply of three kinds of nuts.

The acorns weren't shelled, which was okay. Molly explained that she'd wanted to make flour in the fall, but her arthritis had flared up, and so she'd frozen the acorns with full intention of continuing on to flour. Celeste cut off her apology with a hug. Gathering the acorns was just the first step, true, but Molly assured her she'd tossed out any that showed signs of weevils before freezing them.

Celeste was immensely grateful that the black walnuts were shelled. Just peeling the green hulls was a monumental task that, if not done carefully, left your hands tinted black for weeks. Two pounds of shelled and ready-to-use black walnuts were a treasure.

The hazelnuts made Celeste tear up. She and her mother loved their flavor and spent considerable time every fall picking them from the bushes Brenda had planted in their backyard when Celeste was a toddler. It wasn't Christmas without hazelnut ice cream. And that's where the last of Celeste's stash went following the winter solstice dinner.

Her pack-the-pantry party also provided four types of berry and flower vinegars, wild black mustard seed, a small packet of wild caraway seed, and dried cherries from Trudy's trip to her sister's orchard near Traverse City.

Another gift stood out from the others. Celeste felt the fist-sized lump through the gingham gift wrap. She pulled the green grosgrain ribbon, and the cloth fell away to reveal a knobby wild ginger root. Celeste had lived her entire life on Mackinac Island and never found one. But Sonia, who was in her eighties and never left the island, had.

Celeste felt the strong tips of the woman's fingers against her scalp as she drew her close. "I know you'll make good use of it," she whispered. "Ginger root is like a woman," Sonia said louder, straightening to look at the group. "Smooth to the touch. Curved, but with hidden crevices. And fierce to the taste."

A ripple of laughter went around the room. Celeste reddened and set the root in its cloth on the table next to the other gifts.

It was late, and everyone except Aunt Tilda and Sonia had said their goodbyes. Sonia took Celeste by the hand to the screened porch at the back of the house where Celeste and her mother dried the herbs they grew—she for cooking, her mother for soaps, lotions, and scented oils.

"I have one more gift for you," Sonia said, leaning in close, wisps of her white hair framing her face. Her breath smelled of wine and fresh basil leaves. She'd started chewing them when she quit smoking to become a midwife. Tobacco breath just wasn't helpful when reminding a woman in labor of breathing techniques, she'd explained. Celeste's mother heartily agreed. Sonia had been the midwife at Celeste's birth.

The old woman pulled a tall, narrow jar out of the pocket of her skirt. The industrial stamped lid declared the contents to be gherkins, but as Sonia held it up to the glow cast by white stringed lights, Celeste saw a dozen or so small, peach-colored berries floating in clear liquid.

The jar held summer glory, almost glowing in the soft light.

"Cloudberries." Celeste breathed the words.

They were rare this far south. Unlike blackberries and raspberries, a single berry grew on each branch, held aloft on a crown of leaves. You didn't gather cloudberries by the fistful and dribble them into your mouth to stain your lips and tongue like you did other wild fruit harvests. Cloudberries were to be cherished, one at a time.

"My special gift to you," Sonia said, offering her the jar. "My grandniece found them near Marquette. They're in ice wine. Keep the jar refrigerated. She gave them to me for my birthday, but when I told her about your dinner, she agreed you should have them." Sonia leaned in. "Though I did eat a few. Who can resist cloudberries?"

---

Icarus loaded everything into his plane, pretending to calculate whether the weight of the large cooler, baskets, and her doodled-pirate suitcase were more than what the plane could carry, deciding they were safe only because he hadn't eaten a big lunch. Celeste hadn't planned her menu yet, so she brought everything.

The next day was the start of April. The main kitchen of the Forager Chefs Club was hers to commandeer, Elena told her upon her arrival.

Celeste reacquainted herself with the kitchen, unloading the cooler and baskets. She put the precious jar of cloudberries in the refrigerator.

She went to the smaller adjunct kitchen on the far side of the building that everyone used for their daily meals. That refrigerator had a wide range of ingredients. She pulled out a glass bottle of milk. It was the vintage half-gallon style becoming increasingly popular. She carried it to Elena's desk outside the common room.

Elena wasn't there.

Celeste cradled the milk bottle as she roamed the floor in search of the manager, reacquainting herself with several rooms and alcoves.

She noticed a framed pen-and-ink drawing she would revisit later. When she retraced her steps, she found Elena at her desk.

"How can I help?" Elena said, setting down her pencil on the open ledger in front of her.

"Are perishables delivered regularly?" asked Celeste. "Is there a list of nearby resources? If I want something in particular—something that can't be foraged, I mean—do I request it?"

"Request it?"

"Where do I get local butter? Cheese? And milk." She held up the bottle. "This milk is going to be sour by my competition dinner."

"It's going to be sour long before that if you don't get it back in the fridge sometime soon."

Celeste flushed. "I brought it with me because I wanted to ask you about the address on the label." She leaned in, pointing at tiny green print near the bottom of the bottle. "I don't know this part of Michigan. How far away is this dairy? Do they deliver?"

Elena folded her hands on top of the ledger, blocking the entries and notations from view. "Celeste, this is the Forager Chefs Club. There are lots of ways to forage. Waiting around in hopes of a delivery isn't one of them. At least not here."

Celeste looked again at the label.

"Okay," she said. "So where is Kalkaska, and how do I get there?"

"It's about an hour northeast of us. Can I offer you some advice? You have some exploring to do, Celeste. There are significant resources here on the property and not too far afield for one with the heart of a forager. You left us rather abruptly last month, remember? I'm afraid it may have put you at a disadvantage, particularly since you have the first competition month."

*Which is why I left,* Celeste thought but didn't say. This Elena seemed very different from the one who had laughingly helped her get settled in the kitchen hours before.

"Then I better get going," said Celeste. She went to put the milk bottle back.

Closing the refrigerator, she saw Elena leaning in the doorway, arms crossed.

"You'll want to check out the Gourmet Bait Shop," she said.

"The bait shop. Seriously?"

"The *Gourmet* Bait Shop. It's between here and Bear Lake. There's a pickup truck you can borrow in the barn down the hill. Keys are in the ignition. You can drive a stick, right?"

"I can drive a bicycle, horse cart, and snowmobile. I don't have a driver's license."

Elena's eyebrows went up.

"I live on an island that doesn't allow cars." *Remember? You have a file on me; you and Randall know all about me. Why would you think I can drive a pickup truck?*

"Ah, yes." Elena pursed her lips and tapped them with a manicured forefinger, still leaning against the doorway.

"Do you have a bicycle I can use?"

Three more lip taps.

"That's a good question." Elena looked thoughtful. "I have some foraging of my own to do."

And she was gone.

*Great*, Celeste thought. She opened the refrigerator door again, grabbed the milk bottle by the neck, and took a swig before putting it back. Shutting the door, she saw a different figure in the doorway.

"I've got a car," said Blaise. "I could take you."

Celeste sat in the passenger seat of Blaise's black Audi. Blaise didn't talk or turn on the radio. That suited Celeste. Turning onto the paved two-lane road, Celeste lowered the window, leaned her face toward the opening, and closed her eyes. She liked the feel of the accelerated spring breeze rushing against her skin, skimming the cup of her ear, riffling her short red hair, tickling her scalp. It reminded her of riding downhill on her bike along a winding, narrow, blacktop road of Mackinac Island, descending from the high interior to the shore of the straits. Except she wasn't about to hang her head all the way out the window like a dog, so she only felt the wind on one side, and Blaise's car was a lot faster than her bike. She never closed her eyes when riding her bike because she didn't have a death wish to find herself sprawled against the front end—or worse, the back end—of a Percheron. Still, it reminded her. And that gave her a warm feeling, even if being in Blaise's car or thinking about his offer to give her a ride didn't.

Following Elena's directions, it didn't take long to get there. Blaise sighed loudly, exasperated, and muttered under his breath—his first vocalization of the trip—when he saw the Gourmet Bait Shop. Celeste's spirits rose. This was her kind of place.

It was clear there had once been an ampersand inserted in the space between the "Gourmet" and "Bait" red lettering on the side of the building. A shadow of glue residue was still there for anyone who cared to notice. The one-story, white clapboard building was long and low. A covered porch ran the length of the front, supported by red, turned-wood columns that had been painted and repainted and painted yet again over the years. A red, rust-spattered metal roof provided dubious protection from the elements.

There was a commercial freezer on the far end of the porch emitting a steady hum, its blue "ICE" lettering faded and its metal door held shut by an unlocked padlock looped through a thick clasp. Next to an old church pew of dark wood were banded bundles of split firewood, labeled five dollars each. On the pew, a hand-lettered sign on heavy cardboard let customers know that firewood was also available by the cord: quarter, half, and full (delivery extra, stacking extra-extra). The sign was splotched and faded, a veteran of many seasons. Celeste liked it. It reminded her of home.

Blaise walked past her into the store. Celeste shrugged. Okay, you couldn't eat wood. She could appreciate his focus.

True to its name, immediately to the left of the entrance was a glass-doored refrigerator filled with different kinds of bait. White cylinder cardboard containers of varying sizes were labeled as worms, leeches, minnows, crayfish, crickets, or grasshoppers. The lids were clear. Celeste shuddered and refrained from closer inspection.

"Looks like Chinese takeout," said Blaise, passing her. He threw up his hands in mock defense at the look she threw him. "Kidding! Just kidding," he said. "Same kind of containers. You don't do a whole lot of takeout on that island of yours, do you?"

Celeste walked away, angry that she didn't have a good retort. Eden was likely right: Blaise showed strong signs of being an asshole. And here she was, stuck with him. She glanced at her phone. Two bars. Did they have Uber out here? Why the hell did she bother to keep this thing charged? She should just embrace a totally off-grid lifestyle.

There were a lot of aisles in the close confines of the Gourmet Bait Shop. It didn't take many steps to put some distance between her and Blaise. Celeste slowed and reminded herself that she was foraging. Elena had said this was a good place to start.

Wandering the aisles of wooden shelves in the opposite direction of Blaise, Celeste came to a heavy door, closed to the late March breeze. Movement caught her eye, and she peered through its window.

The backyard of the store was a chicken yard, enclosed with tall seven-foot posts supporting strong horse fencing. Crisscrossed in a grid across the top of the yard was clothesline, flashy hawk-deterrent tape tied at most of the intersections. The tape flapped in the breeze in a kaleidoscope of color. Nearly two dozen chickens of various breeds scratched the bare dirt or perched on large, splayed branches set in the yard. In front of a coop painted a lively green with white trim, four chickens perched on a weathered porch swing hanging from the sturdy branch of an overhanging cherry tree. The swing was hydrangea blue, and the words "Chickens Only Please" were stenciled on it in white. Under a wide overhang on one side of the coop, Celeste saw the ampersand that had once adorned the side of the building. It was metal, about eighteen inches wide and half as long, its red paint faded. Turned upside down, it served as a receptacle for chicken feed. Celeste smiled and continued down the store aisle.

She opened a cooler door and picked up a glass bottle of milk, kin to the one she'd held at the Club. Neatly stacked on the shelves along with the milk were blocks of butter, containers of yogurt and sour cream, smaller bottles of light and heavy cream, and buttermilk. The labels varied, but everything in that cooler came from a local farm.

*Well, not always a farm*, she conceded, noting the large red ampersand featured on the pressed cardboard egg cartons. She selected one, a bottle of heavy cream, and a block of butter. Walking to the front, Celeste's eyes continued to scan the shelves, cataloging. She nearly bumped into Blaise as she rounded a corner.

"Can you believe this place?" he said. He sounded sincere, not at all the haughty and oblivious guy who made snide remarks. "Need some help with those?" Blaise asked.

She nodded at his first question and opened her mouth to say no to the second, but he reached for the cream, precarious in her arms after she'd added a jar of pickled white asparagus.

"They have three types of flour, grown and milled locally. Did you see the cheeses?"

Celeste admitted she hadn't.

"The wine selection is for shit, but the beer isn't bad, and they have ciders and even some mead. I've got my usual sources, but this place is convenient in a pinch."

Along with Celeste's cream and asparagus, Blaise set a bottle of mead, a buxom woman drawn on the label, on the front counter. The woman standing behind the counter could have been a somewhat older model for the label, except she wore a Bob Seger T-shirt, and her graying brunette hair was in a braid that went halfway down her back.

"I love your store," Celeste said, separating her selected items from Blaise's mead on the scarred wood.

The shopkeeper smiled. "Thank you so much. It's actually my uncle's store, but I've been running it for him for the last few years." Her smile became fixed as she looked at Blaise. She reached for the bottle of mead. "That it for you?"

Celeste noticed a *John 2:9-10* tattoo on the underside of the shopkeeper's left forearm.

"That'll do it for today," said Blaise. "Celeste is right—great store."

"Except for the wine," said the shopkeeper, putting the mead in a brown paper bag and setting it in front of him. "Will that be cash or credit card?"

"We're with the Forager Chefs Club," said Blaise, ignoring the barb. "Is there an account?"

Celeste glanced between them. Her mom and Aunt Tilda had each given her some money, and she'd brought some of her own.

The shopkeeper paused. "You're in the competition?"

Blaise nodded. So did Celeste.

The shopkeeper pulled a clipboard out from under the counter, flipped a couple of pages, looked at Blaise, and seemed to consider. "Can I see some ID?" she asked.

Blaise pulled his wallet out from his back pocket and fished out his driver's license. Celeste flushed. She'd left her state ID in her room. The woman took Blaise's driver's license, looked at it, and handed it back. She flipped the clipboard around and had Blaise sign on a lined sheet of paper. He picked up his bagged purchase and headed to the door.

"Meet you at my car," he called over his shoulder.

Celeste's face reddened as she gathered her items to return them to their places. She didn't want to spend money if she didn't have to. "I'm sorry. I don't have my ID with me. I'll come back when I do."

The shopkeeper picked up the bottle of heavy cream before Celeste could add it to her arms.

"No need. I know who you are." Her mouth quirked. "The whole account thing was arranged last month. Elena called a bit ago to say the two of you were on your way. You're the first of the five competitors to visit." She saw Celeste's eyes dart to the door through which Blaise had exited and shrugged. "You make disrespectful comments about my uncle's store in my hearing, I give you shit. It's what makes the world go 'round."

Celeste set the butter and eggs back down on the counter, feeling yet again at home.

The woman made notes on a pad and put Celeste's purchases in a paper bag. "Don't you start out daunted," she said as she wrote and packed. "You'll never get anywhere in the world if you let yourself be daunted." She finished packing, slid the bag across the counter, and held out her hand. "I'm Annie, by the way."

# Blaise

Blaise had explained to his twin brother that they were going out of the city for a few weeks—probably twenty-one days, but maybe longer. It would be colder than in Grand Rapids, particularly in the evenings and overnight. It was likely to rain, and there would be mud. He should bring his boots. And multiple pairs of socks. He could bring as many clothes and books as he wanted because he would have his own room with plenty of space to arrange everything just as he liked. He would have his own bathroom, so no one would bother his toothbrush or razor.

Bradley looked straight ahead the entire drive, not speaking. As was their routine, Blaise made sure the gas tank was full before they left and didn't stop along the way. He didn't turn on the radio and kept his phone on vibrate.

The routine left a lot of space for Blaise's thoughts.

He wanted to focus on the competition, put in order his ideas for his September menu and how he'd leverage time at the Club to his best advantage, but his thoughts drifted to his parents. He wondered—for the umpteenth time—if his mother found more fulfillment raising another man's daughters in a Chicago high-rise than she'd apparently found raising her own sons. He wondered if his father had yet had a heart attack on the golf course of the country club he'd joined after remarrying and moving to Nashville. It was, admittedly, one of Blaise's favorite recurring daydreams.

Pulling up in front of the Club, Blaise disciplined his thoughts away from his parents and to the task at hand.

First, get Bradley settled. He could have left him in Grand Rapids on his own, but—the conversation with Randall notwithstanding—Blaise thought Bradley might give him an edge. His brother would need to feel comfortable in his surroundings, though, to be of any help. That would take time.

Blaise unpacked his suitcase and arranged his toiletries in the bathroom. Bradley's room was right across the hall. He doubted Randall or Elena had planned it, but the view from Bradley's room was perfect. It didn't look out on the dirt-and-gravel lane that led back to the familiarity of Grand Rapids. Instead, the view was the back lawn that bordered the forest of the Club's acreage. Blaise had casually pointed out a trailhead between the trees. He needed Bradley curious to explore that acreage devoid of people.

It was unlikely his brother would come out of his room for the next day or so, but that was okay. The windows were there with their view. Blaise would bring him his meals and cook things for him that were familiar.

He would invest the time and whatever else was needed. He would forgo the income he would make cooking for private dinner parties in Grand Rapids. Fifty thousand dollars and the recognition he was due were on the line.

# *APRIL*

# Celeste

They'd delivered her bicycle. She'd come downstairs to get a cup of coffee, a growing list in her head of things to find, things to prep, when Elena, sitting at her desk, remarked casually that there was a delivery for Celeste on the front porch.

Celeste didn't know who Elena had called or how it had been arranged, but she was grateful. It was robin's-egg blue and chrome, complete with its roomy woven basket and two heavy canvas panniers. She'd spent all her high school graduation money getting it professionally repainted when she got the job at the Grand Hotel, determined not to look shabby when arriving for work.

Since her bike's arrival, she'd made several trips back to the Gourmet Bait Shop, spending time with Annie to learn about additional resources nearby. She didn't want her foraging to simply consist of exploring a store's shelves, regardless of how unique and marvelous that store may be.

Evenings and days too drenching for outdoor exploration were spent in her room at the Forager Chefs Club or in one nook or another, windows open to the sound of the rain and the fecund scent of field and forest, pouring over the decorative border of her month assignment—what her mother had called a "treasure map"—and comparing it to the detailed pen-and-ink drawing she'd found in one of the rooms that looked out on the entrance garden. That garden had come to life in the weeks she'd been here. First, the hellebore blossoms, crocuses, and snowdrops had emerged, then daffodils, their fragrance light but discernible. In the past couple of days, grape hyacinth had bloomed. Sharp, broad green blades and softer, thinner ones poking through the rich soil were the promise of iris, both bearded and Siberian. Celeste wouldn't see those in bloom—even with the gentle, early spring that had come, it would be weeks before they would be in their glory and Mackinac's Grand Hotel opened in May—but she remembered her arrival at the Forager Chefs Club back in February, imagining this very garden bright with the color and texture of irises. Celeste had been surprised not to see any cupped leaves denoting tulips breaching the soft earth but then noticed deer prints among the beds. Tulips never lasted long where deer roamed.

Comparing her treasure map with the drawing she'd liberated and brought to her room—it was April, after all, her month of license for all types of foraging—and then spending hours exploring the Club grounds, Celeste had located quite a few useful landmarks, including a group of beehives. Finding the beekeeper who tended them had taken a bit more work, but she'd had a wonderful afternoon talking with the man who had been tending honeybees for more than forty years and his apprentice grandson. She'd left with two jars of honey, some honeycomb, and a tiny container of bee pollen.

Her latest visit with Annie had Celeste and her bicycle farther afield than she'd ever been. She followed Annie's handwritten directions to Briar Patch Farm, which was two barns down from the turn where the church used to be.

"Trust me. You'll know it when you see it," Annie had said when Celeste asked how she was supposed to use something that was no longer there as a landmark.

Given the reliability of cell service, Celeste figured it was just as well she didn't count on any sort of GPS.

And she did know it when she saw it.

The clapboard church's white paint was faded, chipped, or peeled away, and its shingles were awry or missing. Grasses and weedy sumac trees nearly blocked the building from view. Ivy had a good start taking over one side, and tendrils reaching around the southwest corner announced expansion intentions. Interestingly, the windows were intact. They weren't fancy, but it was nice to know that the people who lived here weren't the kind to break church windows. Annie had said that the congregation had dwindled as children grew up and moved away, and people aged and died. When repairs to the building became too much, the congregation that was left had joined another church. That had been nearly twenty years ago. There were plans to do something with the building, but time had moved on.

Celeste had never attended a church, but seeing this one pulled at something in her. If God lived in churches, what must He be thinking of the state of His home?

As she bicycled past the dilapidated building, Celeste saw a small yard to the side, bordered by decorative wrought iron sections about three feet high, each mostly rusted to a rich, deep orange hue. Inside, the spring grass was trimmed, and bunches of small-blossom jonquils bloomed. Rising from the grass in somewhat regimented rows were headstones—some straight, some slightly askew—perhaps twenty-five or so.

That care—even though those under the stones would never know of it—made Celeste feel better as she pedaled on, seeing in the distance the first of the two barns that marked her destination.

A few yards up the long dirt driveway, Celeste gave up trying to pedal, got off, and walked her bike, her boots squelching in the mud. A wiry woman came out from behind a barn, leaning a bit to one side from the weight of the large, dented bucket she carried. Seeing Celeste, she set the bucket down. She was of middle height and looked like she had spent her entire life outdoors and hadn't worn sunscreen a day of it. She could have been fifty or seventy years old. She wore faded jeans tucked into tall, dark-green muck boots, and her red plaid flannel shirt was rolled up at the sleeves and hung open, a T-shirt advertising a band Celeste had never heard of underneath. Long wisps of hair that were either blond or gray escaped the wide-brimmed hat clamped down on her head.

The woman watched Celeste approach.

Celeste pushed out the kickstand of her bike before turning to introduce herself and explain the reason for her visit.

"You're one of those forager chefs," the woman said.

"I'm not a Club member," said Celeste. "I do forage, back home. And I cook what I forage. I work in a hotel kitchen. But I'm not really a chef." She glanced back at her bike to make sure the kickstand wasn't sinking into the mud. "I'm not even sure why I'm here." From somewhere behind the barn, she heard the squeal of a pig. "I mean, I know why I'm *here* here," Celeste said, indicating the muddy earth at her feet. She then spread out her arms. "I'm just not sure why I'm here." Two ducks wandered out of the barn. The first one poked its head into the bucket, then walked away, disinterested. The other duck followed it. "I mean, I'm here for the competition," said Celeste. "Maybe you heard about it? I was invited. They gave me a room at the Club and everything. And it's really nice. Everyone has been really nice. Well, pretty much everyone. Most of the time. I just wonder sometimes if they made a mistake since I'm not really a chef. But I do forage and cook, so . . ."

The wiry woman reached down and picked up her bucket.

Celeste stuck out her hand.

"You can call me Celly."

Celeste left Briar Patch Farm with a small sack of potatoes, several turnips, two celeriac bulbs, and a thick bundle of carrots that were only a little bit hoary in her bicycle basket. These had come from the farm's root cellar, dug into a hillside with a thick wooden door of indeterminate age and a doorway so short that Celeste had to duck to enter. She also had two stewing chickens packed in plastic bags with ice, one in each of her bicycle's panniers.

The woman waved away payment. "Annie vouched for you. I'll

settle it with her," she had said.

She had never offered her name, and Celeste felt it would be an imposition to ask while tromping all over the woman's farm. She seemed to take it as a given that anyone who found her farm knew who she was.

Celeste walked her bike down the farm's muddy driveway to the blacktop road. Pointing it back in the direction she'd come, she climbed on the seat and started to pedal.

Celeste was nervous. She felt twitchy. This irritated her because the forest was where she always went as a remedy for nervousness, twitchiness. Like when pretty much everyone yelled at her that first month in the Grand Hotel kitchen—okay, well, maybe *yell* was a strong word, but you *could* yell without raising your voice. She'd often wondered in those early weeks why the hell she'd let Aunt Tilda talk her into taking the job. She could have been delivering UPS packages, except she wouldn't have shooed away kids who were daring enough to hop a ride on the back of her wagon; she'd have just pretended not to see them, maybe winked at them as she picked up one box or another to take into its destination, and her colleagues would have been two Percherons, which was preferable, frankly, to people in high-stress kitchens. When she wasn't in the kitchen, Celeste had escaped to the fields and forest of her island. And it had been medicine, walking among the trees, eyes keen for edibles to bring home to preserve or make into a meal for her and Mom, thoughts far from the wants and needs of hundreds—no, thousands!—of tourists hungry for food for their stomachs and Instagram accounts.

Here she was now, on acres of forest and field at the Forager Chefs Club. Birds flitted and filled the air with sound, intent on nest-building and mate-wooing. The light spring breeze barely touched Celeste, but far above her, new leaves rustled as they tasted the air coming off Lake Michigan. Red squirrels ran energetic forays among last fall's leaves, sometimes taking a clutch in their mouths to carry up a trunk to cushion nests high in the trees. She couldn't see them, but Celeste imagined the extended population in the woods: deer, raccoon, fox, rabbit. *What else?*

All this was exclusively hers for the foraging, if only for this one month, April.

It was a treasure.

And yet here she was. Nervous. Twitchy.

What. The. Hell.

She needed to forage ramps from the patch she saw sprouting earlier in the month. And wood sorrel. She needed to find wood sorrel. Tomorrow was the last Saturday in April. Tomorrow was her competition dinner.

Celeste's stomach lurched at the thought. She stopped, leaned one arm against a tree, fingernails digging into the rough bark, braced her legs, and waited.

She didn't throw up.

Damn.

Celeste closed her eyes, turned to put her back against the tree, and slid down to the forest floor. Just a few minutes—that's all she needed. A few minutes to center herself. To think about her island, to draw strength from it, even with it so far away. Instead, she got a picture in her mind's eye of her mother using a familiar long-handled, broad wooden spoon to stir a clump of wool in a dark-green dye in the huge copper pot that had been a fixture on their small kitchen stove for as long as Celeste could remember.

*Never let challenges daunt you. Focus on what you believe, what gives you strength. Draw from it. Draw deep. Rally what you know to be true—your experiences, the relationships you've built—and make those your armor—your weapon, if you need one. Think about how you will enlist all those things to help you move forward on the path you've chosen. Don't ever, ever let anyone or anything daunt you.*

Daunt. Who talked like that? Who used *daunt* as a verb?

Her mom, that's who. And Mom *had* used that word. After hearing Aunt Tilda's story—her confession, really—her mom's words had an even deeper meaning.

Someone else had used the word "daunt" in advice to her recently. Where? Who? Oh, right. Annie at the Gourmet Bait Shop that first time they'd met.

Celeste stood up. The hell with nervous and twitchy.

She looked around, orienting herself. There was the deer trail, almost invisible if you weren't looking for it. She hitched her canvas gathering sack over her shoulder and checked the foraging knife tucked in her belt.

"Time to gather the ramps," she said to a squirrel that had paused in its own task to regard her. The squirrel looked at her for another moment and then continued up the trunk of a large maple tree.

Following the deer trail, Celeste went over the positives: the list of things that were completed and ready for her competition dinner tomorrow night. There were a lot of positives. She'd finalized her menu yesterday, after she was sure she'd get her hands on all the ingredients. Or as sure as she could be. Elena had said she'd type it up and print it out for the judges.

She had almost all the ingredients on that menu. She'd foraged morel mushrooms over the past few days, spending what seemed like hours bent at the waist, stepping carefully, pushing aside last year's leaves with a walking stick, delighted when she found a grouping of three or four. It was because of the morels that she was a tad late in giving Elena the menu. She'd had to be sure she could find enough before including them.

It had taken her three days, a couple of hours being completely lost on two of those days, and nearly abandoning her left boot in riverbank muck before she'd found the wild asparagus she sought. But she *did* find it. Annie had laughed when Celeste related her tale, then pointed to a basket of spears harvested that morning from a neighboring property. Celeste laughed with her. But she was glad she spent that time foraging the asparagus for her dinner on her own. And she suspected Annie respected her for it too.

The fiddleheads had been a bit easier. Her map had a drawing of fern fronds near a bend in the river that marked the western boundary of the Club's property. Celeste found the spot earlier in the month and confirmed from the U-shaped stems of last year's fallen fronds that these were the right species, the edible ostrich ferns. It had been a waiting game to see if the weather would cooperate—stay mild enough for the roots to send out their tightly wound tendrils wrapped in their brown papery wrappings in time for her dinner. It had, and they did. She'd collected what she needed, careful to snap off no more than half from any one crown.

Foraging ramps and wood sorrel were the tasks for today. The fresh fish was the only true question mark and out of her control, but she had a plan and a backup plan and a backup plan to the backup plan. She wanted lake trout—had put it on the menu—but could make do with perch if she had to. If everything went to hell in a handbasket, Annie had local trout in her freezer and had set aside enough if Celeste had to call in plan C. She'd already made stock from the Briar Patch Farm chickens. The Club had an excellent dehydrator, and she'd make good use of it—her salted dandelion petals were done, as were her sugared redbud blossoms and wild violet petals. She'd arranged with Annie for the delivery of eggs, cheese, and heavy cream the morning of her dinner. On that trip, she'd found nettles in the field behind the chicken yard and carefully harvested what she needed after confirming with Annie that she didn't use any pesticides. Celeste had made her own cornstarch for the pavlova—Michigan grew corn, lots of it—since she hadn't found a source of ready-made cornstarch actually produced in Michigan. It wasn't that hard, just time-consuming. Celeste was determined not to use any of her three available "exceptions." She needed any edge she could get.

Ramps were an edge, she hoped.

Then again, who knew what the judges were looking for? And who were they, anyway, these judges? She thought of the faces on cookbook jackets and restaurant reviews in newspapers and magazines. Would the judges come from among that august group? Who the hell were the members of the Forager Chefs Club? She'd searched, but she'd not found a clue in the nooks and rooms of the Club. Thinking about it, Celeste felt a bile of panic rise again in her throat, and she forced herself to swallow it. She paused on the deer trail to pull out her water bottle. She took a long pull.

*Don't be daunted*, she reminded herself. *Focus.*

She put the water bottle back. Ramps. She was in the woods to forage ramps.

She liked ramps well enough. They were the first pungent spring edible to be found in the forest—a wild leek with a taste that was a cross between garlic and onion—and so brought fresh flavor to a diet that was historically largely game and whatever was left in the root cellar by this time of year. But that wasn't why Celeste had spent so much time locating them for her competition dinner. Ramps had become trendy. She'd seen them featured in cooking magazines she'd leaf through (but not buy; who had money for that?), and she made side income in the spring harvesting ramps for some of the small, upper-end restaurants. But trendy could also be destructive. Ramps weren't prolific on the island, and she'd been taught to be careful, never to harvest too many, never ever pull up the entire plant, take only the leaves sometimes, and, at most, use her sharp knife to slice through the bulb below the earth's surface, leaving half the bulb and its root intact to grow and propagate. Trendy, she'd learned, could be the death of a micro-ecosystem.

Celeste knew where to harvest ramps at the Forager Chefs Club—she'd identified a patch earlier in the month, shoots coming up through the earth not too far from where she'd later harvested morel mushrooms. She'd collect the ramps she needed and then go a different route to a meadow she'd located on the map. Hopefully, there, she'd find wood sorrel—it was a fairly common plant that she just hadn't stumbled on yet here—but it was early in the year. Wood sorrel, looking almost like clover but with tiny yellow blossoms, would give her salad dressing the subtle lemony tang she wanted.

Celeste's steps slowed as she approached the patch where, after hours upon hours of searching, she'd found ramps.

There was someone there.

And that someone was digging up her ramps.

He was on his haunches, turned mostly away from her, but she recognized the wide-set shoulders, the strong profile of his face, and the thick, black hair.

Blaise.

Celeste felt disbelief, followed by a surge of anger. *That one is an asshole,* Eden had remarked to her that first evening when Blaise had taunted Christian because of his job driving a salt truck in the winter. She'd been cautious of Blaise but then thought maybe Eden was wrong when he'd given her a ride to the Gourmet Bait Shop. And then he'd made his asinine comment about Chinese takeout when he saw the white cartons of fish bait in the coolers.

Blaise was staying at the Club. Celeste noticed him from time to time, though they rarely spoke. She didn't know why he was there—Blaise's competition dinner wasn't until September. But he, like she, were the guests of the Forager Chefs Club this entire year, able to come and go as they liked, for whatever length of time they liked. Celeste had been doing her best to give Blaise the benefit of the doubt.

But this, *this,* crossed the line.

"You can't be here," she called out. She hoped her voice sounded strong and stern.

Blaise ignored her.

"I mean, you can be here, but you can't forage."

As soon as the words left her mouth, Celeste wished she could pull them back. There could be no room for negotiation in this. Her dinner was tomorrow night. She had no time to find another patch of ramps—if there even was one. And she shouldn't have to. "It's April. April is mine."

Blaise stood up and turned to her but didn't look directly at her. Celeste looked at his cloth bag in one hand, the lower third clearly full, a sharp foraging knife in his other hand. Celeste lifted her head, willing herself to show no uncertainty, no fear of a man with a knife in the woods out of earshot of anyone. She didn't think he'd use his knife or physical strength against her. She could be wrong in that assessment. Her mom had been wrong once, back when Celeste was fifteen. It had been just the two of them—Celeste and her mom—since then. *So weird how the brain works. So many thoughts in such a short span of time*, Celeste thought, with ambitious Blaise standing a few yards away, his face betraying no emotion, holding a knife, in violation of a rule that could get him kicked out of a competition worth fifty thousand dollars.

She drew a deep breath, the way she had when the man who was supposed to be her mom's "guest" for the summer had climbed into Celeste's bed with whispers and groping hands. She'd come out of sleep abruptly, feeling him crawling on top of her, shoving one knee between her legs, his breath hot against her skin.

She'd tried to push him off, but he was heavy, so heavy. She'd tried to scream, but he'd put his large, tanned hand over her mouth, murmuring to her: this was good, it was good, it would all be good. Celeste had reached out, grasping, flailing, managing to reach her foraging knife on her bedside table. She hadn't remembered why she'd left it there but was glad she had.

She'd grasped it as a lifeline. Lifted it high. Stabbed it into his shoulder. Felt it sink into meat, then hit something hard and skitter a bit to one side. There had been a roar, then yelling, screaming—his voice, then her mother's. But the pressure of his knee trying to push her legs apart had been gone.

Celeste drew a deep breath and forced her mind to put the memory aside. This was not the same. She was standing, alert, and in control.

She held a knife. That part was the same.

Whatever Blaise had found, whatever he'd foraged, was hers to find, hers to forage. It was April.

*He won't use physical force against me*, she told herself again. She had her knife or could run away if she was wrong. She suspected Blaise preferred other weapons. Celeste braced herself for the curled lip, the snide remark that always seemed to come so easily to him. She knew how his look, his words, his disdain, could cut.

Instead, he didn't respond to her challenge. He didn't seem to want to meet her eyes. That gave her confidence. Celeste spread her feet apart and crossed her arms while keeping a grip on her knife. Why was he acting so different? Guilt? She didn't know Blaise well, but from their interactions, guilt hadn't seemed to be in his repertoire. He was also dressed unexpectedly. More relaxed—faded jeans that were a little baggy, a long-sleeved waffle-woven shirt that was misshapen from many, many launderings, and worn hiking boots. His bag was cotton with handles, the logo of a Grand Rapids bookstore emblazoned on the front.

Not exactly the catalog-perfect picture she'd come to associate with Blaise. But this was the woods, and they were foraging. Or—Celeste corrected herself—*she* was foraging. He was trespassing.

"Well?" she said.

He shuffled his feet and looked up toward the treetops. She resisted the urge to follow his gaze. After a few moments of silence, he took a few steps toward her, halving the distance between them. She uncrossed her arms but waited. Willed herself not to step backward.

He held the cloth bag out to her.

After a moment, she stepped forward and took it. Her hand grazed his, and his head turned, his green eyes meeting hers briefly. Then he moved past her and walked away, his empty arms swinging at his side, going back the way she had come. His steps were quiet on the soft leaves and loam. She watched him until he disappeared over a small rise that she knew would take him down to the stream and back along a path to the Club. He never looked back.

She opened the bag. Ramps, expertly sliced through the bulb that would have left the root intact in the soil, the foraged food an ombre of color: rich green from the tops of the broad, flat stems to white at the bottom of the firm bulbs.

She looked again at the path Blaise had taken. Why had he been foraging here, in April, when he knew, *he knew*, it was against the rules? She could raise a fuss about it—possibly get him kicked out of the competition. If she'd been only twenty minutes later in arriving, finding this patch already foraged, would she have then denuded it just for one dinner? She put that thought aside. Instead, she focused on what it meant to have found Blaise here. Did he think she was that much of a threat that he needed to sabotage her? Celeste shook her head. That didn't make any sense. Blaise was a well-known chef, at least around Grand Rapids. People sought him out. But still . . .

Celeste looked again in the bag, then back at the cluster of ramp plants that remained. Blaise had foraged well: ethically and sustainably. Not too much from any one spot, not disturbing the earth any more than necessary. From what he'd foraged, she probably had enough ramps for her dinner. She counted again. Well, close to enough. And this was *her* foraging dinner. She set down the cloth book bag and her sturdier oiled canvas bag and knelt to forage a few more ramps, enjoying the feel of her fingers in the soft earth, mindful of the gift it was giving her.

# PERSEPHONE'S RETURN DINNER

AMUSE BOUCHE:
Under the Earth Vichyssoise
*Potatoes, root vegetables, crisped nettles*

FIRST COURSE:
Emerging from Below Flatbread
*Crisp flatbread with fried morels, black mustard seed paste, goat cheese, ramps, and salted dandelion petals*

SECOND COURSE:
The Return of Spring
*Pan-seared trout with ginger root shavings and toasted hazelnuts
Wild asparagus and fiddlehead ferns with wood sorrel dressing*

THIRD COURSE:
Demeter's Joy
*Pavlova topped with sugared violets, redbud blossoms, ice wine cloudberry, bee pollen, and honeycomb*

# Celeste

Celeste lifted a tasting spoon to her lips, let the soup rest on her tongue for a moment, then pressed it against the roof of her mouth. The potato had little taste, was there to give body, and was just as she wanted: smooth, creamy. The puréed root vegetables—turnip, celeriac, carrot—carried the flavor, along with the chicken stock she'd made, simmering, straining, and skimming for two days until it had been reduced to culinary liquid gold. The result was rich with layers of flavor.

It was a Vichyssoise soup, served cold. For the story of her dinner, Persephone's Return, this was her take on coming up from below the earth, rising to the surface, still cold from the winter that represented the mourning of the goddess Demeter, Persephone's mother. Hades, forced to release his kidnapped prize, if only for a while. And to accentuate what he must have felt, Celeste had included nettle in this dish. The leaves, harvested so early in the season, washed and blanched, wouldn't produce the sting and itch an encounter with the plant typically would—but anyone reading the menu would know nettle's reputation. After washing and blanching the nettle leaves, she'd salted them and put them in the dehydrator. They'd come out curled and crisp, the perfect topping for her soup, adding texture and a shadow of color.

Her Under the Earth Vichyssoise was an amuse bouche: a taste, a preamble to the meal, a gift from the chef. She would have it served in the bulbous glasses typically used for digestifs—port, Madeira, and the like—set on small saucers. No spoons.

She had all the dishware she'd use for service stacked and ready on a side table. Randall and Elena had said the Club was hers for the foraging, and she'd taken them at their word. From various cupboards, shelves, a small dirt-floor cellar room under the oldest part of the building, and a treasure trove of dusty attic space in one of the wings, Celeste had collected a menagerie of chargers, plates, glassware, and flatware. Her favorite find was a set of twelve glass-and-metal napkin rings nestled in a hinged box lined with satin. One of the rings had a crack in its glass, but Celeste only needed five. The asymmetry of the mismatched dinnerware would add to the atmosphere she wanted: natural, organic. If she ever had her own restaurant, she'd never have everybody-gets-the-same-thing place settings. And tonight, if only for this one night, the Forager Chefs Club *was* her restaurant.

Celeste looked at the clock. She had hoped the trout would be here by now but had taken a chance in arranging to have today's catch—not yesterday's. And she absolutely didn't want anything frozen. Annie had been skeptical at cutting it so close, reliant on the whims of weather and chance, but helped her get in touch with three different local fishermen. It was trout season. At least one of them was bound to have enough luck to come through.

Right?

Celeste picked up her handwritten list of tasks and timing, going down her checklist. She'd started grinding the wild mustard seed with a mortar and pestle but ended up relying on a food processor to get it fine enough that adding a bit of salted vegetable oil created a paste. The hazelnuts were toasted. The dandelion petals, redbud blossoms, and violets had received their wash of flavored egg whites—salt for the dandelions, sugar for the flowers—and had spent time in the dehydrator. On one of the prep counters, the ginger root was wrapped in its gingham cloth; next to it was the honeycomb and bee pollen.

Everything else—except the trout—was either foraged or delivered from the Gourmet Bait Shop and staged in the refrigerator, including the crowning glory of her pack-the-pantry party: the cloudberries preserved in ice wine. Those would highlight her dessert. Celeste had been checking every day to make sure that precious jar was still there in the back of the Club's main kitchen refrigerator.

Celeste picked up the gingham cloth from the prep counter and unwrapped the ginger root Sonia had given her. She lifted it to her face, closed her eyes, and inhaled deeply through her nose, a moment of respite from the turmoil in her head. Preparing the ginger for its role in her main course would take her mind off waiting for the trout.

She smiled, remembering what Sonia had said at her birthday gathering. *Ginger root is like a woman. Smooth to the touch. Curved, but with hidden angles and crevices. And fierce to the taste.* For some reason, that made Celeste think of her encounter with Blaise the day before. He'd been so different. Maybe because he'd perceived her as fierce? She felt a blush bloom in her cheeks. She picked up a paring knife and then set it down. She pulled out her pocketknife instead. Settling herself on a tall stool next to the butcher block, Celeste went about the task of peeling the ginger and slicing it into wafer-thin shavings with a practiced hand.

A woman who looked to be about her age arrived at the kitchen door twenty minutes later. She wore faded jeans, a T-shirt from a Billy Joel concert before either of them was born, and an optimistic smile.

"I have your trout," she said cheerily. "Is there someone who can help me bring the cooler in?"

They lugged it in together from the back of her dad's pickup truck, Celeste learning along the way that the woman's name was Jo—short for Josephine, not Jolene, no offense, she said, to Dolly Parton—and that the trout had been caught by her uncle and older brother on Lake Michigan that morning. Apparently, Annie had done her own outreach regarding the fishermen Celeste had contacted.

"My grandaunt Christine was Annie's Girl Scout troop leader

the year Annie sold more boxes of cookies than anyone on this side of the state. Annie's kind of a legend around here when it comes to getting things done. So when she let Grandaunt Christine know that she really, really wanted you to have enough lake trout for this dinner of yours—and caught on the very morning of the dinner!—well, Grandaunt Christine told her son, my uncle Vic, so he and my older brother Evan were out on the water extra early today to do what they could to get you what you need. Plus, the weather cooperated," Jo added pragmatically as she fetched a garment bag from the truck cab. "I suspect Annie sweet-talked Mother Nature somewhere along the way too. April weather can be iffy for fishing." Jo headed down the hall to the bathroom, clearly familiar with the way. "You made a good friend when you made friends with Annie Tate. Be right back."

Celeste was well into filleting the fish when Jo returned to the kitchen, her long brunette hair pulled back from her face and confined into a messy bun on the top of her head, dressed in black pants and a white collared shirt, wrapping the long ties of a white apron around her trim waist.

"So, what do you need?" she said.

Celeste paused in her filleting. "Need?"

"Yeah, need."

There was a space of silence as Celeste racked her brain for what Jo could possibly mean. The fish was delivered. That was the last ingredient.

A shy look crossed Jo's face.

"I'm not just here to deliver fish, Celeste. I work special events at the Club. I've been hired by Elena to be one of your two servers tonight. But since there's some time between now and when I need to start serving, I thought I could maybe help here in the kitchen." She lifted one shoulder. "Nothing big, of course—but I could chop vegetables or stuff like that? Unless you'd rather I not? That's okay too. I'm not a professional or anything, just a wannabe cook who watches a lot of Food Network. So I'm okay if you'd rather I just help with service. I know this is a big deal, this competition dinner." Jo shrugged again, working very hard to look nonchalant.

Celeste remembered her first weeks in the kitchen at the Grand Hotel: her failed attempts at finding someone to teach her, to take her under their wing. A restaurant kitchen was competitive, she'd learned. And observation helped only so far. She'd brought her copy of the *Saucier's Apprentice* to the Club.

"I would absolutely love your help getting this dinner ready," she said.

Thirty minutes before service, a young man came into the kitchen. He wore black pants, a white collared shirt, and a lot of freckles.

"Sorry I'm late," he said. "Car trouble."

"As in you couldn't get Tiffany out of it?" Jo said, setting out the amuse-bouche glasses on one of the side counters.

The young man's freckles nearly disappeared into his blush. Celeste busied herself at the sink. She knew what it was like to be a redhead and blush. Your face basically matched your hair, making your head one round, red globe.

"Only thing better than a breakup is the makeup," said Jo in a singsong voice. "Celeste, this is Joe. He's the other server for tonight. Joe, this is Celeste."

Celeste turned from the sink. "You're kidding. Jo and Joe? How are you going to know who I need to do what?"

Joe, his face redder, if that was possible, indicated the back door with a hitchhiker thumb. "Do you want me to leave?"

"No, of course I don't want you to leave. We're serving in thirty"—she looked at her watch—"twenty-five minutes. And that's not even the point." She let out a breath of air. "Do either of you have a nickname?"

Silence.

"I could call you Josephine," Celeste suggested.

Jo looked at the floor. "Sure, Chef," she said.

"Just call me Red," Joe said, a taste of resignation in his tone. "A lot of people do."

Jo hugged him around the neck and whispered something in his ear. He seemed embarrassed but pleased.

Celeste sighed. "Fine," she said. "If that's settled, can we get on with serving dinner?"

"Oh my gosh, Celly, the room looks gorgeous," Jo said. "When did you have time to get all the flowers?"

"Flowers?" asked Celeste,

Jo held out her phone.

Celeste turned, the tasting spoon of wood sorrel dressing just leaving her lips. It was just as she wanted it. She'd have preferred olive oil but was sticking to her guns of not using any of her three exceptions. Instead, she'd found a sunflower oil sourced in Michigan at Annie's Gourmet Bait Shop. Paired with the wild raspberry vinegar from her pack-the-pantry party, handfuls of foraged wood sorrel reduced to a paste in the food processor for a hint of lemon, plus a touch of salt, it had just the taste and consistency she wanted to dress her salad of delicate, steamed wild asparagus mixed with prepared fiddlehead ferns. Cleaned of their papery coverings, thoroughly cooked, then lightly sautéed in butter, the fiddlehead fern heads added a bit of crispiness for texture.

Jo smiled and thrust her phone out.

Never taking her eyes off the image on Jo's phone, Celeste set the spoon aside. She reached for the phone, and Jo gave it to her. Celeste scrolled through several photos and then handed the phone back. "Is there anyone in the dining room?" When Jo shook her head, Celeste left the kitchen through the door leading to the dining room.

The dining room for her competition dinner was alight with the rays of a sunset still more than an hour away. It streamed through the room's one large window of a dozen panes of antique, wavy glass, touching the flames of candles of various colors, sizes, and shapes placed in an asynchronous, almost random, pattern on the oak trestle dining table, the deep built-in shelves, and the two pine sideboards. In juxtaposition to this, three vases were set on the long dining table, none the same but somehow harmonious—like a trio of daughters—each holding a messy but gorgeous array of daffodils, grape hyacinth, crocus, branches of redbud, and newly budded beech leaves.

"There must be nothing left in the front garden," Celeste said, breathing out. She'd had no idea that this was part of what the Club would provide for each competition dinner. *Elena*, Celeste corrected herself, *what Elena would provide*. There was no doubt in her mind that anything provided by "the Club" had Elena and her management skills at its core. Celeste had given her the menu, so Elena must have devised this perfect way to decorate the dining room for the "Persephone's Return" dinner to give it the ideal setting and mood. Of course, Elena would do the same for all the other contestants, but that was fine. Looking around the dining room again—the beauty of the candlelight coming from different levels and angles, how the flowers spoke of April, the asymmetry of it all denoting the natural resurgence of spring—it was what she should have done herself. But she'd been so focused on the meal—on foraging for it—that she'd completely forgotten how important the meal's environment was to the whole experience. But Elena hadn't. And, efficient as always, Elena had created this gorgeous ambiance for Celeste's competition dinner.

She heard footsteps on the pine planks behind her. Celeste turned. It was Elena. A smile bloomed on Celeste's face. She opened her mouth to express her gratitude. She stopped, seeing Elena's expression.

"Wow," said Elena. Her eyes were wide, and she smiled in genuine enjoyment. She nodded as her gaze scanned the room, the lit candles perched in unlikely places, the three overflowing flower vases perfectly spaced on the trestle dining table. "Did you do this yourself or hire someone local?"

Randall came into the kitchen just before the seven o'clock start to remind Celeste that she wasn't to enter the dining room while the judges were present. Jo and Joe weren't to take any photos or relay to Celeste any information about the judges or their reactions. The two of them were here to serve the Club's guests—not play a role in the potential outcome of the competition.

"I'm very serious about keeping a level playing field," Randall said. "And that means no intel regarding who the judges are, their conversations, comments, or reactions going anywhere beyond that dining room."

Celeste immediately thought of Blaise freely roaming the Club grounds. Possibly talking up the judges over cocktails right now. Where was he?

Randall appeared to read her mind. Or, more realistically, Celeste thought, her face.

"I advised Blaise earlier today that he and his brother would need to either spend the evening in their rooms or off property."

*Wait*, thought Celeste. *His brother?*

"Good luck," Randall said, one hand on the swinging door that opened onto the short hallway that led to another door, beyond which was the dining room with five people who could change Celeste's life.

The dinner itself was a bit of a blur.

Jo and Joe—she ended up not using Joe's nickname because she communicated with eye contact and pointing, and any words were directed at the both of them—were quick and efficient. Dishes removed after each course were taken to the adjunct kitchen, so Celeste didn't even have the benefit of seeing if they came back empty or with barely a bite taken.

She was happy with her "Emerging from Below" flatbreads. She'd made them without any yeast, forming them with an upturned edge and monitoring the oven so they would come out with the edges crisp and a bit scorched, the centers soft and chewy. She put a thin smear of wild black mustard paste across each, then juxtaposed puddles of tangy goat cheese. Over these, she artfully placed the morels and ramps she'd sautéed in butter. A few more minutes in the oven to give the cheese a gloss, and the flatbreads were nearly ready to serve. Jo looked over Celeste's shoulder as she sprinkled on each flatbread the dandelion petals she'd salted with an egg white wash and dehydrated, adding an additional spritz of petals in an arc on the plate's rim. Celeste set the first three plates on the serving tray Jo held, Joe right behind her with an identical tray for the last two.

"Wow," Jo said after watching Celeste. "I never saw that on Food Network. Eating dandelions?"

"Ever read Ray Bradbury?"

"Who?"

"We'll talk later. Go."

Celeste got nervous and burned two of the trout fillets but had enough to replace them, sending silent thanks to Uncle Vic, Evan, and the benevolence of Mother Nature. From her foraged dinner plates, she selected those in patterns of blue and red, setting the green ones aside. She wanted her fish, adorned with ginger root shavings and toasted hazelnuts, paired with wild asparagus and fiddlehead ferns dressed with the wood sorrel dressing, to stand out on the plate, not blend into it. Watching Jo and Joe carry the trays through the swinging door, Celeste felt a note of misgiving. *Would the judges think the effect garish?* The door swung shut. Celeste squared her shoulders. Done was done. It was time to plate her dessert.

Her hand was shaking so badly as she placed the sugared redbud blossoms and violets on the delicate meringue pavlova that she had to hold her right wrist with her left hand. She then set a trio of small cubes of cut honeycomb on one side of each plate and added a drizzle of honey around the edges. She thought of the beekeeper, his apprentice grandson, and an afternoon spent among brightly painted hive boxes on a sunlit afternoon, watching the comings and goings of honeybees, listening to their golden hum.

She then took up the gherkins jar she'd set out from the refrigerator that afternoon. Celeste pictured Sonia's grandniece in a cloudberry patch near Marquette, picking each with care, planning a particular gift for her grandaunt. Agreeing later that it should, instead, come to her. Specifically for this dinner.

That grandniece, whom Celeste had never met, believed in her because Sonia did.

Celeste twisted the lid open. Perfection floated in ice wine.

"What's that?" The first words from Joe, back from delivering the main course.

"Cloudberries," said Celeste, focused on anointing each of the five pavlovas in front of her with a single, perfect berry. She poured a small puddle of the cloudberry-enhanced ice wine on each dish, finished with a drizzle of honey.

"There are a few left," she said, dabbing a drip on the edge of one plate. "You can taste when we're all done if you want." She looked at him. His eyes roved between the plate she'd just wiped and the jar, ten or so cloudberries still floating in it.

"What do they taste like?"

Celeste shrugged as she added, with tweezers, the barest dusting of bee pollen among the sugared flowers and cloudberry. "You'll have an opportunity to find out, after we're done. And, no, you can't take any to Tiffany. This is a one-time offer for you—but only after we're done. And only if you deliver these safely to the judges in the dining room."

She watched her two servers leave the kitchen on their way to the dining room, each carrying a tray of her final course: Demeter's Joy. Jo turned to her as the door swung shut. Her expression reminded Celeste of the way she'd felt when she found *The Saucier's Apprentice* in the St. Ignace thrift store.

The door closed. Celeste waited three breaths and then slid her back down the butcher-block table until she felt the floor beneath her.

She leaned her head against the leg, closed her eyes, and let out long, pent-up breath.

Her competition dinner was done. She'd given it her all. Now it was just a matter of what her competitors did—if they could do more, do it better than she just had.

She opened her eyes.

Blaise had a brother?

# MAY

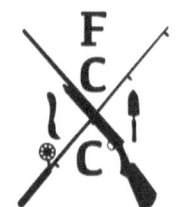

# Bradley

Her name was Celeste, Bradley now knew. She lived on Mackinac Island, which was between Michigan's Lower and Upper Peninsulas. He'd never been there. She worked in the kitchen of a famous hotel.

That was about the extent of what Blaise could tell him when they'd played their latest game of Questions.

Questions was a game his brother made up when the two of them were in middle school. Bradley didn't like conversations. It was hard to know what to say when people said random things and then expected you to say something back. To help him practice, Blaise made up the Questions game. Blaise almost always started. He'd ask a question, and Bradley would answer it. Then Bradley would ask a question, and Blaise would answer it. They were adults now, but Blaise still initiated the Questions game from time to time, for practice, he said. The toughest part most of the time was coming up with a question to ask his brother.

But not this last time they'd played.

Blaise had seemed surprised when Bradley said he wanted to play Questions. Bradley rarely initiated the game. But he had wanted to know about the girl in the woods. The one who was angry. He'd seen her around the Club, though he'd never spoken to her. He watched her from time to time, so there were things he already knew.

He knew she liked to read by an open window; though, when it rained, she seemed to forget about the book in her lap and would just look out at the rain falling. When she did that, he'd look out a window too. Maybe it could be something they could talk about if they ever spoke. How the rain looked, smelled, sounded—she from the perspective of her window and he from his.

She rode a bicycle the color of a robin's egg. It had a woven wicker basket attached to the handlebars that was always empty when she rode away from the Club but typically full when she came back. He knew she liked flowers and budding branches and other growing things from the garden and woods because he saw her bring them into the Club. She would arrange them in containers she gathered from shelves and dusty forgotten places of the Club and then carry them up to her room.

Depending on the light, her hair was the color of strawberries, ripe or nearly ripe. It was short and curly, and she was petite in a way that reminded him of British illustrations of sprites and fairies that live in flower blossoms.

He hadn't known the color of her eyes until they met in the woods.

Bradley also knew she was part of the dinner contest his brother was involved in. Blaise told him there were a lot of rules. One of the rules was that neither of them could forage on the Club property during a month that was assigned to another contestant.

April was assigned to the girl with strawberry hair.

He hadn't realized it was still April when he went to the woods with his bag and knife. It had been April for such a long time already, he'd thought it was over. He should have checked; he knew that now. He'd realized his mistake when she'd spoken to him while he was foraging ramps, the makings of a dish forming in his mind. It was the first time she spoke to him, and she'd been angry. All the words he'd planned to say to her someday had dried up in his throat when he'd stood up and turned to see her there in the forest, like a fierce sprite ready to pronounce judgment for a serious transgression.

Which was why he'd given her his bookstore foraging bag with the ramps in it. Their hands had touched briefly when she took it from him, and he'd felt butterflies in his stomach at the contact, a jolt in his chest when he'd looked into her eyes for all of a heartbeat. They were the color of a deep lake, and he felt underwater, unable to make sound. Unable to breathe. She hadn't said anything when he gave her the bag. She'd just watched him. He could tell she was ready to fight him—verbally or physically—or run. He didn't want her to do any of those. He would've liked to look at her eyes longer, but that always made him uncomfortable, even when people weren't angry. So he'd walked past her and back to the Club, playing the scene over and over in his head. Once back, he'd gone in search of Blaise and, after a time, said he wanted to play Questions.

So now Bradley knew that the strawberry-haired girl with lake-blue eyes who loved watching the rain and reading by windows and gathering flowers and branches for her room and riding her bike and cooking meals from things she foraged was Celeste.

She lived on an island where no one drove cars and worked in a kitchen at the grandest hotel on that island.

In turn, Blaise knew that his brother had broken one of the contest rules—an important one, apparently—although it had been an accident. Bradley's last question was whether his mistake could get Blaise kicked out of the competition. Blaise wasn't sure. It might depend on whether Celeste was still angry.

It was Bradley's secret that he'd decorated the dining room for Celeste's competition dinner as an apology. He'd done it the way he imagined she'd like it, with all sorts of different flowers and budding branches arranged as though they'd grown with the intention of one day being there, that evening, in that room. He'd enjoyed doing it.

Roaming and gathering outdoors—his own thoughts, the rustling of animals in the underbrush, and the songs of birds in the trees his only companions—had long been among his favorite things. Typically, his time outdoors was spent noticing and harvesting ingredients that could be made into a dish—something else he enjoyed. When he foraged for food, Bradley's imagination and senses wandered, considering and coalescing how different tastes, textures, and smells could weave and meld to create something delicious. This time, of course, it was Celeste who had created something delicious to eat. He'd helped her—he hoped—when he gave her his bag of ramps. He'd been careful in the harvesting, he'd planned to say. But then their fingers had touched, and the thought had left his mind.

The candles had been a final addition, foraged from different rooms and storage shelves and closets around the Club. The dining room had looked beautiful in the way she was, Bradley decided when he was finished.

There were chairs for five around the table. Leaving the room, he'd imagined what it would be like to have just two chairs at the table. And what game of Questions he and Celeste might play over a dinner.

Bradley was drinking his morning coffee in the common room when Celeste walked in.

"You're Blaise's brother, aren't you."

She made it a statement, but technically, it was a question.

"Yes," said Bradley. He groped for a question that wasn't the obvious one—the one he and Blaise most needed answered.

"You're the one I met in the woods on Friday." She glanced around. No one else was in the room. "You were foraging ramps," she added quietly.

Bradley shifted in his seat. Those weren't questions.

"Yes," he said anyway.

She tilted her head. She wasn't smiling but didn't seem angry.

"Why?" she asked.

He wanted to tell her the truth—that the air had smelled of spring and had given him an idea of a dish that needed ramps—but he didn't want to make her angry again.

"I thought April was over."

She folded her arms.

"I know I should have checked. I'm sorry."

He had to come up with a question. He didn't want her to leave, and she might if she ran out of questions and he didn't have one.

"Did you like the flowers?" he asked. It was something he wanted to know. He wished he could have seen her when she first entered the room.

"Those were from you?"

He nodded, not looking at her.

"They were gorgeous. And the candles were perfect too." She indicated the other end of the couch. "May I?"

His breath caught as she stepped around one of the overstuffed chairs to sit, only one empty cushion between them. She was close enough to touch.

"I'm Celeste," she said.

He nodded again.

"What should I call you other than Blaise's brother?"

Of course. His name.

"I'm Bradley," he said.

"Nice to meet you officially, Bradley. I think I've seen you around the Club, though now I'm not sure if it was you or Blaise I was seeing. I didn't know he had a twin. Do you cook? Like your brother?"

This was two questions in a row. The answer to the first was easy. The answer to the second was more complicated. Blaise had said the game of Questions was to help him practice having a conversation. That's what this was—right?

"Yes, I like to cook. Blaise went to culinary school, so he cooks like culinary school. He cooks like a chef. I cook . . ." Bradley searched for the words. "I cook what I taste in my head." He paused. "Sometimes it comes out like it tastes in my head. Sometimes not."

Celeste seemed to take this in. "I get what you're saying. Sometimes, when I come across something unexpected when I'm foraging or when we're down to meager pickings in our kitchen at home, I come up with ideas of things to make with what's around. It can sound really good in my head. Sometimes, the actual dish matches what I envisioned." She shrugged and laughed. "*Aaand* sometimes not. What were you going to make with the ramps?"

Celeste wasn't revisiting his mistake in the woods. She was interested in talking with him. Interested enough to ask another question.

"I didn't have it all worked out," Bradley said. "Something in a cast-iron skillet. Someone had delivered fresh eggs. And goat cheese."

"That would have been from Annie. My order was brought to the main kitchen, but there was an order for the adjunct kitchen too. The delivery guy got them mixed up, but I caught it in time."

"I went looking for morels," Bradley offered. "But then I saw the ramps." It was getting easier to keep this conversation going. Celeste was different from other people who talked to him, who wanted him to respond quickly and say the things they expected him to say. He looked into her eyes, a brief interlude of lake-blue, then looked away again.

"There are morels pretty close to that ramp patch," Celeste said. "I collected enough for my dinner, but there were a good many more."

"I'm sorry about the ramps," Bradley said. "Did you use them in your dinner?" He hated the thought that maybe they'd gone to waste.

"I did. I harvested a few more after you left. And apology accepted," Celeste added. "Thank you for making the dining room look so gorgeous." She pulled her knees up under her chin and looked thoughtful. "A skillet dish, huh?"

"Yes." His turn. But she spoke again before he could think of another question.

"Y'know, it's now May," Celeste said, "And May isn't assigned to anyone." She lifted her chin from her knees. He was reminded of a sprite deciding judgment. "I haven't had breakfast, and I'm not getting picked up for the airport until mid-afternoon. I know where we can forage morels. And we can't harvest more than a few ramps from that patch, but maybe enough for a skillet dish? There are still plenty of eggs and goat cheese. Wanna cook with me?"

Bradley felt a swelling in his chest. Yes, he very much would like to cook with her. He met her eyes again. Held the gaze longer.

# Eden

"Have you decided on your menu yet?"

"Not yet," Eden said to her grandma. She carefully tamped around the tomato seedling with her fingertips. There had been a gentle rain shower in the morning, followed by bright sunshine that made her glad she'd worn her garden hat with the wide brim. The soil was moist and warm, the deep color evidence of years of composting. Its fragrance was a fecund spring elixir.

A lot of the homes in Idlewild had vegetable gardens, some larger, but none produced more delicious or varied vegetables and herbs than Perseverance Ross's—Perci, to her friends. Eden and her grandma were already harvesting peas and lettuces that had been planted in mid-March. A variety of radishes, carrots, cucumber, squash, and other seeds had been planted earlier in the month. But the tomato seedlings—sprouted from the seeds of a half-dozen heirloom varieties gathered every summer and into the fall, then planted and nurtured in trays in the southern-facing sunroom—were not set into garden soil until the third weekend in May. It was tradition.

Eden reached for another seedling.

"I have some ideas. I've already talked to Mrs. Abrams because I know I want to use butter, cream, and cheese from her cows. I've been writing notes to myself as I get ideas. I just have to gather them all up, winnow them down, and coalesce them into a menu."

Eden saw one of the hens run away from the others, a sizable grasshopper clasped in its beak. The chickens roamed her grandparents' property, feasting on bugs, clover, and other delicacies, including the occasional mouse or vole if they could catch it. She remembered explaining to an aghast, disbelieving group in culinary trade school that chickens were omnivores, and making them vegetarians through an enforced manufactured diet did *not* result in eggs "the way nature intended." The debate had been so heated that she half expected to find her tires slashed when she went out to the parking lot that evening. There were more than a few people in her class, she'd discovered, who never had close contact with the origins of their food. If she ever started a cooking school, she'd include mandatory curriculum for students to get down and dirty. If they wanted to cook it, they should learn firsthand what it took to get it to their kitchen. She saw the chicken that caught the grasshopper in a tug-of-war with another hen. The insect tore, and the hunter settled for gulping down the half it retained.

"Grandma," said Eden, "could I take a couple dozen eggs with me? I don't know how—or if—I'll use them, but as you always say—"

"Better to have it and not need it than to need it and not have it," her grandma finished for her. "Of course, child, take all the eggs you want." She stood and straightened her back. "Time for a break. I've got iced tea in the fridge." She patted Eden's shoulder as she passed by. "And you can tell me why you avoided your father's phone call earlier today."

"He wants me to run for Detroit City Council," said Eden.

She set a glass of iced tea in front of her grandma and poured one for herself. She put the pitcher back in the refrigerator and sat down.

"And what do you want?"

Her grandma reached for the sugar bowl on the kitchen table. Eden watched her add three heaping spoonfuls. The spoon clinked against the glass as she stirred.

"To make a difference. Apparently, he thinks I'm not doing that now." Eden drank from her glass. The cold tea felt good going down her throat. Dirt under her fingernails and unsweet tea suited her mood.

"I doubt he thinks that. Do you think you'd make more of a difference being a politician than cooking at the mission?"

"I do more than just cook at the mission."

"But what lights your inner fire is the cooking. Orchestrating those Thursday night dinners. Those are special." Grandma set down her spoon. "Aren't they?"

"He said I could keep doing the Thursday nights—that it would be strong optics for my campaign."

"Optics. What else did he say?"

"That I could do a lot of good. Draw attention that could fix some of the things that need fixing. Affect a lot of people. He has a group of pastors who would support me. They feel the time is right for a younger generation on the council."

"And yet here you are planting tomato seedlings with me."

"It's the third weekend in May, Grandma. Where else would I be?"

"Maybe taking a call from your father? We get cell service in the garden, you know."

Eden picked up her grandma's discarded teaspoon and fiddled with it. "He wants an answer. And I don't have one yet. I've got other things on my mind."

"Like your menu? Your competition dinner is a few weeks away."

"Five. And the election isn't until next year." Eden set down the spoon. "Let's say I do decide to run. Fifty thousand dollars in my campaign coffer would mean I needn't be beholden to anybody. I could run my campaign the way I want. Not owe favors."

"So what are you going to do?"

Eden downed the rest of her iced tea.

"I'm going to go plant the rest of those tomato seedlings."

# JUNE

# Eden

Eden spat toothpaste into the porcelain sink. Taking a mouthful of water and agitating it from cheek to cheek, her eyes strayed to a note she'd written in lipstick on an upper corner of her bathroom mirror: *cuke blossoms painted with cheese?* She'd written it there a few days ago, an inspiration in the shower with no pencil or paper on hand. She spat out the water and ran her hands through her hair a few times, finger-combing it to a semblance of how she liked it. Lifting her phone, she took a photo of the lipstick note.

It was time. She'd been letting ideas percolate. Today, she would settle on the menu she'd cook for the most important meal of her life.

Eden put on jean shorts and a V-neck T-shirt. Before pulling the quilt back into place that she'd cast aside when she arose that morning, she ran her hand under the pillows. No notes. Thumbing through the small notebook she kept on her bedside table, she found two she wanted. She ripped the pages out and put them in her pocket. Remembering drinks in Detroit with a friend the prior weekend, she rummaged through her purse and found an idea scrawled on the back of a cardboard coaster.

In the kitchen, she poured a cup of coffee from the pot Grandma had already brewed and went out to her truck. It was the motherlode. It was how her creativity worked. The long miles between Idlewild and Detroit gave her time to think, for her imagination to wander along woodland trails, meadows and fields, and the farmers' markets she frequented. Her notes helped her recall conversations with people who had been cooking from the land for longer than she'd been alive, as well as record her thoughts from techniques learned at trade school and from what had gone right—or wrong—in her own experimentations with food. From the visor, the center console, and the glove compartment, Eden collected various scrawled notes. She kept a notebook in her truck, but sometimes it strayed, accompanying her into the mission kitchen or elsewhere, unavailable when inspiration hit her. That's when she wrote on the backs of receipts, carryout menus, and ads for tarot readings or mattress sales that she'd occasionally find under her windshield wiper and didn't want to toss into the street. When she had an idea, she wrote on whatever came to hand, with whatever would write. Lipstick, in a pinch.

Eden sipped her coffee, remembering a camping trip a half-dozen years back. She'd woken just after sunrise with an idea and concocted a new recipe, kneeling on the ground outside the tent, writing with her finger dipped in the ashes of the campfire from the night before on the T-shirt she pulled off her body. No, she hadn't been wearing a bra—it was a camping trip! Yes, there was photographic evidence. She loved that photo, taken by her then-boyfriend when he emerged from their tent and saw her before she noticed he was there. He'd gifted her with a framed eight-by-ten. On the back, he'd written, "This is the essence of who you are."

They'd broken up amicably six months later—different paths, different goals. But she'd kept that photograph. It was her muse.

She was alone in the house. Grandma was with a group of ladies planning lunches and snacks for the church's upcoming Vacation Bible School. Grandpa was doing his weekly visitations with those who couldn't make it to Sunday services.

Eden went to the sunroom, less crowded with the tomato seedlings planted. She taped the various odd bits of paper and Post-it notes to the cedar siding wall. On a window ledge, she positioned the photograph.

Sunlight streamed in, and the mild June breeze made the affixed notes flutter. Two broke free and drifted to the floor. Eden picked them up and attached them more firmly to the sunroom wall.

"You don't escape consideration that easily," she said. She glanced at her phone. "I won't forget you're there. It's all under consideration."

She looked at the photograph and called to mind the intensity she'd felt dipping her finger into cold ashes to write on the shirt she'd stripped over her head, leaving her half naked. The morning light had been new and gentle, the breeze a chill on her exposed skin. She remembered there had been birdsong and the familiar fecund scent of the forest floor. But her focus had been on the tactile feel of her index finger first against the soft ashes and then against the rougher cotton fabric of her shirt as she traced out the inspiration in her mind.

With both hands cradling her warm coffee cup, she strolled the room, roaming her eyes from the photograph to the taped notes to her phone set on the small side table. Through the open jalousie windows, she could hear birdsong and smell the morning breeze and earthy scent of leaf mulch—echoes of that other morning. She wanted to resurrect that feeling of passion, of intensity.

"It's time to settle on a menu," she said out loud.

# Christian

"I'm stuck."

A nose poked around Christian's shoulder and sniffed the sauce he stirred with lackluster motion, startling him. He'd thought he was alone in the Flint kitchen with his thoughts and dinner preparation.

"More garlic," said his mother. "And maybe some red pepper flakes."

The nose receded. Christian replayed the past few minutes, trying to recall what else he may have said aloud as his mind wandered down well-trodden paths of would'ves and could'ves. He didn't want to add the Forager Chefs Club competition to the lengthening list, but . . .

He reached for the red pepper flakes and another two cloves of garlic as his mother sat down at the kitchen table.

"Why stuck?" she asked as Christian expertly peeled the cloves and then crushed them with the flat of his knife against a scarred cutting board, releasing their fragrance. He scraped them into the sauce and added several generous pinches of the flakes.

"Not stuck anymore. You're right. Garlic and red pepper flakes. It just seemed to need something. Wasn't sure what."

"Hmmm. Well, sometimes it takes a fresh nose."

Christian slowed the tempo of his wooden spoon to envelope the new ingredients into their companions in the saucepan, introducing them like an experienced host at a cocktail party. He inhaled deeply as they obligingly mingled, and the enhanced fragrance rose. He'd used one of the few remaining jars of preserved tomatoes from last season's harvest. In another couple of weeks, he'd be able to sink his teeth into a fresh tomato from their garden. He imagined plucking it, the slight snap of the stem as it gave way to release the sun-warmed fruit to his hand, biting into it like an apple, feeling the dribble of juice and seed run down his chin even as the rich, ripe taste of summer spread over his tongue. His mouth watered at the prospect.

Christian reached to the repurposed ceramic Maille mustard jar beside the stove for one of the half-dozen or so teaspoons he kept there, gleaned over time from abandoned houses. He dipped the teaspoon into the tomato sauce and raised it to his lips, careful to blow on it so as not to burn his mouth. He inhaled, exhaled, and closed his eyes.

Then, he tasted.

The sauce tasted of childhood gatherings in his grandparents' backyard, the uncles playing bocce ball flavored with good-natured taunts, the aunts exchanging neighborhood and family gossip and observations. And him, running to avoid being tagged "it" by one of his cousins, skirting along the basil border of the large vegetable garden, his hands open and grasping as he went. When he thought no one was looking, he had always stopped to smell his hands. Earth, sage, and oregano from where he'd crawled and hidden. Basil, from running through it, his hands outstretched and reaching because, well—it was basil.

Opening his eyes, he selected another spoon and brought a taste to his mother. She, too, inhaled and exhaled and then closed her eyes before opening her mouth for his offering. He watched her. Almost immediately, her lips curved in a smile, her eyes still closed. She nodded.

She never asked him what memories he saw behind closed lids when he tasted good food, so he had never asked her what she saw. It seemed a private thing.

But he did wonder.

"How are you stuck?" she asked again.

He turned to another wooden cutting board on the counter, his homemade gnocchi waiting there like plump, dollhouse-sized pillows. They wouldn't take long to cook. He lowered the flame under the saucepan even further. He'd started the sauce that morning but would let it simmer another half-hour. He reached for the open bottle of pinot noir on the counter and topped off his squat café glass. He gestured toward his mother. At her nod, he took another glass from the cupboard and filled it.

"I told you. Not stuck anymore. The extra garlic did the trick."

He sat, glad she was in the kitchen with him. The smell of cooking sometimes made her feel ill; other days, she said it nourished her. Today was one of the good days. He wanted to savor it, not cloud it with all his doubts and regrets.

His mom sipped from her glass, waiting, and Christian was reminded yet again that his intentions almost always gave way when she had a different plan.

"Could you hand me paper and a pencil?" she asked.

Christian got up and opened a drawer. He shuffled through loose AA batteries, a roll of Scotch tape, a tube of superglue, a pair of reading glasses, some clothespins, and other assorted items until he came up with a pen, the logo of the local bank emblazoned on the side. Remembering his last encounter with the bank and his close call with getting arrested—okay, he'd been angry, but there was no reason for everyone to get so spooked by a couple of overturned chairs—he tossed the pen to the back of the drawer and rifled around a bit more until he found a pencil. He held it out to his mom, then realized the graphite tip was at a forty-five-degree angle to the rest of it. He tossed it back in the drawer and rummaged until he found another pencil. This one had its tip intact. He handed it to his mom, along with a sheet from a thin pad affixed to the refrigerator by a magnet from a long-ago field trip to the Greenfield Village Museum.

"Thank you, Son."

She bent her head and started writing.

Christian looked at the dishes in the sink and decided the clatter of cleaning up could wait. He opened the drawer again and fished out the pencil with the broken tip. He pulled his folding knife out of his pocket, the one he always kept with him for foraging, and began to sharpen the pencil, letting the wood shavings drop into the shallow prep bowl he'd used for onions.

Stuck. Why had he said that out loud? She'd asked him to accept the invitation. And so he had. He'd figure it out. He always did.

Christian continued to scrape away at the pencil, the *snik-snik* of his knife letting her know he was in no hurry.

It was already nearing the end of June. Eden's dinner was just over a week away. He needed to give some serious thought to his menu for August. What was something uncommon and foraged that he could get his hands on in August? He could barter for squab from the guy down at the farmers' market. Quail would be better, but he didn't know where to source it. Squab, he could get, and there was a recipe from a 1920s cookbook that he'd tweaked to his liking . . .

His mother set her pencil down and held the paper out to Christian.

"What's this?" he asked.

"Shopping list. I'm going to cook dinner tomorrow. Or maybe the next day. I have a menu in mind, and this is what I need."

Christian took the list. Today had been a good day, but that didn't mean it would carry over to tomorrow—or the next day.

"Quite eclectic. Rabbit?"

"Is that a problem?"

He scanned the rest of the list. He knew where he could find everything, but it would take him a while to do it.

"Not at all, Mom."

Christian folded the list and tucked it into his jeans pocket. He sat down, picked up his café glass, and held it out. She picked up hers, and they clinked.

"I want you to take the camera," she said. "I want photos from all the places you go to get the things on that list."

The camera was a small, 35mm instamatic. No fancy lenses—just point and shoot. It looked like something from the nineties. *It probably is*, Christian thought. It wasn't digital—it required actual film. Looking at the little window on the back, Christian saw there was a roll of film in it already, two of the available twelve photos used. He rummaged around in the cabinet and found a pristine box of film. He scrutinized it. The expiration date was the same year he'd gone away to culinary school. *Appropriate*, he thought. He shrugged. He knew of a place downtown that still developed film.

The blackberries were easy enough to gather. One street over and down a block. He remembered riding his bike down this street as a boy, past the small but pristine lawns with shrubs that skirted the squat brick houses, borders of flowers along the concrete walkways that led to a front stoop or a small, covered porch where husbands and wives would sit in the evenings and chat and watch the neighborhood wind down toward nightfall.

He stopped in front of the house, remembering the couple who had lived in it. They'd been older—but then everyone was when you were ten years old. They didn't have kids, but they hadn't yelled at him or his friends when their bikes sometimes veered off the sidewalk and onto their lawn as they raced each other with daring passes. He remembered one time when they cheered as he maneuvered past Jeffrey, clipping handlebars but both staying upright. He'd never talked to them, but he knew in his heart they were good people. They'd left the neighborhood quite a while ago. He didn't know the circumstances. There had been a for-sale sign in their front yard for a while. Christian mostly kept tabs on the perimeter right around his mom's house, but he had a soft spot for this place. He'd decorated the living room with one rather large shotgun hole two years ago when he'd gotten word of a group setting up shop. They'd moved on. He couldn't be here all the time, though, and somewhere along the way, the scrappers had visited, ripping out the copper piping, the hot water heater, and even some of the doorknobs. Christian didn't have his gun with him now, but everything seemed quiet. He strode up the cracked concrete of the driveway. The rusted metal latch of the gate in the backyard's chain-link fence screaked as he lifted it.

The grass was long, and grasshoppers took flight as he stepped into what had once been the manicured backyard of a proud homeowner. A good third of the yard was blackberry canes laden with fruit. At one time, it had likely been two or three tended plants, but in the years since the couple had left, the canes had had free rein. Even the chain-link fence delineating this yard from the next was ignored as the blackberries expanded their domain.

On the far side of the yard, between two dwarf plum trees dappled with unripe fruit, was the skeleton of a children's swing set, its rusted limbs reaching for the sky and empty chains dangling. Faint vestiges of green and white candy-cane swirls of paint were still visible on the metal poles. He wondered about that swing set every time he came here to forage blackberries or plums. He had never seen kids at this house. Had they grown up and gone away? Had something happened to them? Or had there maybe never been any? He couldn't remember anyone ever being on the porch other than the two of them, smiling and chatting with one another, her holding a tall, frosted glass, him a bottle of beer, as Christian and his friends hurtled by on their bikes.

Christian pulled the camera from his rucksack, raised it to his face, looked through the viewfinder, then lowered it. He didn't want just a photo of the blackberries. That story was one of resilience, but it wasn't the only tale here. He moved through the tall grass and past a broken concrete birdbath to stand with his back against the canes. He looked through the viewfinder again. Small splashes of immature plums amid leaves of green looked youthful against the gray-brown gnarled branches. The trunks of the plum trees were laced with flakes of gray and green lichen and had split in places, dried sap filling the crevices. The two trees stood sentinel for the desiccated swing set, the dull chains, speckled with rust, swaying ever so slightly. In the background of it all was the house: orange-red brick and solid still but with windows so glazed with grime and time that they seemed to stare out at the yard with a cataract gaze that didn't really see what had become of what was once tended and nurtured.

Christian pressed a button on the top of the camera and heard the click of the shutter. He lowered the camera. He turned, backed up a few steps, and took a close-up photo of the blackberry canes, lush leaves, fruit, and stems filling the viewfinder. Then he put the camera away. He'd give his mother the photo of the blackberries but thought he might keep the other one for himself. Not show it to her at all. There was a fine line between poignant and sad, and he didn't want to cross it with her. He glanced at his watch, pulling a cotton bag out of his rucksack. Then he joined the insects and birds in harvesting blackberries.

# Eden

"It's a sprain, not a break," said Mrs. Abrams. "And I've got plenty of help from the neighbors. So don't you worry." She patted Eden's arm with the hand that wasn't wrapped up in a sling. "I had them set aside milk for your daddy's mission supper. You'll have all the milk and cream you need for your dinner. And take whatever you want from the cheese cave. There's butter too. I wouldn't let you go into that competition without anything less than the best my girls can provide!"

Eden managed a smile and a nod. She felt guilty that she hadn't known about Mrs. Abrams's injury until arriving to pick up ingredients for the Sing His Praise dinner and arrange for the dairy she'd need for her competition dinner two days later. Grandma would be aghast if she knew Eden was here without so much as a casserole or pound cake in hand.

Mrs. Abrams seemed to read her mind. "Do you want some banana bread for the road? The neighbors and church have brought by so much food that I'm going to have to feed it to the chickens pretty soon just to make room in the house! Now, I know I'm always your last stop. So tell me who you've been visiting this week. Don't tell me what you went *for*," she admonished. "Just tell me who you've visited, and lemme guess. Wait," she said, "I gotta sit down first. This wrist sprain tires out my legs after a while. Pour us a cup of coffee, will you?"

Eden went to the sleek machine on the kitchen counter. Mrs. Abrams hadn't wanted the modern dairy churn her son had tried to gift her, but she apparently did like the fancy coffee maker he'd bought her instead. Sitting down at the kitchen table with two mugs of fresh coffee, she watched Mrs. Abrams add a good helping of cream to hers.

Eden inhaled the aroma rising from her mug before sipping. She always drank it black. She didn't want anything to dilute the perfection of a well-roasted coffee bean. She closed her eyes and sighed in contentment. He may be away in Chicago doing legal battle with corporations, but Thea Abrams's son always made sure his mother had good-quality coffee. God bless that man.

She opened her eyes and saw Mrs. Abrams looking at her expectantly, a smile playing on her lips. She knew the coffee was good.

Eden set down her cup and started counting out on her fingers.

"Eddie Walker, Henry Louis, Jennifer Blessing, Explorer Troop 961," Eden rattled off. "And Jem Spaulding, though I'm not sure yet if I'll actually use for the dinner what I got from him."

Mrs. Abrams nodded at each name. She sipped from her cup and tapped the table with her fingers that extended from the sling.

"Eddie Walker," Mrs. Abrams said. "That man is constantly in the marshes. You gonna serve frog legs?"

"Well, there's a thought, but no," said Eden. "He's made cattail flour. And you know how much time and work it takes for that. I thought it would be a good starch to include, given the whole 'forager' theme, although it definitely has a distinctive taste. I don't want to overdo it. I thought I might mix it in with some of Grandma's crop to make duchess potatoes. Basically, mashed potatoes piped and browned to look fancy," she added.

"Ah! And what goes with potatoes but some good beef! So you're getting beef from Henry Louis."

"The best tenderloin in this part of the state."

"Even farther afield if you ask me. And Jennifer? It's too early for apples."

Eden held up a finger. "Ah, but not for apple cider vinegar."

"Good point."

Mrs. Abrams lifted her cup to her lips.

Eden knew she was buying time; the Explorer Troop would be the tough one.

"Okay, you've got me stumped. I don't think you need anyone to spread mulch, and it's the wrong season for raking leaves or shoveling snow. What on earth do a group of ten- and eleven-year-old boys have to do with your competition dinner?"

Eden savored the moment. It wasn't often she stumped Thea Abrams. "I'm paying them a dollar for every live crayfish at least four inches long they can deliver to me by noon on Friday." She held up a finger. "That's still alive, of course."

"And Jem Spaulding. It's his dandelion wine, right?"

"Yes. I'm just not sure how to use it yet. Jem only let me have one bottle and made me promise not to use it for cooking."

"So pair it."

"I thought of that, but I'm not pairing any of my other courses. And I'm not sure dandelion wine would be right for that, anyway." Eden got up and refilled her cup. "I like that it's unique, but is it maybe too 'down home'? Too country?"

"Too 'Idlewild'?"

"Too reminiscent of homebrew and the wrong side of the tracks."

"I've got a book I'm going to lend you. It may change how you think about dandelion wine. There are a lot of dog-eared pages. Pay particular attention to those. I know you're not supposed to do that, but they're my books, so I'll do as I please."

Mrs. Abrams met Eden at her truck as she finished loading ingredients for the mission dinner. The cover of the book was worn, but the words *Dandelion Wine* by Ray Bradbury were still clearly legible.

"Don't let ingredients define you, Eden," said Mrs. Abrams as she leaned in to give her a one-armed hug, the other cocooned in its sling. "Cook from your heart, your knowledge, your passion. Don't limit yourself to others' notions of what fits where and when. And that advice doesn't just apply to cooking either."

"She's definitely been talking to Grandma," Eden muttered as she pulled out of the driveway.

"You haven't left yourself a lot of time," said Elena from her desk in the Club's reception area as Eden came in two days later.

"Time for what?" said Eden.

Elena looked up from her ledger, bemused, and set aside her pencil. It reminded Eden of her fourth-grade teacher's reaction when she walked to the front of the class to deliver her memorized poem and announced her selection. Her eight-stanza selection.

"Time to get to know the grounds," Elena said with the same patience that echoed Eden's fourth-grade teacher.

Had Eden memorized the entire poem? To recite it incorrectly would be disrespectful. If she didn't intend to recite the entire poem, she should tell the class the portion she would recite. Which portion would that be? "All of it," Eden had responded and then went on to recite Maya Angelou's "Still I Rise."

"I don't need to get to know the grounds," said Eden. "I just need to know the kitchen. I did that back in February." She paused. "May I have my room key?" she asked, meeting Elena's steady gaze with one of her own.

"Of course." Elena opened a drawer, pulled out a key linked to a brass disk engraved with "Ironwood," and handed it to her.

"Thank you," said Eden. She hoisted her overnight bag over her shoulder. "I parked my truck by the side of the front entrance. I have some coolers and other things I need to bring to the kitchen. Do I need to move my truck to the back of the building to bring those in?"

Her tone bordered on bitchy, but she couldn't seem to help herself. She was edgy. The four pastors of her father's prayer group had shown up for yesterday's mission dinner. They offered the opening prayer together. She knew what they wanted—what her father wanted—but she wasn't ready to give them an answer. At least not the one they expected. *He shouldn't have invited them. Not this week. Not two days before my dinner.*

But Elena didn't need to know any of that.

All Elena needed to know was that Eden didn't require the largesse of the Forager Chefs Club acreage to create a memorable, competitive dinner. She had her own resources. And while she liked Randall—he had smiled to see the children dance and tipped the band—Elena was just so damn . . . *White*. She reminded Eden of the hostesses in the fancy restaurants and members-only clubs in Detroit and its rich suburbs. Tall. Slim but curvy. Blond hair, blue eyes. Dressed in that White-girl way of knee-length skirt and a blouse that seemed all prissy and virginal but still teased in the way the fabric of the skirt clung and the way the blouse seemed strained to contain the pert bosom within, just one undone button away from wanton.

"At the Forager Chefs Club," Elena said in her pleasant, hostess tone, "everyone is welcome through the front door. I'll arrange to have your coolers and whatever else brought to the kitchen for you. Is your truck unlocked?"

Eden trekked those coolers between Idlewild and Detroit and parked her truck behind the mission building and on downtown streets. She always locked her truck cab and the cap that enclosed the bed. It seemed a bit of overkill out here in the middle of nowhere, but some habits were engrained. She reached into her pocket, pulled out the keys, and gave them to Elena.

"You're a bit behind the curve, but please let me know if there is anything I can do to help."

"And why would you think I'm behind the curve?"

"Other contestants have taken advantage of the Club's generous offer to spend time here, explore the acreage, and learn what is here to forage. It's surprising that you would arrive literally the day before your dinner."

"The Forager Chefs Club doesn't have anything I don't already have or can't get on my own," Eden said.

Eden sat in her favorite pajamas on the wide window ledge of her comfortable room at the Forager Chefs Club with a glass of white wine from Michigan's Old Mission Peninsula and looked out at the moon-tinged landscape.

She hadn't meant her words to Elena to come out harsh. She hadn't meant to be harsh with her father, either, when she told him she wasn't ready for an announcement. Her father had been on her mind, and so her words to Elena had been about more than just ingredients and foraging.

From Elena's response, the Club's manager knew it too.

*Then, why are you here?*

Eden thought about having recited that poem—flawlessly—when even her fourth-grade teacher—her Black fourth-grade teacher—didn't think she could do it.

She'd taken a chance and jumped on the pendulum Grandpa had described when she signed the contract for this competition. Four months later, with coolers and crates in tow, she was ready to cook. To leap off the pendulum. Like him, she now felt like she'd landed on one foot. Who—or what—would help steady her if she reached out her hand? Or would she just teeter there on her own until she either steadied herself or fell over?

She'd made good use of the daylight hours since she arrived. Everything was *mise en place*—unpacked and ready, the bowls, pans, and other kitchen tools she'd need selected and set out. Whatever could be prepped was prepped, including fresh mascarpone cheese that she made with Thea Abrams's cream and Jennifer Blessing's apple cider vinegar rather than lemon juice. For her sorbet, she'd used one hundred fresh lemon verbena leaves from Grandma's garden, steeping them in heated milk before straining the mixture.

The mascarpone was draining in cheesecloth in the refrigerator next to the chilling lemon verbena sorbet mixture and yet more cream, milk, and butter. The beef tenderloin was wrapped in butcher paper and secured with twine on a separate shelf. In the refrigerator's two vegetable bins were plucked squash and cucumber blossoms, a half-dozen large watermelon radishes, an array of wild and garden greens, and juicy blackberries picked that morning. On one countertop, the crayfish were still alive in their tub, next to a vase of delicate elderflower blossoms, the tall bottle of dandelion wine, a small paper sack of potatoes, and a braid of garlic. Unwashed eggs for the merengue—nature's protective "bloom" precluding the need for refrigeration—sat on another counter next to an apple crate holding containers and jars of various sizes and sorts, including one of cattail flour.

She'd be back in the kitchen early in the morning, but for now, she'd earned a respite. Eden sipped from her glass, enjoying the crisp taste of the wine—citrus and green tea with a hint of mineral undertone. The windows had been open when she arrived—the Club didn't have air-conditioning. She liked that. The only place she preferred air-conditioning was in the city, where closed and locked windows meant added security and a muffle to urban noise. Here, she listened to familiar forest sounds, the wind sweeping tree branches in an arrhythmic tempo. It reminded her of camping nights near Idlewild—not too far from here, actually—lying under the stars, her dog Samson snoring at her feet, sometimes with a friend or two chatting well into the night, more often just she and Samson. She missed that dog.

It was June. Her month. And maybe she should have spent more time here, getting to know the lay of the land, but she'd been busy and had responsibilities elsewhere. She was here now. And in the space of just a few hours, she'd laid claim to the most important square feet of the entire acreage of the Forager Chefs Club—the kitchen. Tomorrow, she'd make a dinner in it the likes of which those judges, whoever they were, had never tasted. Eden sipped from her glass.

And felt steadied.

# "THIS FINE FAIR MONTH"

APERITIF:
Essence of "This Fine Fair Month"
*Dandelion Wine*

FIRST COURSE:
Artist's Palette Blossoms
*Squash and cucumber blossoms painted with fresh mascarpone and filled with meadow greens puree*

SECOND COURSE:
Michigan Surf & Turf
*Pan-roasted beef tenderloin in blackberry au jus*
*Crayfish mousse on watermelon radish disks*
*Duchess-style cattail potatoes*

THIRD COURSE:
Blossoms & Herbs
*Elderflower merengue with lemon verbena sorbet*

# JULY

# Daniel

Daniel's first thought when he drove up the winding, rutted lane hemmed in by trees that ended at a clearing fronting the Forager Chefs Club was that Thistle would have loved it. The building was an eclectic patchwork of log and stone and stucco and plank, each section obviously built decades or more apart but crafted to mesh with what was already there, creating an ever-larger shelter that was both stalwart and welcoming.

His truck had barely come to a stop before Ethan unbuckled his seat belt and hopped out the door, Biscuit close behind him. Ethan lifted both arms and sounded a loud *whoop!* to the sky and slammed the door shut before running up the front steps of the wide, covered porch. Biscuit followed, only stopping long enough to lift a leg to an iron post supporting a carved sign before bounding after Ethan. Both stopped before the closed, broad door, the boy suddenly shy. They turned back to look at Daniel, still sitting in the truck.

Daniel rolled his eyes at the slammed door but decided not to say anything about it. It had been a long drive. He couldn't blame his son for being glad to feel ground under his feet again. To reach their destination for this July.

For the last three years, they always went away for July.

Daniel had told his son about the cooking competition—that they were making a longer trip, both in distance and duration, to explore and prep. Ethan was excited to help with scouting the grounds of the Club. Daniel had locked up the cabin and loaded the truck with what he thought they'd need to be away six to eight weeks.

He didn't tell his son that the last time he'd been this far downstate was the year he'd stood with Ethan's mother on the bank of the Au Sable River and promised to love her for as long as he lived.

He glanced at the weathered, carved sign on the iron post as he walked up the porch steps. He'd take some time later to discern the elements of the emblem associated with the Forager Chefs Club.

The room just inside the front door felt like an upscale hunting lodge but without animal heads mounted everywhere. There was no one to greet them, no obvious hotel reception area, just an elegant desk of blond wood with inlay and a vase of flowers in one corner. Daniel and Ethan exchanged a glance. Daniel shrugged his shoulders. Ethan returned the shrug and went to explore an adjacent large room with deep chairs and a long leather couch facing a stone-framed fireplace that took up most of one wall. Biscuit followed, his toenails clicking on the wide, plank flooring. After a couple of minutes, Daniel did too. They'd been invited, after all.

Ethan was stretched out on the leather couch. Biscuit was investigating the room, nosing everything his snout could reach.

"Look, Dad! It's long enough to be a bed!" Ethan threw his arms up over his head, and the backs of his hands landed on the broad armrest. He scooched his body down until the soles of his shoes touched the opposite armrest. He put his arms over his head again. Now the tips of his fingers of his left hand touched the armrest, those of his right not quite. "See? I can even stretch all the way, and I still fit! Can I sleep here?" He wriggled. "It's really comfortable."

Daniel wandered around the room, taking it in. It reminded him of the hunting lodge the Royal Trolls owned near Escanaba—rustic but refined. Whoever this Forager Chefs Club was, they had money. Not as much as the Royal Trolls, Daniel noted with a practiced, somewhat jaundiced eye, but enough to put his mind at ease that this competition was legit.

"Are you saying you need a nap?"

Ethan shot upright on the couch. "No! I'm not sleepy! I meant later. Nighttime. When it gets dark."

"Dark? Your bedtime is before it gets dark, dude. It's July. And I'm sure they'll have a room for us. Maybe it's up in the rafters. Wouldn't that be cool?" Taking in a wall of framed maps, both historic and topographical, Daniel stopped in front of one that was different from the others. It was done in pen and ink, with small splashes of watercolor. It reminded him of the drawings of the Hundred Acre Wood in the Winnie the Pooh books Thistle had read to Ethan, but this map was far more detailed. He leaned in. Daniel heard high heels clicking against the plank floors and turned.

"Welcome! I'm so sorry I wasn't here to greet you when you arrived."

The tall, slim woman in the timber-framed doorway was smiling, her hands clasped demurely at her waist. Ethan looked at her and ducked his head, suddenly shy. It's what he always did when a pretty woman spoke to him. He'd been tongue-tied for a solid week when his kindergarten class got a new teacher's assistant. Daniel saw the woman notice Ethan's reaction. She winked at Daniel and took a few steps into the room. Biscuit immediately came from the corner he'd been investigating and placed himself between the woman and Ethan. He didn't growl, and his tail was up, but it didn't wag. She stopped, keeping her eyes on the dog and her hands clasped at her waist. Daniel opened his mouth to call Biscuit away, then closed it when he didn't see any sign of aggression and that she wasn't afraid.

"It's okay, Biscuit. She's nice," said Ethan. "You *are* nice, right?"

"I try to be nice to guests," she said. "If you are who I think you are, you're definitely guests, and I hope we can also become friends—including your four-legged guardian here. I'm always nice to friends. You're Ethan, right? And this is your dad?"

Ethan nodded but, still shy, didn't move from the couch.

Biscuit advanced to sniff the woman's shoes, working his way up her legs until he nudged the hem of her skirt.

"Be polite," she admonished, her tone calm and friendly.

Biscuit withdrew his nose, stepped back two paces, and sat down. His tail swept the floor three times before he looked over his shoulder at Daniel. He still blocked the path to Ethan.

The woman followed the dog's gaze.

Daniel thought it was probably time he said something. Maybe he'd delayed because of the wink. He wasn't sure how he felt about a wink from an attractive woman he didn't know in a place he was planning to stay with his son for a month or two.

"Hi. Hope it's okay we just settled in. Biscuit, heel."

The dog immediately came to sit at his left side.

The woman lifted her eyes from the dog to meet Daniel's with a steady gaze.

Yeah, he probably should have called the dog over right from the get-go. This wasn't his house. She belonged here. He was a guest.

Old habits.

"I'm Elena," she said to Ethan. "I'm the manager here at the Forager Chefs Club. I've been so looking forward to meeting you. It must have been a long drive. Are you hungry?"

Ethan shook his head.

"Well, maybe in a little while. We have a nice room reserved for you and your dad—and Biscuit, is it? Do you want me to show you where it is? Once you're settled, you could explore the Club and grounds a bit. There's a kitchen just down the hallway"—she pointed to a doorway on the far wall—"called the adjunct kitchen, and I've made sure it has a lot of snacks. Would that be okay?"

Ethan nodded, finally meeting her gaze from beneath shaggy blond bangs.

"It's a pleasure to meet you too, Daniel. I work with Randall. Let me know if there is anything you need. Randall is away this afternoon, but I know he's looking forward to personally welcoming you. Can I show the three of you to your room?"

This time, there was no wink. Elena's look and tone were purely professional. He wondered briefly if maybe he'd imagined the wink. He followed her, gathering Ethan from the couch on the way. Biscuit quickened his pace to move beside the boy, the two climbing the stairs in tandem.

Their room was a suite, tucked under the eaves at the back of the main section of the building above what Elena said was the common room, facing a trimmed lawn and the forest beyond. The hallway door opened to a sitting room with doors to two bedrooms, each with its own bathroom. Under the roof overhang and running the length of the suite was a balcony with sliding glass doors accessing it from all three rooms. Heavy, light-blocking curtains ensured guests wouldn't be awakened by sunlight unless they wanted to be.

"P-E-T-O-S-K-E-Y," Ethan spelled out, pointing at each letter on the brass disk attached to their heavy room key as he sat on one of the two double beds in his room.

"Sound it out," said Daniel, unpacking Ethan's suitcase.

"Pet. Os. Skey. Pet-os-skey. Petoskey! Like the stone!"

"Good man. That's exactly right."

"Why did they name our room after a stone?"

"Maybe they like Petoskey stones. They're cool, right? Remember the ones we found on the lakeshore? And when you own a place, you can name it whatever you want."

Ethan nodded, thoughtful. "I like Petoskey stones." He looked up. "We own our cabin. Does it have a name?"

Daniel paused and continued unpacking. "It does," he said. "Your Mama named it Heaven's Glade." It had been their private name. He walked to the sliding doors and opened them to the summer breeze and birdsong. He carried a stack of Ethan's shirts to the dresser and slid open one of the drawers.

"Mama is in heaven, right?"

"Yes, she is."

"So if our cabin is Heaven's Glade, why isn't she there with us?"

Daniel shut the drawer and sat on the bed beside his son.

"She *is* there, Ethan, in a way. She'll always be with us. Maybe that's why she named it Heaven's Glade before she had to go. Because she loved that place so much and wanted it to be a home for you. It's like an echo of heaven—a little piece of it—and part of her will always be there. It's ours, and it's special. Because she made it special."

Ethan considered this, his fingers tracing the engraved name on the brass plate of the room key. Finally, he nodded.

"I like our room name. Can we go fishing now?"

Daniel felt a tightness in his chest that he hadn't realized was there relax. He ruffled the hair on his son's head. He'd need a haircut again soon. It was good they could have these conversations and then move on, right? Daniel recalled the pen-and-ink map he'd seen on the wall in the common room. They wouldn't have to drive to Bear Lake. There was a good-sized stream on the property.

"Sure, let's go fishing."

# Eden

It felt very decadent to drink wine mid-afternoon, particularly after not doing much of anything for most of the day. Eden closed her eyes and lifted her face to feel the dappled sunlight. She reached one bare foot to the ground to give the wide bench swing another push. The chains looped around the strong beech branch above her creaked a bit. She sipped her wine. So this is what a vacation felt like. It felt decadent.

Decadent felt good.

Well, and she'd earned it.

Eden looked out over the landscape of the Forager Chefs Club, the lawn speckled with dandelions, clover, and wood sorrel sloping down from the back of the building to the edge of the woods, a narrow, worn trail curving and then disappearing into the shadows. Follow that trail, she knew, and beyond her sight was a sizable stream with deep-cut banks that marked the property boundary on the west side, curving east farther along. She'd gone for a walk that morning, as she had the past few, exploring the acreage, immersing herself in its beauty and bounty.

On that first walk—the day after her dinner—she'd found a patch of wild raspberries and made them her breakfast, right there among the birdsong and rustles of small animals in the undergrowth. She'd found a small grove of wild pear trees, their fruits still round and hard. The day after, she'd gathered some hen-of-the-woods mushrooms she found and fried those up in butter for her lunch.

She hadn't gathered anything on her walk today. It was July now. And July was not her month for foraging. She didn't know if it belonged to anyone—back in February, it had been up for grabs for the mysterious fifth contestant. She supposed she could ask Elena. *Maybe later*, Eden thought, stretching out her legs, enjoying the sway of the swing, the tartness of the wine on her tongue, the luxury of not being needed immediately by anyone, anywhere, for anything. Her cell phone had no bars. The pastors and her father could wait. She was on vacation.

Due to the Fourth of July holiday, there was no Sing His Praise dinner this week, so Eden had decided to do what she hadn't before—take the Club up on its offer to spend time here. A little break would do her good.

Her dinner had gone well. After a lot of consideration, she'd started with the dandelion wine, taking a line from the book Mrs. Abrams had lent her to title her aperitif—her whole dinner, in fact. June was the first month of summer, and nothing said summer more than dandelion wine—except maybe watermelon. She'd decided early on that she wasn't going to serve watermelon.

The mascarpone cheese for her first course had been thicker and a little more difficult to "paint" onto the interior of the squash petals than she'd liked, but she'd thinned it by mixing in more whey with a wooden spoon. Hers somehow wasn't as silky as Mrs. Abrams's, but she'd made it work. Eden had originally planned to stuff the squash blossoms with a pesto made with a mix of foraged and garden greens—garlic mustard, chickweed, purple dead nettle, wood sorrel, dandelion, and wild onion, along with milder lettuces from Grandma's garden to tame the pungency—but traditional pesto meant olive oil and pine nuts. Eden had decided to see how far she could develop flavors without using any of her exceptions. So, instead of pesto, she called it a puree. She'd seasoned it with thyme, basil, and the allowed sea salt and piped it carefully into the blossoms. The taste of the bright green paste was a little acrid, but Eden thought the mild mascarpone toned that down enough—and better a stronger taste than bland, at any rate. She'd melted butter and gently sautéed the stuffed blossoms, just enough to take them from raw but not so much as to lose their gorgeous yellow-orange color. The cucumber blossoms were too small to stuff. These she'd breaded in a flour and a sage herb blend and sautéed until crispy, scattering them artfully on the plate for texture, along with dots of the bright green "meadow" puree.

She'd cooked the beef tenderloin medium rare. In a last-minute decision, she'd taught one of the two servers assigned to her—a tall young woman named Jo who had shown up early and was eager to learn—how to tilt the cast-iron pan and spoon the browned butter over and over the meat before setting it out to rest. With multiple pans going, it helped ensure all five plates were done at about the same time.

Cleaning and preparing the crayfish had been a labor, but Eden felt she'd given a good, strong nod to her rural roots. Besides, she liked the idea of "surf and turf" as a theme. The Great Lakes were inland seas, albeit fresh rather than salt water. The large, colorful disks cut from Grandma's mild watermelon radishes had been the perfect vehicle for the "surf," providing a crunchy texture to juxtapose the spoonful of creamy crayfish mousse as well as just a hint of bite alongside the beef.

Eden had mixed Eddie Walker's cattail flour with her egg-yolk-rich potato mixture in a 1:4 ratio before piping them duchess-style and baking them until golden brown. The cattail flour had given the dish a wild, nutty flavor that she hoped the judges appreciated.

Her elderflower meringues had nearly been a disaster. Elderflowers were big and plate-shaped, made up of tiny blossoms, each at the end of its own tiny, tender branch. Perched atop shiny merengue and then baked in a low-temperature oven for a couple of hours, they were delicious. She'd carefully cut what she needed from an obliging neighbor's bush and brought them to the Club in a large vase she placed on the kitchen counter. Coming downstairs the morning of her competition, Eden had been dismayed to find the stems drooping and a good number of the blossoms littering the countertop. Collecting them a day ahead had been a risk that hadn't paid off. She'd gone outside in search of a cell signal—she remembered Christian's frustration with no bars on his phone. Maybe Grandma could pick some new blossoms for her and have someone deliver them—the distance to Idlewild wasn't that far. Roaming around the building grounds, her eyes on her phone, she turned the far corner on the backside of one of the building's two wings. If she hadn't stumbled against a gutter spout leading rainwater away from the building, she might have missed it. Anchoring a long bed of perennials was an elderflower bush—more like a many-branched tree, really—rising twelve feet in the air and amassed with blossoms.

So she had foraged something from the Club's acreage after all, Eden mused as she drank wine in the middle of a July afternoon on a wide wooden swing beneath a beech tree and enjoyed her first vacation in years.

A young boy—maybe six or seven—was making his way toward her across the wide lawn, carrying a fishing rod twice as tall as he was with a large, shaggy dog keeping pace.

Well behind the two of them, she saw Christian. He was talking with a man roughly his same height, though broader across the shoulders. The newcomer's hair was the same wavy blond as the boy's, though a bit darker. Both could use a haircut. The dog left the boy's side and bounded to her, then stood just beyond arm's length. It lifted its snout and sniffed, nostrils flaring.

Eden met the dog's eyes and pushed her foot against the ground to reinvigorate the swing's motion. She took a drink from her glass. She was on vacation.

"Whatup, dog?" she asked, keeping her voice light.

The dog wagged its tail slowly—once, twice, again—as though considering. Then it sat, still just out of reach. It looked over its shoulder and let its tongue loll.

"His name is Biscuit." The boy came up beside the dog, planted the butt of his fishing rod against the ground, and put his arm around the dog.

"Well, hello, Biscuit. And what do they call you?"

The boy met her eyes, flushed, then dropped his head. His fingers moved in the dog's hairy coat. His lips moved, perhaps answering, but no sound came out.

"That must be your dad coming with Christian," Eden said to cover the boy's shyness. "Or maybe he's your uncle?"

The boy looked up at her from beneath shaggy bangs. "He's my dad." He looked over his shoulder, reassured by the approaching proximity of the two men. "I'm Ethan," he said.

"Nice to meet you, Ethan. I'm Eden."

"Our names sound kind of alike."

"They do, don't they? We better not be late for dinner. If they call us in from outside, it'll be hard to tell who they're calling, right?"

Eden was pleased to see that made the boy grin. "My dad has to call me a lot. Sometimes, if it's taking too long or if I don't hear him, he'll call Biscuit. Biscuit always comes when my dad calls, and since we go together almost everywhere . . ."

Ethan shrugged.

"Sounds like a good system."

"Do you have a dog?"

"I used to. My dog went with me pretty much everywhere too. He'd come with me when I went camping. His name was Samson."

"My dad and I go camping a lot. What happened to your dog?"

"He died. He got pretty old."

"My mom died too. But she wasn't old."

The boy said it so matter-of-factly. Eden searched for something to say, but by then, Christian and Ethan's dad were close enough to hear their conversation, so she looked up to greet her competitors instead.

"Christian! Good to see you!" She put her foot to the ground to push her swing a bit more to make it clear she wasn't getting up. "And you must be the mysterious fifth competitor. I've just been chatting with your sous chef."

"That would be me," the man said. "I'm Daniel."

She judged him to be in his midthirties. He stood with one hand in the pocket of his jeans, a fishing rod in the other, with a lidded woven basket looped over his shoulder and his feet spread apart in an easy stance. He looked like central casting for a backwoods trail guide in a rom-com—rough around the edges, but he likely cleaned up nicely.

"Eden. Nice to meet you."

"So?" said Christian to Eden. "How did it go?" He looked at Daniel. "Eden is Miss June."

Eden raised her eyebrows. It made her sound like she was in a beauty pageant or the centerfold of a men's magazine. Christian wasn't a misogynistic asshole, though, she'd decided back in February. They'd spoken a bit before heading back to their respective lives. She'd told him about dividing her time between her grandparents' homestead in Idlewild and the mission in Detroit. He'd told her about taking a break from culinary school to look after his mom, tending their large garden in Flint, and taking on odd jobs to make ends meet. Eden had read between the lines, though, and had a lot of respect for what he was doing. Flint wasn't an easy place to be these days, especially as the primary caregiver for a terminally ill parent. And you don't just walk away from a prestigious culinary school and expect to pick up where you left off later.

She saw Daniel look between Christian and her. The corner of his mouth had quirked at the "Miss June" remark. Now he was waiting to see if she would take offense. Daniel was a watchful sort, she decided. And he was her competitor.

They both were.

"It went really, really well," Eden said. "You should be nervous, Mr. August."

She turned her gaze to Daniel. "Are you cooking this month? Are you Mr. July or Mr. October?"

"October. With school out, I thought Ethan and I could spend some time downstate."

"Downstate. And where's home?"

"Upper Peninsula. Escanaba. You?"

"Idlewild." At Daniel's blank look, she gestured roughly east with a hitchhiker's thumb. "Not too far from here."

"Sorry," he said. "It's been a long time since I was this far south."

"That's a shame. Some of the best ingredients are this far south."

"Yeah, maybe. You trolls tend to think so."

Eden laughed, nearly spilling her drink, as much at the remark as the horrified look on Christian's face.

"What, you've never heard that before?" she asked him.

"What, calling you a troll? No, gotta say never have."

"No offense to the lovely lady," said Daniel. "Trolls are you here in the Lower Peninsula."

"We live under the bridge," finished Eden. "If it makes you feel any better, Christian, call him a Yooper."

"Dude, I highly advise you don't use 'troll' as part of any pickup line down here 'under the bridge.'" Christian used his fingers to make air quotes.

"Duly noted," said Daniel. "So what *is* the best ingredient available only here under the bridge?" he asked Eden.

She looked at him over the rim of her glass. Christian was also paying close attention.

"You want incredible dairy? You won't find it from cows that spend five or six months of the year in pasture—and only pasture—and then in barns or paddocks eating hay the rest of the year. And that's all I'm going to say." Maybe it was the wine, but she felt empowered. Her occupation was dominated by men, and here were two hanging on her every word about the best ingredients for a competition-worthy meal.

Daniel tipped a make-believe hat.

Ethan pulled on his father's sleeve.

"Right," Daniel said. "Dinner won't catch itself." He nodded at

Eden. "It was a pleasure meeting you." He turned to Christian. "You got a pole? Want to join us?"

"No and yes," said Christian. "How about next time?"

Daniel smiled at Eden. "How about you? Want to trade in your wineglass for a fishing pole?"

"Not a chance. I'm savoring some well-earned downtime." She lifted her glass to the man and his son. "As my grandpa would say, I wish you fish."

Daniel held out his hand to shake Christian's before nodding a farewell to Eden and heading toward the wood line path that would take them to the stream, Ethan keeping pace with short runs and hops and the dog loping around and through the forest underbrush to take point.

*Definitely central casting*, thought Eden, aware of Christian watching her as she lifted her wineglass to her lips and pushed her bare foot against the ground to again set the swing in motion.

# Daniel

"We found currants!" Ethan was exuberant. Daniel looked up to see Eden standing in the doorway of the main kitchen, her morning coffee in hand.

"You did! I see!" Eden responded, equally effusive.

*Ethan has that effect on people*, Daniel thought, not for the first time. You couldn't help but share in his enthusiasm. That came from Thistle, he knew.

"We're making currant jelly. Do you want to help? It's for the October competition dinner!" Ethan clapped his hands over his mouth. "Oh, I forgot," he stage-whispered to Daniel. "Was that part a secret?"

Eden laughed out loud. "No worries, Ethan. Your secret is safe with me. I already had my competition dinner."

Ethan's concerned eyes stayed on Daniel.

"Not to fret, bud," he said. "None of our ingredients are a secret. The ingredients on their own don't make the meal. It's how you prepare and serve them."

"Very true," said Eden, sauntering into the room. "But as I said yesterday, it's not just *which* ingredients but the *quality* of the ingredients that make the difference between a good meal and an eye-roll, oh-my-god-that-is-de*li*cious meal." Eden made a mock swoon that set Ethan giggling and Biscuit's tail wagging.

"True enough," said Daniel. "What better source than the fields and forest?" He pointed to the colander of fresh currants they'd collected on their way back from fishing.

"What indeed? Particularly the forest. Have fun, boys!" she said and left.

"I like her," said Ethan, mashing currants through the chinois.

"Me too," said Daniel, his mind puzzling through what he knew of Eden, where she lived, and how those juxtaposed with possible dairy-in-the-forest sources.

# Blaise

Blaise felt uneasy. He rotated the cut-crystal wine glass in his hand, feeling the hard edges of its pattern against his fingertips. Took a sip. A moue of distaste crossed his lips. He got up from the couch, went to the kitchen, and dumped the rest down the drain.

His apartment kitchen was pristine. That was part of the problem, Blaise reflected as he picked up the wine bottle he'd brought home from his latest visit to the Forager Chefs Club. He was confident there was some good Michigan wine out there. He just hadn't found it yet. He refused to cook with a wine that he wouldn't serve at the table. Not that there was much cooking going on at the moment.

Blaise looked down the hallway to his brother's shut bedroom door. Bradley hadn't wanted to cook this evening. Or yesterday evening. Or the evening before that.

It was something they did together. The thing that had first served to salve the wound of their parents' abandonment. The divorce announced two weeks after they graduated from high school. Weddings, in different states, before that year was out. Clearly, his parents had decided long before graduation that their marriage was done, pursuing their separate lives while maintaining the charade of a life that included Blaise and Bradley. Agreed to wait until after the twins were out of high school—and eighteen years old, legally of age—to let them in on the truth. They'd been good at keeping it all hidden. Those first few months, Blaise had spent a lot of time going over it in his head, sorting through memories, trying to see what he had missed. His parents had been good, very good, at giving the appearance that all was well. All was normal.

Which had been a lie.

His parents had sold the family home but paid for Blaise to attend the Culinary Institute of America—the renowned CIA—in Hyde Park, New York. Provided a monthly stipend for his and Bradley's support, even now, ten years later. That would end in two years. Once he and Bradley were thirty, they would be on their own. *But of course,* Blaise had not said aloud to his father, *you've got another family to provide for now, new heirs.*

Blaise opened the small wine fridge and selected a bottle of Pouilly-Fuissé. He should try a couple of the other bottles of Michigan wine he'd brought back as samples from the Club's wine cellar, but his mood was too dark to risk another mediocre glass.

He uncorked the bottle, chose a new glass, and poured. Took a sip. Better. Much better.

But the kitchen was still pristine, the range top and ovens cold. Not what he'd wanted—or expected—for tonight. Or yesterday. Or the day before that. He went back to the couch.

He thought they'd be cooking. Collaborating. Inventing.

He didn't have his competition dinner menu set yet. He had some ideas, but his jotted notes for three courses would require at least seven exceptions to the foraging rules. He had to get that down to three. Or figure out a way to mask a few of them, get by the mandatory ingredient check. He held his wine up to the light. A beautiful thing, French wine.

It was still July—the tail end, but still July. He had plenty of time before the last Saturday in September. But he liked to feel ahead of the game. July and August were slow for his épicerie de blaise business. Most of the clientele who could afford him were at their beach homes or vacationing in places that required a passport to reach. He didn't have any engagements booked until after his competition dinner. That should be a good thing—time to experiment, come up with new recipes with Bradley, perfect their execution on his own—but his kitchen was cold. So he was at loose ends, trying to find a decent glass of Michigan wine and waiting for Bradley to come out of his room and want to cook.

He opened and then shut random kitchen cabinet doors, seeking inspiration from the ingredients within, hoping that the sound might travel down the hallway and slip under Bradley's bedroom door, pique his brother's curiosity enough that he might venture out, decide he was hungry and wanted to cook. Blaise paused at the sight of several tins of anchovies. Cooked down in a sauté pan, they liquefied, adding a unique, salty depth of flavor. But they weren't a freshwater fish. Yet one more ingredient he couldn't use without expanding his exceptions list even more.

Blaise wondered how the salt truck driver was doing. Christian's dinner was in August. He'd been surprised to learn that he and Christian had attended CIA at the same time. If their paths had crossed, it hadn't been memorable. He didn't know—and frankly didn't care—why Christian had left before completing the program. A lot of people couldn't cut it. The fact that the guy was now driving a salt truck in Flint spoke volumes. Christian wasn't really competition at all.

Blaise took another long sip of Pouilly-Fuissé.

Maybe he'd drive back to the Forager Chefs Club tomorrow. Sitting around here certainly wasn't getting his menu created. He glanced again down the hallway at the closed bedroom door. Bradley might be more in the mood for some brotherly bonding in the kitchen after being left to himself for a few days.

# *AUGUST*

# Christian

"Dude! Shit. I almost didn't pick up, thinking it was one of those 'your car warranty has expired' calls! So you finally decided to rejoin society and get a cell phone again!"

"Yeah, good to hear your voice too, man," Christian said. He hadn't been sure this was a good idea, calling after no communication for almost two years. But there was no way he had the time—or gas money—to drive to the Upper Peninsula, and it was William who had the contacts he needed anyway.

"So what are you doing these days? Please tell me you got out of Flint and are running your own kitchen in a restaurant that's such a dive, it's actually trendy."

"Nah, still keeping the lights on in Flint." Christian kept his voice nonchalant. How to tell his friend—the one who had raced bikes with him along the neighborhood's sidewalks—that the cancer had spread, was eating away at his mom's memory, that moving her from the house where she'd come as a bride would be too disruptive and disorienting?

"Will the last person to leave Flint please turn out the lights? Shit, man, that's you?"

"Apparently. What're you up to?"

William laughed, and the years vanished, taking Christian back to beers and bars where they'd mapped out schemes and dreams.

"Waddaya think? I'm running a kitchen in a restaurant that's such a dive, it's trendy. Oh, and I got married. Got a little one on the way."

"That's great, man. Really great. Congrats."

There was a pause. "How's your mom?"

"Hanging in there. She doesn't want to leave Flint."

Another pause.

"You're a good man, Christian. Seriously. Give her my best, will you?"

Christian doubted his mom would remember William, even though she baked the cake for his eleventh birthday. "Sure. I will."

Another pause. How to bridge the years? Best to get to the point. The reason for the call.

"Hey, William. I got a favor to ask. You still got that contact at Michigan Sea Grant?"

# Blaise

Bradley had the patience of a rock. Or maybe just the sheer stubbornness. The stubbornness of a big rock in the middle of a stream, making everything go over or around. Or maybe his brother was just oblivious. Oblivious as a big rock in a stream, making everything—and everybody—go over or around.

Blaise didn't like going over or around. And he shouldn't have to. Bradley was his brother. Not just his brother—his twin.

Why didn't he want to cook together anymore?

Blaise had stayed at the Forager Chefs Club for three days before guilt got the better of him and he drove back to Grand Rapids to make sure Bradley was okay—that he was eating, that he wasn't staying in the same clothes, that he hadn't lapsed into an obsolete routine and gone back to the restaurant that had fired the two of them.

The apartment had been pristine, but Blaise had noted there were fewer eggs in the refrigerator, the ground lamb was gone, the loaf of artisanal rye bread was half gone, they were down to one stick of butter, and they'd be out of milk soon. Good, so Bradley had been eating, doing a little cooking.

Now, two days later, it was clear that Blaise's absence hadn't budged Bradley into wanting to create anything new in the kitchen with his brother.

A rock. In the middle of the stream that was Blaise's life.

His brother was sitting on the couch in their living room, gazing out the window. A book from the public library on flower arranging was open on his lap.

"Let's play Questions," Blaise said, sitting down in an upholstered chair across from him.

Bradley didn't say anything but glanced at him before looking away. He shut the book.

This was assent.

"What did you do while I was gone?"

A pause. "I read," Bradley said. "I walked to the library. And I played chess."

"With whom did you play chess?" Technically, this was a breach in Questions protocol—it was Bradley's turn for a question—but Blaise wanted to know if someone had been in the apartment with his brother while he was gone. Maybe there was a chess set at the library?

"Nobody. I switched seats. It was a long game, but I won."

"Excellent. I won't ask black or white because it's your turn for a question."

"Where did you go?"

"To the Forager Chefs Club."

"Why didn't you take me with you?"

Again, a breach in the game's protocol, but Blaise was glad. It meant Bradley cared about the situation; it was important to him.

"I didn't think you wanted to leave your bedroom."

That wasn't entirely true, but close enough to keep the game going without sounding petulant.

"Would you have wanted to come?" he asked.

Bradley considered this. "Was Celeste there?"

Again, a breach in protocol to ask a question without first answering the one before. This *was* interesting.

"She wasn't. Do you only want to come to the Club if she is there?"

A pause.

"Yes."

"Why?" The hell with protocol, with the game. He and his brother were having a conversation, a real conversation. This was good. It was more than good. And he was learning something very important about his brother. The silence stretched. Blaise tried again.

"Why do you want to be at the Club when Celeste is there?"

A pause.

"I like her." He turned his head and met Blaise's eyes. "We cooked together."

Blaise blinked. *They cooked together? When?*

"Is that why you won't cook with me?" he asked instead. "Because now you only want to cook with Celeste?" His throat felt tight as he asked the question. He remembered Bradley asking about the redheaded girl the day before her competition dinner in April. They'd played Questions, one of the few times Bradley had initiated the game. Blaise had been pleased—had taken it as a sign that he'd done the right thing in bringing his brother to a new environment. He had been less than pleased to learn Bradley had foraged during her month—and she caught him. It seemed she'd forgiven Bradley—by extension, forgiven Blaise. Unless she was holding that card to use later. Transgressing the foraging rule could kick him out of the competition. Now he tried to remember everything he'd told his brother about the girl from Mackinac Island.

"I'll cook with you," Bradley said. "Can we cook at the Club when Celeste is there?"

Blaise recalled his conversation with Randall back in February: "*The terroir contest invitation was extended to you. Not to you and your brother. You have publicized yourself as a solo chef, and it is as a solo chef that you must compete.*" Practicing at the Club with his brother would raise all sorts of red flags. The fact was that Randall's perceptions—the rumors—were uncomfortably close to reality. "*There are stories of the dishes the two of you created together at the restaurant before you went solo—his creative use of ingredients combined with your structure and discipline. You have the technical skills that bring your brother's innovation and imagination to the plate."*

"How about we practice here so you can show Celeste when we go to the Club?" offered Blaise.

Bradley didn't answer. He opened the book on his lap.

Three days later, they made the drive from Grand Rapids to the Forager Chefs Club. Blaise had told Bradley that Celeste would either already be there or would arrive soon after. He wasn't sure if that were true, but he'd done what he could to make it true. It had been enough to get his brother into their apartment kitchen the last two days. Bradley may have the stubbornness of a rock, but water did eventually wear away even the hardest stone.

# Celeste

"It's just not in the cards, Celly," Chef said. "I appreciate your efforts at self-teaching sauces, and I know you have a reputation with the locals as a good foraging cook, but that's different from what we do here. If you're looking for a path to grow your career, maybe consider moving to the mainland. More restaurants, more options, particularly downstate." He spread his hands in an apologetic gesture as if that would ease the sting. "Think about it."

Celeste nodded, the lump in her throat blocking words, even if she could have thought of any. She went to her station to cut vegetables. Ten minutes later, she cut herself. It wasn't deep, but it bled a lot. She left the kitchen, avoiding everyone's eyes. When she returned, bandaged and gloved, she saw someone had cleaned up her mess for her. She felt a tap on her shoulder.

"Call for you in the office. A guy," said Keith, one of the kitchen porters. "Better make it quick. Chef doesn't like personal calls."

Celeste tamped down her panic. Who would call her here? Several curious looks followed her out the kitchen door.

It took her a moment to recognize Blaise's voice. It took a little longer to comprehend what he was asking her to do.

"Just for a week or so," he said and then, more tentatively, "And maybe another couple of weeks in September?"

"Let me get this straight," said Celeste. She kept her voice low.

"You want me to come stay at the Forager Chefs Club so that you can practice cooking without worrying about Bradley because he doesn't want to be at the Club unless I'm there, and then again next month so you can focus on beating me in this competition? Do I have that right?"

There was a pause.

"He hasn't been himself, Celeste. Not for a couple of months now. He's been asking about you." Another pause. "He's been asking *for* you. He says . . . he says you cooked together." There was something in Blaise's voice—just the barest tinge of accusation, as though she'd crossed some line.

"I'll think about it," Celeste said. Don't call me at work again." She hung up and went back to her station, ignoring Chef's steely gaze and her coworkers' glances.

It had been early May, just a couple of days after her April competition dinner, when she found out that Blaise had a twin brother. Bradley had told her he'd collected and arranged the flowers, set the candles for her dinner—all as an apology for foraging her ramps. He hadn't met her eyes when he said it, but he seemed sincere, nonetheless. She'd accepted his apology, offered that they make lunch together— May wasn't assigned to anyone so they could forage as they liked.

They'd taken the trail into the woods. They'd been among the trees, not speaking, eyes scanning the ground for edibles, when Celeste had stopped, put a hand to Bradley's arm, and pointed. A fox stood on a fallen log several yards away, posed as though for a photograph, sunlight streaming down through the branches of new spring leaves. The fox and the humans watched each other until a rustle in the underbrush had broken the spell, and the fox had bounded with lithe grace after the sound. Celeste had turned to smile at Bradley, and this time he had held her gaze, not skittering it away like that small animal in the underbrush. Celeste hadn't known at the time that Bradley had autism, but she'd understood that this was different, that perhaps it didn't happen often.

They'd found the morel patch and then harvested a few more of the ramps, mindful in their selection and manner of cutting. Back in the kitchen, they'd chopped and sautéed, adding this and that from the refrigerator and the pantry shelves and the baskets she'd packed for her return home until they'd gone through a dozen tasting spoons and decided the dish was ready. They'd scooped it into shallow bowls and eaten while sitting on the wide bench swing hung from a beech tree behind the Club, sharing a bottle of white wine from the Leelanau Peninsula that had a colorful court jester sitting in a boat on the label. They hadn't talked much, but not much needed to be said. It had felt companionable and romantic. She soaked the label off the bottle before she left and took it with her. She used it as a bookmark.

"It's crazy, I know, to even think of dropping everything here and going," Celeste said the next morning after telling her mother about her conversation with Chef, Blaise's call, Bradley, the beauty of the room he'd prepared for her dinner, her confronting him, their foraging walk, and then cooking together and sharing a meal. "I have a good job. I'm always going to be just prepping unless there's a change in head chef, but it's still a good job."

"There are always more jobs."

"Yeah, but Aunt Tilda pulled some strings to get me this one."

"And she can pull more if it comes down to you needing them—which I don't think you will." Her mother sipped from her teacup, a delicate piece that didn't match any other in the house. "She lives for that kind of thing, you know."

Celeste remembered the pizza delivery after dark last February. "True."

"Put aside what your head is telling you. What is your heart telling you?"

Celeste dropped off her handwritten resignation letter that afternoon.

The garden in the front courtyard of the Forager Chefs Club was a riot of the late-summer colors of Echinacea, coreopsis, salvia, and bee balm. Parked in one of the visitor spots was a car she remembered from her first trip to Annie's Gourmet Bait Shop.

Elena stood up to greet her as she came through the door, pulling her pirate-doodled suitcase behind her.

"Celeste! Welcome back! How are you?"

"Unemployed. But happy to be here. I think."

"Well, I'm delighted to see you. I have your key, and your room is clean, restocked, and ready for you." She handed Celeste the familiar, heavy key with its brass label of *Leelanau* and a posey of flowers.

The posey was a tight cluster of blooms, their stems enveloped in a complex weave of three different colors of ribbon tied at the bottom in a bow. Celeste raised it to her nose and inhaled. The fragrance was sweet and spicy.

"Wow, you've outdone yourself with the welcome this time, Elena. Thank you."

"Oh, that isn't from me. A certain gentlemen gathered them and did the ribbon work. He reluctantly let me be the steward when I told him that I most certainly would not let him into your room."

Celeste held the flowers against the lower half of her face, feeling her cheeks redden. "Is anyone else here?"

Elena counted off on her fingers. "Well, Blaise and Bradley, as I'm sure you've guessed. Christian is here. His dinner is just over a week away, so no foraging on the property, please. Oh, and Daniel is here with his son Ethan. I don't think you've met them."

Celeste lowered the bouquet, interested.

"The elusive fifth contestant?"

"The very same. He came down from Escanaba at the beginning of July. Ethan is his six-year-old son. I believe they plan to stay until school starts in a couple of weeks. And, of course, they'll be back for Daniel's October dinner. Oh, and they brought their dog, Biscuit. He's a sweetheart. You're not afraid of dogs, are you?"

"Only if they hate redheads." A few years back, there had been a dog owned by someone who'd rented one of the lakeshore houses for the summer that apparently had a distinct dislike for anyone with red hair. The dog got loose one day. After a harrowing race—she on her bike, the dog hot on her heels—Celeste had avoided the lake path on that side of the island for the rest of the summer. "So everyone is here except Eden?" Celeste felt a pang of disappointment. She'd have liked to see Eden again, spend some time with her. She knew she should think of Eden only as a competitor, but both their dinners were in the books now, so maybe there was room for conversation or even friendship. Eden was so confident. Celeste would have welcomed any advice the woman could give her about what she should do next with her career.

"Everyone except Eden," Elena confirmed. "She spent a bit of time here after her June dinner and met Daniel and Ethan. She hasn't told me of any plans to come back, although she's welcome. And we'll see you all in December."

December. The judges' decision would be revealed that first week. She'd have to make some decisions about what to do with her life—both if she won and if she didn't. But that could wait, at least for a while.

"It's good to be back," Celeste said. She headed toward the stairs that would take her to her room, carrying her bouquet in one hand and pulling her secondhand suitcase behind her with the other.

# Christian

Christian sorted through the pots and found the small, heavy one he wanted for the sealed package on the counter. William had come through. The package of Manoomin wild rice had been waiting for him when he arrived at the Club yesterday. Technically, Manoomin wasn't rice but rather came from a grain-producing grass native to the Great Lakes and Canada. To grow, it needed shallow, quiet, fresh waters, like those where streams and rivers emptied into the Great Lakes. It had been an important food source and cultural touchstone for the Ojibwe tribes, but loss of habitat, degradation of water quality, and other factors had had a severe negative impact. Manoomin was making a comeback, though, and Christian wanted to include it in his competition meal. It had a nutty, complex flavor that would complement his entrée, and there wasn't anything more native to Michigan than Manoomin.

He held the package, feeling the weight. Harvesting Manoomin was arduous and done by hand. It wasn't something you picked up in the local grocery store. He had enough in this package for the five servings he needed for his dinner with that many more to spare. It had been a while since he'd had Manoomin. He was going to cook some for his lunch to reacquaint himself with the taste and texture.

He added water to the pot and measured in the Manoomin. Three-to-one, rather than the usual two-to-one of rice. He turned on the gas burner and set the pot over the flame.

The doctor and the visiting nurse said it was time for hospice care. They'd been saying it for about a month, but this past week, they were more insistent. There were days that his mother didn't leave her bed. Christian had promised her he wouldn't make her leave her home.

He'd made that promise shortly after his father left. The man had lived his whole life in Flint, but then had come the repeated stints of unemployment in a city that seemed to be dying by inches. Finding out his wife had inoperable cancer was more than he could handle. On a day that should have been an ordinary Tuesday, Christian got a call. It was the last time he'd spoken with his father. And the last day he was a student at the Culinary Institute of America.

Christian had intended to get his mom settled and then go back to school, keep in touch more often but continue with his last year of training. Instead, he found the mortgage two months in arrears, the roof leaking, a notice that the electricity would soon be turned off, and not much more than packages of dried ramen noodles and canned soup in the pantry.

He'd waited until his mother was asleep to call Rachel. Yes, they'd made plans, but plans weren't really promises, and promises weren't vows. Vows were made before God—were made *to* God. They were sacrosanct. Like when someone took an oath of office. Or became a priest or a nun.

Or when you spoke marriage vows. *In sickness and in health.*

What he wanted—whatever plans he'd made—had to bend when a broken vow left his mother stranded.

He'd promised his mom that he wouldn't make her leave her house, the one she'd come to as a bride.

A promise wasn't a vow.

But this one sure felt like it.

It had taken three years of working full-time following high school to save enough money to attend the CIA. It hadn't taken long for what was left to be depleted. But he'd brought the mortgage up to date, made the necessary repairs to the house, and set about making sure that his mother had nourishing food and whatever else she needed.

He'd made another promise to her, this one just the week before.

*Promise me you'll finish this competition.*

*Mom . . .*

*No, you must promise me. I took culinary school away from you. I don't want to take this away too.*

*You didn't take culinary school away from me. It was my choice to come home.*

*Promise me.*

He promised.

Her church was a godsend. Two retired nurses divided their time to stay with her when he was at the Club since he couldn't afford to pay for the care she needed when he wasn't there to provide it. He felt guilty coming to the Club a full five days before his competition dinner. But he needed the time to gather his ingredients and perfect his menu if he were to have any hope of beating his competitors. He was glad he had William ship the Manoomin to the Club rather than to Flint, where packages frequently got waylaid by porch and mailbox thieves. That thought brought him back to the pot on the stove, the simmering water.

The salt! Damn, he'd forgotten to add salt.

He grabbed a dish towel and lifted the pot lid with one hand as the other reached back to the salt cellar on the counter. Even as his fingers scooped up the portion he wanted, his mind started screaming at him.

*Wrong! Wrong! Wrong!*

The urgent message from the nerve endings in his fingertips didn't outpace the message that his brain had already sent to his hand. His fingers released the salt into the pot before his brain could process what, exactly, was wrong and send the signal to his hand to stop.

Christian looked in horror as familiar, large, rough, blue-tinged crystals of industrial salt settled into the simmering Manoomin.

# Celeste

They'd been sitting for a while on the couch, close but not touching. Celeste had brought *The Saucier's Apprentice* with her to the Club, determined to continue her self-education. She had it open to the chapter "Sauces Derived from Fish Fumet and Velouté," the book positioned on her lap so that Bradley could also see it, the wine label bookmark tucked near the back, the smiling face of the court jester peering at them above the paper.

"I want to try this one next," Celeste said, pointing at the recipe for bretonne sauce.

"You! Asshole!"

The rough shout from the doorway held more rage than anything Celeste had ever heard outside of a movie. She turned to see the source, aware of Bradley leaning forward.

Christian loomed in the doorway, breathing hard, one hand bunched in a fist at his side, the other pointing a long finger at the two of them on the couch. He looked like a post-apocalyptic survivor whose last hold on sanity had just snapped. He was looking past her. He was looking at Bradley.

Bradley noticed this and stood, taking a long sidestep to stand between her and the rage in the doorway.

Christian lunged.

Celeste screamed.

# Daniel

He was halfway up the short staircase leading from the Club's back entrance to the main level, Ethan and Biscuit close on his heels, when Daniel heard the scream.

"Stay here," he ordered Ethan, who had stopped, eyes wide, at the sound.

Biscuit barked.

"Biscuit, guard!" commanded Daniel, pointing at the dog and then at his son.

Without waiting to see if he was obeyed, Daniel vaulted up the stairs. Elena was standing behind her desk, talking hurriedly into a walkie-talkie, her chair fallen behind her against the floor. Grunts and screams were punctuated by the sound of breaking wood from the common room.

Daniel ran in and saw the heavy leather couch tipped on its back, two men grappling on the floor, Celeste scooting back from a broken side table to cower under the trestle sideboard that held glasses and the tray of decanters. It was the wrong move. Just as he reached the two men, one of them thrust out a leg, seeking purchase to turn the other on his back, knocking one side of the sideboard hard enough to send the decanters and glassware tumbling. Celeste screamed again. Daniel felt the sting on his arm of whiskey and glass shards skipping up from the floor as he braced his legs and, with his left hand, grabbed the collar of the man on top and put his right arm around his neck. He heaved him off and threw him to one side.

"Stop!" he roared.

He looked at the one he'd thrown against the upended coach. Saw it was Christian. *What the hell?* Turned to see the other man on his back, arms outspread, breathing heavily, not looking at him. Not looking at anyone. No, not true. He was looking at Celeste, but oddly, his eyes touching on her then away, over and over again. He looked familiar. Blaise, he remembered. They'd met briefly when the man had come to the Club a week or so ago. He was the September competitor.

"Don't fucking move, either of you," Daniel said, legs braced, breathing hard. "Or I swear I'll put you through that window."

"No one is putting anyone through a window. Whatever it was, this is over." The sharp voice of command came from behind them.

Daniel turned to see Randall in the doorway. Just past him was Elena, her hands on Ethan's shoulders, his face white, eyes large. Biscuit stood in front of the boy, hackles up, a low growl emanating from his throat.

Daniel put his hands up in surrender and nodded at Randall. He turned to Celeste and held his hand out to her.

"Don't put your hands on the floor. There's a lot of glass," he said, stating the obvious.

She nodded and took his hand in both of hers, coming out from under the table without putting her knees on the floor. She had a cut on her cheek and another on her neck, he noticed. They both seemed to be shallow. She looked scared. She went to crouch next to the man lying on his back. He seemed unaware of anything else in the room, just continued to watch her, his eyes flitting to and away as she approached.

"Are you okay?" she asked him.

Daniel heard a harsh laugh from Christian. He turned, ready to prevent any further mayhem. The mayhem came from a different quarter, though. Celeste took three strides, moving past Daniel, and kicked Christian in the ribs. He groaned and doubled up.

"What the hell?" she screamed. "What was that for? We were just sitting here!"

"Enough!" roared Randall as Elena came into the room and took Celeste by the shoulders.

"You want to know what for?" snarled Christian. "Ask Blaise." He pointed at the man lying on his back among the shards of glass.

Celeste pulled her leg back again for another kick, but Elena drew her closer by the shoulders, forcing her to set her foot down to keep her balance.

"You asshole! That's not Blaise. That's Bradley! His brother!"

Christian closed his mouth and lifted his head to look at the man he'd attacked.

From the doorway came Randall's crisp voice.

"You, you, and you. In my office, now," he said, pointing to the three men in turn. "Elena, could you please see to Celeste? It looks like she has a few cuts. I would like to speak with you, Celeste, once I'm done with these gentlemen."

"Ethan, could you and Biscuit help me with Celeste?" said Elena. "No, no, stay where you are. We'll come to you."

Daniel patted his son's shoulder and glanced back at the common room before leaving to join the other men in Randall's office.

What a waste of good whiskey.

# Christian

*The asshole has a brother? A twin brother?* Christian swallowed hard as he followed Randall. He'd beat the shit out of the wrong guy. This was more serious—far more serious—than losing his temper and overturning a few chairs in a bank office. He was almost certainly thrown out of the competition. He vaguely recalled some wording in the contract he signed about *decorum* and *embracing the tenets* of the Forager Chefs Club. Well, he hadn't really been in the running to win anyway, right? The culinary school dropout from Flint? So, kicked out of the competition. What else? Well, at a minimum, paying for damages. He pictured in his mind—slow motion, like in a film—all those decanter bottles and glassware crashing down. God, what was that going to cost him? And, of course, there was always the possibility that this guy—whoever the hell he was—would press charges.

Christian's last thought before Randall started speaking was to wonder if he'd turned off the range flame before stalking out of the kitchen. If not, that pot was burned and ruined by now.

*Add it to my tab*, he thought.

# Daniel

"Okay, so we're going to do this the old-fashioned way," said Randall. "Do not speak unless spoken to. By me."

Randall's office was not large. He sat behind his desk, but there weren't enough chairs for the other three to sit, so they stood. Randall pointed to Daniel. "Mr. Metsja. Recite. To the point. No elaboration."

Daniel cleared his throat. *Recite?*

"I was coming in from the back with my son and dog. We weren't foraging, just taking a walk, noting where things are . . ."

"To the point, Mr. Metsja."

It was rare for him to be told to be *more* direct.

"We were on the back stairs when we heard a scream. I told Ethan to stay where he was. I ran to the common room and saw these two in a fight. Celeste was trying to stay out of the way. I broke up the fight."

*There*, he thought. *That to the point enough for you?*

Randall pointed at Blaise's brother.

"Bradley, what happened?"

Bradley looked at Randall's desk, his arms loose at his sides. Daniel could see a dark bruise forming on his cheekbone, and his shirt was ripped. He didn't show any sign of having heard Randall. He just simply stood and looked at the desk, blinking occasionally.

After several moments, Randall turned to Christian.

"As you may have surmised by now, the man to your left is not

Blaise Strooth. He is Bradley Strooth. Through special arrangement, he has been welcomed as a guest of the Forager Chefs Club. Please, do explain why you attacked a guest of this Club."

Christian raised an open palm in supplication, then let it drop again. He turned to Bradley.

"I'm sorry. I thought you were your brother. I was out of my head. I know it probably doesn't mean much, but I am so sorry."

"And why would it make a difference if it had been Blaise in the common room and not Bradley?"

"Because Blaise swapped my sea salt for industrial road salt, and I used it in my practice dish before I realized it. It ruined a key ingredient for my competition dinner—an ingredient that I can't easily replace."

Randall picked up the walkie-talkie on his desk and turned his back. Daniel heard the unit crackle but couldn't discern Randall's words or the response.

"And how do you know it was Blaise who did this?" Randall asked, turning again to the men before him and setting the walkie-talkie on his desk.

"Ask him. He's made it clear that he doesn't think I belong here." Christian lifted his chin. "I drive a salt truck during the winter. It came up back in February when we were deciding our group exception. I said that the only salt in Michigan was mined salt, that it has a blue cast, and that it's used as road salt. He's brought it up a few times since then."

Randall looked at Daniel.

Daniel met his gaze but said nothing. He hadn't been there when that conversation happened. He didn't care if Christian drove a salt truck or dug ditches to make ends meet. Hell, he plowed driveways and parking lots in the winter. And anyway, Randall hadn't asked him a question.

"It's not up to Blaise whether someone does or does not belong in this competition," Randall said. He looked at Bradley, who was looking off into the distance above Randall's shoulder. "Bradley, would you like to say anything?"

Bradley turned his head to look at Christian.

"You scared Celeste. She got cut," he said.

"I did scare her, and I'm sorry for it," Christian agreed. "I lost my temper and was really angry at what your brother did. I didn't mean for Celeste to get hurt. I didn't mean to hurt you. I thought you were your brother. I'm sorry. When I see Celeste, I'll apologize to her."

Bradley nodded once, his gaze steady, then turned back to again look over Randall's shoulder.

"Gentlemen, you are excused," said Randall. "Christian, I believe you know where the broom and dustpan are in the kitchen. You've got some cleaning up to do. I have a few calls to make. You and I will speak again about this."

# Christian

Before he got to the kitchen, Christian heard the whisk of a broom and the soft scrape of glass being moved across the wood floor of the common room.

"Here, let me do that," Christian said to Celeste.

She handed him the broom. He saw the shine of ointment on the scratch on her cheek, a Band-Aid on her neck.

"Celeste, I am so, so sorry."

"I know."

"Blaise swapped out my sea salt for blue highway salt. I didn't notice it until—well, it doesn't matter. I lost my temper, and I shouldn't have. Especially not toward you and Bradley."

"I heard about the blue salt. I was with Elena when Randall called over the walkie-talkie to ask her to bring the salt cellar to his office." She sighed. "You're probably right about it being Blaise. I'm sure he thought it was just a joke."

"Yeah, well, the joke is definitely on me."

"What did Randall say? What's he going to do?"

"He sent me to clean up this mess," Christian said, indicating the broken glass, whiskey puddles, and overturned furniture. "He said he had to make a couple of calls."

Christian swept together broken glass to join Celeste's pile. "They'll kick me out of the competition."

"That's harsh. What about Blaise? What happens to him?"

"I don't know. Maybe nothing. He could say it was just a prank, a joke, like you said. Did he break an actual rule? And I can't even prove it was him. I'm pretty sure me attacking someone breaks a rule. And breaking a rule gets you kicked out."

Celeste looked thoughtful.

"I found a cardboard box to put the broken glass in," she said. "And not all the decanters broke, so that's good."

It took a half-hour or so to sweep up all the glass and put the room back in order. Christian took the box of broken glass out to the trash and hosed off the broom bristles and dustpan before putting them back in the kitchen closet. He came back to the common room to see Celeste standing with Bradley, who still wore the torn shirt. She was talking with Blaise.

Christian shoved down a surge of fury.

"Oh, man, I'm going to have your ass in a sling for this," spit out Blaise.

"No. No, you're not," said Celeste, interrupting the retort on Christian's lips. She held up a hand toward Christian. "You stay there. I don't want to have to sweep up this place again." She pointed at Blaise. "And you, back off. You've done enough harm already."

Blaise sneered and took a step toward Celeste. "Since when—"

He cut off mid-sentence when Bradley took a step forward and put his hand on his brother's chest.

"Stop," said Bradley, his tone flat.

Christian felt a hand on his shoulder. It was Elena. His stomach dropped at her expression: sorrow, empathy. This was it, then. She had come to tell him to pack his bags, to leave.

"Christian, I'm so sorry," she said. "There's a call for you. Randall said you should take it in his office."

His heart skipped a beat. Cell service being what it was, his mother had the Club's landline number. As did the two retired nurses from church and her doctor. He followed her back to Randall's office.

The phone receiver lay on the desk, waiting for him. He heard Elena shut the door behind him.

# Randall

Randall sat on a high stool pulled up to the main kitchen's butcher-block work island, a glass with two fingers of bourbon close to hand, the rest of the bottle not much farther away. It was the last Saturday in August, and the kitchen was cold. It shouldn't have been. That was one of the three things that were currently wrong.

He took a sip of bourbon and again picked up the handwritten sheet of paper that had been left behind when Christian made his hasty exit earlier in the week. He'd been in the kitchen, working on his dishes, practicing the timing of his menu. And then he'd added salt to his dish—except it hadn't been the sea salt he expected. Randall scanned the menu again with a practiced eye. Somewhat ambitious, not overly so. He set the paper down with a sigh and looked around again at the kitchen. It should have been a flurry of activity. It wasn't. No one was cooking at the Club tonight. The judges who had arrived as scheduled were now dining together in Manistee. Which was the second of the three things that were currently wrong.

The phone call had come while Randall sat at his desk, alone in his office, looking at the salt cellar filled with rough crystals of an ever-so-faint blue hue, trying to decide what to do. It should have been obvious. Christian had attacked a guest of the Club. But it didn't feel obvious, looking at that salt cellar, knowing the personalities involved. Meek people rarely made good chefs. And if he eliminated Christian from the competition, what to do about Blaise, who set the tirade in motion? It was a prank at best; it was flagrant sabotage at worst. He couldn't eliminate two of five. Or could he? Should he?

And then the phone rang. Randall picked up, knowing Elena was with Celeste.

Randall took another sip from his glass, thankful that he hadn't decanted this bottle of orphan barrel bourbon. It hadn't been part of the smashed ruin that had strewn the floor of the common room.

Elena had kept in touch with the woman who called. She was a retired nurse, a friend from Katherine's church. She'd asked for Christian. It was imperative he come home. Immediately.

He'd made it in time, Elena had relayed to Randall the next day.

Which led his mind to the third thing that was wrong, so very wrong, about today. Katherine Koch Gallo—the vibrant woman who had drawn pictures with colored pencils of her dishes rather than write out a menu, who had brought to one memorable potluck dinner the best beef Wellington Randall had ever tasted, who would likely have been a member of the Forager Chefs Club, probably of the Founders Circle, had she not instead married Thomas Gallo and moved to Flint—had died today.

And he'd never told her he loved her.

She hadn't recognized him when he'd stood at her front door back in January.

Randall tipped the glass to his mouth and downed its contents. He thought he heard a footstep and turned his head toward the door. He wouldn't have minded if Elena joined him. But she was seeing to the judges' dinner, he remembered. The doorway was empty. He reached for the bottle that he'd set next to the framed photo, the one he kept locked away and never displayed, and poured another two fingers of bourbon.

He sipped from the glass and pondered what he would have

decided to do about Christian and Blaise and the competition dinner that should have been prepared in this kitchen tonight had the phone call summoning Christian not made the decision for him.

MICHIGAN DINING AT ITS FINEST ↙ change title?

FIRST COURSE:

TRIO OF HERBAL BUTTERS, WHITEFISH SPREAD, PESTO, SELECTION OF BREADS, LOCAL CHEESES, FRESH BERRIES

SECOND COURSE: ↙ call Leonard to confirm brother coming to Bear Lake Friday

SQUAB STUFFED WITH PLUMS, DUCK + VEAL DEMIGLACE

MANOOMIN WILD RICE

GLAZED BEETS WITH CHERRIES

THIRD COURSE:

HAZELNUT TART WITH LIQUER-INFUSED WHIPPED CREAM  (FRANGELICO? ↗ 3RD exception)

exceptions: pine nuts + olive oil for pesto

# *SEPTEMBER*

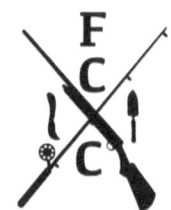

# Blaise

Blaise realized he'd been approaching it all wrong. He'd let himself get tangled up in Randall's words back in February about not relying on Bradley for inspiration—could he deliver as a solo chef?

Yes. The answer was yes. He could.

Blaise didn't need to create a meal nuanced with unexpected pairings and foraged flavors to win this competition—he didn't need Bradley. He just needed to do what he did very well: plan, prep, and cook an exemplary dinner sourced locally. He had the skill. He had the local contacts. The immediate goal wasn't to stand out among *all* chefs but to outcook just four people and thereby win fifty thousand dollars and acclaim. Three people, he corrected himself.

He took a sip of the French Bordeaux he'd brought with him from home. The only one who could even be considered competition had been Christian, and only because he had attended the CIA. The rest hadn't any *real* culinary training. Blaise had confirmed from a source that Christian hadn't been kicked out. He'd simply packed up and left—walked out on the premier cooking school in America!—choosing instead to drive a salt truck in Flint. Unbelievable. But it didn't matter; the man was now out of the equation.

Blaise had reconnoitered the main kitchen on the last Saturday of August, just to be sure. The only person there was Randall. Blaise had pulled up short of entering the room, seeing him there. He'd been sitting on one of the tall stools at the work island, a glass and bottle near to hand, looking at a sheet of paper.

Blaise had been waiting for the summons to Randall's office. He'd decided he would deflect any questions and instead demand to know what was being done about the attack on his brother. No one had seen him swap out the salt. He'd meant it to unnerve Christian, remind the dropout that he was out of his league, make him wonder if maybe the new guy, the one from the Upper Peninsula who had his kid in tow, knew it too and was sending a message. The fact that Christian actually put the blue salt in his dish just underscored his incompetence, his lack of attention in the kitchen. That was on him, not Blaise.

The summons hadn't come. Blaise didn't know if Christian had been officially kicked out, but it didn't matter. The only person who'd been in the kitchen the last Saturday in August had been Randall, hunched on a stool, morosely contemplating the gas range devoid of any pots or pans, the cold oven. And now August was a calendar page in the past, and Christian hadn't cooked for the judges during his assigned month.

Blaise added more wine to his glass. Held it up to the light, admiring its color.

It was September now. And September belonged to him.

# Christian

Christian squared the hole and made it a little deeper. Someone else may turn the soil here one day, and he didn't want anyone to inadvertently dig up what he was about to bury. Satisfied, he set the shovel aside and fetched the items he'd left on the chaise lounge.

He hadn't had enough money for a burial. He hadn't really had enough for the cremation, either, but what did it matter now if the mortgage fell behind?

He'd selected a spot along the herb border. He poured her ashes in the hole first. Then, he carefully set the other items in, one by one, stretching to reach the bottom of the hole. Her favorite coffee mug, the worn image of Tahquamenon Falls barely visible after years of washings. The small, white Bible she'd received on her first Communion. He wasn't sure it was okay to bury a Bible in the dirt, but he'd take that up with God when the time came—he wasn't interested in the priest's opinion. A four-by-six photo he'd found in her nightstand drawer. It showed a group of seven people at a campfire, the remains of what looked like a feast around them. Christian had peered at each face when he'd found it during his hunt for the Bible. He'd been able to pick out his mother—she looked to be in her early twenties—but hadn't found his father. Maybe he was the one who had taken the photo. Maybe it was before they met. He'd never know. He placed in the hole one of the tasting spoons from their kitchen, a token of all the cooking they'd done together. He added the photo of the wild blackberry canes he'd taken back in June when she'd sent him out foraging with her grocery list. He'd gone back to that yard to pick plums the morning of his last trip to the Forager Chefs Club, intending them for his squab entrée. He supposed the plums were still there at the Club, along with the package of Manoomin, the small glass Pyrex of frozen demi-glace he'd spent four days making last winter, and two mason jars of preserved pears from their basement stores. The last item to go in the hole was her box of colored pencils. He opened it and, seeing how short so many of them were, remembered his plan to buy her a new set. Yet one more thing he hadn't finished. He closed the box to add it to the grave, then stopped. Opened it again. Selected the shortest one, a fresh green that reminded him of young lemon verbena leaves. It was the scent she loved, though holding it to his nose, he only smelled old pencil wood. He closed the box, keeping the green pencil, and set it into the hole.

Eschewing the shovel, Christian filled the hole back in by hand, letting the dirt sift through his fingers, taking his time. It took a while, which didn't matter because there was nowhere he had to be. No claims on his time at all.

When the earth was smooth where the hole had been, Christian pulled out of his back pocket three small envelopes. He spread cosmos, bells of Ireland, and wild verbena seeds, tamping them down and sprinkling additional soil on top. These varieties of annuals self-sowed, and he'd collected the seed himself. They'd lie dormant through the fall and winter, and then, hopefully, sprout in the spring, become established enough to self-sow, and come back, year after year.

He wondered if he'd be here to see it. He could be, he supposed. Did he want to be? He'd fulfilled his promise to his mother—the one that had felt like a vow. His mother had died in her own bed. Had not been made to leave her home in the neighborhood where she'd lived for almost thirty years.

Christian went to the kitchen, washed his hands, and took two beers out of the fridge. He carried them back outside and settled onto the chaise lounge. He scanned the vegetable garden. Still some tomatoes, quite a few cucumbers, and beans. The beetles had decimated the summer squash plants, but the acorn squash on the far side of the garden was thriving. He'd pick what was left tomorrow. Take it to the food bank. He remembered a conversation with Eden back in July about the mission in Detroit where she worked, the dinners on Thursdays. She could probably use the produce too. But he didn't remember the name of the mission and didn't want to suddenly appear on her doorstep anyway. No, the food bank in Flint would make good use of the produce. There were plenty of people right where he lived who would welcome fresh vegetables.

By the time he twisted the cap off the second beer, he had his plan. He'd drop off the food, let the neighbors he trusted know to help themselves to whatever else ripened, and lock up the house. Rely on his reputation to keep the squatters and scrappers out.

Randall hadn't told him he was kicked out of the competition. He might have missed the opportunity to cook, but until someone told him otherwise, there was a room reserved for him, cost-free, for the rest of the year at the Forager Chefs Club.

It was September. Blaise's month. The asshole better not be cooking his Manoomin. Christian took another swig of beer. Only one way to find out. He was going to drive out to the Club.

Stay a while.

# Blaise

"What are you cooking?"

Bradley didn't reply.

His brother could be ignoring him—he'd been doing that off and on since Blaise overheard Celeste explaining why Christian had been so angry, why, when he'd apologized, he'd said it was because of what Bradley's brother had done. Blaise had stepped in to stop *that* conversation as soon as he realized the topic, the two of them sitting on the top step of the Club's front porch, coffee cups in hand. He'd thought they were admiring the flower garden. He'd thought they looked cute together. Instead, the no-talent redhead had been working to put a wedge between him and his brother. His *twin* brother, whom he'd looked after since they were kids.

He confronted Celeste right there. She hadn't backed down, hadn't apologized.

*I'm explaining.*

*Explaining from your side, you mean.*

*I don't have a side. I'm just telling him what I saw, what Christian said. What have you told him about what happened?*

Nothing. Bradley hadn't asked him; there was no need to bring it up unless and until he did. He didn't tell Celeste that. He told her to mind her own business—well, maybe he said it a little differently—used two specific words—but it's what he meant.

She'd looked at Bradley then, and he at her. His brother never looked anyone in the eye, not for long, anyway, but he did look at her. She put her hand on his forearm, squeezed it, and then stood up and went inside.

She left the Club later that day.

Getting a response from his brother was always hit or miss, but it had been more challenging since then. Blaise walked into the adjunct kitchen. On the counter beside Bradley was an open hardcover book, page edges slightly yellow with age. A piece of plastic wrap protected the paper from any errant splashes, and a wooden spoon lay across, keeping the book open about halfway in. Blaise stepped nearer but didn't touch it. He saw the recipe for *huitres Bercy* on the left-hand page and sauce bretonne on the right. Fished-based, then. As Blaise watched, Bradley added stems of various greens and herbs to the mixture simmering on the range top. Seeing no oysters at hand, Blaise knew he must be making sauce bretonne. But that recipe called for leeks, celery, onion, and mushroom caps, along with fish velouté—not the greenery Bradley had just added. Whatever his brother had found in the forest or fields wasn't among the traditional ingredients for the classic sauce.

"Which are you making?" he asked again.

When Bradley didn't answer, Blaise put his hand out as though to shift the book to read it better.

Without turning his head, Bradley moved his brother's arm aside with his own and pointed to the bretonne title.

"Ah," said Blaise, withdrawing his hand, deciding not to comment on the eclectic additions to the saucepan. "That's a good one. I'll have to consider it for my September menu."

Without looking to see if that got a reaction, he turned to leave. Reaching the doorway, he pulled his cell phone out of his back pocket and took a photo of Bradley engrossed in his work. He made sure the photo included the open book on the counter. He planned to take a trip into town today and would send the photo with a text message when he got there. He went on to the main kitchen, thoughtful. Sauce bretonne *was* a good idea. He had the framework of his menu, and it would enhance the whitefish quenelles he'd been contemplating. Sauce diplomate was his first choice, but you needed lobster for that.

He came to the main kitchen and stopped short. Christian was sitting on the same high stool where Blaise had seen Randall two weeks before. He had the brown paper package of Manoomin beside him on the butcher-block work island, along with the half-bushel basket of fresh plums from the fridge, the small glass Pyrex container labeled with Christian's name that had been left in the freezer, and two quart-sized Mason jars of home-preserved pears similarly labeled. He didn't look morose the way Randall had, though. He didn't look angry either. He looked brooding. And intent.

Intent on what?

"I thought you were gone," Blaise said when the silence stretched long enough for him to know that Christian wasn't going to break it. He took a few steps into the room but stayed out of lunging distance.

"Did you, now?" Christian lifted a mug to his lips without breaking eye contact.

"This isn't your kitchen anymore. You missed your date. It's September, and September is mine."

"True. But these aren't. I hope you weren't planning to include them in your menu."

He had planned to use the Manoomin, actually. Had done some Googling during his last trip to town. It was a good ingredient—and not typical. Finding it here in the kitchen had been a stroke of good fortune.

"I'd considered it," Blaise said casually. "Found it here in the kitchen—in September. There are a lot of ways to forage, you know."

"Yeah, I know," said Christian. He got up from the stool and emptied what was left in his cup into the sink. He soaped up a sponge and washed the cup, then dried it with a fresh towel he pulled out of the first drawer he opened. He folded the towel and hung it through a stainless-steel ring on the wall. He put the cup in a small corner cupboard that had a collection of similar cups. He then walked to the butcher-block work island. He placed the plums on the island to accommodate the two Mason jars and Pyrex container in the bottom of the basket, then put the plums back and set the brown paper bag of Manoomin on top. He picked up the basket in both hands. "Lots of ways to forage. Thievery shouldn't be one of them," he said.

He stopped in front of Blaise and waited. Blaise tamped down the urge to smack the Manoomin off its perch. He wanted the man gone. Out of his kitchen. It was *his* kitchen this month. Christian continued to stand in front of him, no more than two feet separating them. There was room for Christian to go around him, but Blaise knew he wouldn't. He stepped aside, much as it grated.

Christian continued forward, leaving the kitchen.

Blaise flipped him the bird to his back.

He wished it felt more satisfying.

Blaise felt satisfaction as he emptied the contents of a bottle of Michigan red wine into the town park's flower border that separated asphalt from grass. In the near distance, he could see children on a playground—climbing, running, laughing, and calling to one another as adults sat on nearby benches and chatted. No one took notice of him. He uncorked the bottle of French Bordeaux and, with a small plastic funnel, transferred the French wine into the Michigan bottle. He firmly corked it. He dropped the now-empty French bottle in a recycling receptacle, got in his car, and started the engine.

He felt pent-up tension leave his body as he drove back to the Club. Pouring French wine into a Michigan vineyard's bottle was sacrilege—and against the rules, of course—but he'd done the right thing. He couldn't control Bradley and his infatuation with Celeste. It was necessary to assert control where he could. He didn't want to edit his menu any further, and now he wouldn't have to. He had just winnowed his exceptions to the acceptable three.

# Celeste

"So that's where it went," Celeste said, enlarging the photo on her phone to be sure.

Sure enough, it was her *Saucier's Apprentice* on the counter beside Bradley. She hadn't realized she didn't have it with her until she was unpacking her overnight bag at home. She'd left the Club in a hurry, seething. She peered more closely, but there was no way to know to what page he had it open. It was about halfway through the book. She reached out and touched his face in the photo. He was in profile, intent on the saucepan as he stirred.

*Just in case you were looking for your book, it's in safe hands,* the text read.

Blaise didn't give a damn about her book.

He did give a damn about her being at the Club.

She considered that for a moment, then typed a reply.

*I'm sure what you meant to text was an apology.*

She put her cell phone away. She did want her book back, and she missed Bradley, but she could let his brother stew a while.

# A HARVEST OF LAKE AND LAND

FIRST COURSE:
*Whitefish quenelles in sauce bretonne*

SECOND COURSE:
*Smoked duck breast in red wine and cherry reduction sauce*
*Rabbit coquettes*
*Fig-glazed brussels sprouts*

THIRD COURSE:
*French apple tart with sauce Anglaise and caramel*

*Exceptions: Balsamic vinegar, lemon, white peppercorns*

# Blaise

Blaise was edgy. After almost two weeks, edginess was taking its toll. He'd twice salted the fish velouté he'd made earlier that week. He'd had to throw it out and drive back to the wharf on Lake Michigan to get more fish to start again. Ironic that of all the possible ingredients, it was salt he'd accidentally added twice.

That wasn't the only mistake. He'd ruined his first batch of white bread to make panko breadcrumbs—rookie mistake. Baking wasn't his forte, but by this point in his career, he should be able to make bread in his sleep.

The problem was Christian.

Ever since their conversation in the kitchen, it seemed that Christian was always around. He didn't say anything to Blaise, didn't do anything that could be construed as threatening and therefore reportable. He was just *there*, turning up in unexpected places and at unexpected times, sitting, standing, walking—that intent, brooding look on his face. Every now and then, he'd meet Blaise's eye, and the hint of a humorless grin would tug at one corner of the man's mouth.

He was looking for an opportunity. Blaise knew it.

Like when Blaise walked down the hall toward the main kitchen earlier that week to see Christian just leaving it. What had he been doing in there? Blaise had spent valuable time checking all the different ingredients he'd need that day to make sure the salt truck driver hadn't switched something out—put baking soda in the baking powder container, for instance, or swapped the heavy cream for light.

Now, on the day of his dinner, when he should have been calm and focused, he'd spent twenty minutes searching the main kitchen for the caramel he'd made yesterday—had started measuring out sugar to make it again—before remembering he'd stored it in the small refrigerator in his room for safekeeping.

He had all his ingredients collected and sorted. He was sure that everything was what it should be—no swaps. Everything was under his eye. Everything except Christian. Today was the last opportunity to make something go sideways for Blaise, to keep him from winning. It must be obvious to Christian, to everyone, that Blaise was the frontrunner. This *terroir* competition was his to lose.

He wondered where his brother was. Likely roaming the Club grounds. Blaise had reminded his brother they were in the last few days of September. October belonged to the Yooper and his kid. He didn't want a repeat of April. He could have had Christian barred from the Club if it hadn't been for Celeste reminding him about Bradley's rule violation.

Celeste wasn't here either. Blaise had snorted when he saw her return text. Hadn't texted back. She hadn't returned to the Club. Which he knew his brother considered his fault, though Bradley didn't come out and say it.

It didn't matter. He didn't need Bradley to cook. It would have been nice to know what Bradley had added to his sauce bretonne. Blaise had tasted it, and the herbal hint would have complemented his whitefish quenelles. But Bradley wasn't interested in talking about the greenery he'd added to the classic recipe, and Blaise had already lost a full day when he had to remake his fish velouté. He couldn't afford time to experiment with different combinations of whatever could be gathered in the fields of the Club.

Casting a glance around the kitchen, he hesitated. He needed to go outside to check the duck breasts he was smoking. But to leave these measured ingredients unattended meant he'd have to check them all again when he came back. Then again, the duck breasts were unattended. What if Christian had unplugged the smoker? Blaise glanced at his watch. His dinner was just hours away. It would be nice to have Bradley here in the kitchen—not cooking, just . . . here. Christian wouldn't do anything with a witness. But Bradley in the kitchen on Blaise's competition day would raise questions with Randall.

Blaise checked the French apple tart that he'd baked that morning. He already had three exceptions on his menu, and vanilla and cinnamon would have been noticeable additions, so he had to forgo them. He hoped three different varieties of apples would make up for it. He'd check the duck, then make his sauce Anglaise.

---

"Suttons Bay," said Randall, picking up one of the three wine bottles Blaise had on the counter. "Good location. I take it this is for the wine and cherry reduction sauce?" He pointed at the preserved whole cherries. "Are these measured out? Or may I?"

"Help yourself," said Blaise. "I have more than enough."

Randall pierced one with a small fork. "My aunt and uncle had a cherry orchard between Sleeping Bear Dunes and Traverse City," he said.

Blaise focused on stirring and looking unconcerned as the Club's director conducted the ingredient review. Two of the three bottles on the counter were uncorked, and the one that was half-full no longer held Michigan wine. He had selected his three exceptions with care and eliminated cinnamon and vanilla from his tart, but he couldn't bring himself to use anything but French wine for his signature wine and cherry reduction sauce.

Randall set the fork down and finished his perusal of the ingredients on the counter. He opened the refrigerator, took out one item, and then another, noting labels.

"The Gourmet Bait Shop is a good resource, isn't it?" he said.

"It is," agreed Blaise, glad to see the man's attention on something other than the wine bottles. "It would have been a hike for me to get the dairy and rabbit from my usual sources. I got the apples, sprouts, and vegetables for the velouté and bretonne at the farmers' market," he added.

"Yes, we got the invoices," said Randall, closing the refrigerator door. "Along with quite a large one from the wharf. What happened there?"

"I had a do-over for my velouté. Is that a problem?"

"Not at all. It happens. Better early in the week than today, eh?"

"Speaking of today, I still have time, I think, to get a couple of my usual staff . . ."

"No, Blaise," Randall interrupted. "Each competitor gets the same staff, and that staff knows the rules. They serve; they are not allowed to tell you the judges' reactions or relay anything else about the dining room. At the end of each course, plates will be removed to the adjunct kitchen. You are welcome to have them assist you with meal prep if you like."

Blaise nodded curtly. No one was going to touch the food in his kitchen but him. He'd plate and then see each of the two servers to the swinging door. There was just the short hallway where they would be alone with his dishes before entering the dining room. Practically no opportunity for sabotage. Should he ask them to empty their pockets? Or would that be perceived as weird? Chefs were allowed to be eclectic. . . . He realized he'd missed Randall's last remark.

"I'm sorry. You said?"

"I said, this all looks in order." From a manila folder tucked under his arm, he pulled out Blaise's handwritten menu. "Elena will get this printed for the judges. Exceptions are balsamic vinegar, lemon, and white peppercorns. Is that correct?"

Blaise didn't look at the wine bottle on the counter.

"Yes," he said. "That's right."

# OCTOBER

# Daniel

Daniel checked his small stack of three-by-five cards again, adding due dates to each in red pen, which wasn't common but not unheard of. The due dates were necessary. This was his grocery list for his competition dinner—things he couldn't easily get himself and would have to find elsewhere if the Escanaba Exchange didn't come through. He was confident the Exchange would, given what he was offering in return—venison roasts, sausage, and jerky and snowplowing come winter. He had developed a reputation of offering fair, quality barter. Well, Thistle had, he amended. He just continued what she'd started.

It was Thistle who had found out about the then-newly formed Escanaba Exchange, made friends with Rug and Abby Trimble, and won their trust. In time, the childless couple had come to look upon Thistle as a daughter. In turn, though she had never said so, Daniel thought maybe his wife had thought of Rug and Abby as the parents she wished she'd had—accepting of her lifestyle and the choices she made.

It was Rug who'd come out to his house three months after the funeral. It had been a rough time. Ethan was home from the hospital, but Daniel couldn't leave a three-year-old home alone to go hunting for the meat that was vital to carry them through the winter. The vegetable garden had gone to weed and seed, food mostly unharvested. The three gnarled apple trees had been picked over by the deer, the wild berries long since eaten by birds and bear, and the nuts hoarded by the squirrels. He did have some pasta dishes and casseroles left in the freezer, gifts in the days and weeks following the fire. Someone—Daniel suspected Stan and his wife Marty from the Mercantile led the effort—had cleared up and hauled away the wreck that was the bee shed where the fire happened.

Rug had arrived on his doorstep on an October morning not dissimilar from this one, Daniel reminisced. The older man hadn't said much—didn't in the best of times—but his eyes had been red-rimmed. Daniel hadn't wanted to accept what he brought—it felt like charity—but short of physically throwing him off his property or burning the lot, he was informed there wasn't an alternative.

"Not charity," Rug had said gruffly. "Thistle left two handmade quilts at the Exchange. And quite a bit of that herbal soap she made back in June. She listed what she wanted for the barter. That's what she got, fair and square, and that's what I've brought."

He'd put one hand on Daniel's shoulder after they finished bringing in the boxes of home-preserved food, two kinds of flour, oats, three bacon slabs, two smoked ham hocks, a half-dozen frozen roasting chickens, and a small wheel of cheese. His foot on the bottom step of the porch, he turned.

"Abby asked me to say to you that it would do her heart a lot of good if you'd let her babysit Ethan now and again."

Daniel's throat tightened, and he didn't respond. After the quiet space of a deep breath, Rug went to his truck. He opened the door. "It sure was nice when Thistle brought the boy with her to the Exchange. He was constantly underfoot. I can't even count how many times Abby or I told him to get down or get outta something he was gettin' into." Rug climbed into his truck. "I sure do miss that." Then he started the engine and drove away.

Daniel had lain awake a long time that night, thinking about what Rug had said, listening for the voice of his wife. By then, the phone calls from his in-laws demanding custody had been replaced by certified letters and one very unpleasant visit from a lawyer threatening to take him to court as an unfit parent.

But he trusted Thistle's judgment, and so Daniel had been able to get in some hunting that fall after all.

The Escanaba Exchange was housed in a sizable portion of the Trimble's large bank barn. Plank boards separated the Exchange from their goats, watched over by two Anatolian Shepherd dogs.

The Exchange was divided into specific areas, almost like the Mercantile in town. People would leave nonperishable items they were willing to barter and a three-by-five card attached or nearby with what they were seeking in return. The twelve-by-twelve wooden posts that supported the hand-hewn beams that held up the barn also had their designations. On these, people tacked cards of the services or goods they had—or would have—to barter and what they'd like in return. Services might be anything from help with shearing sheep or castrating cattle to the use of an ice fishing shed or tutoring for an upcoming SAT exam. Goods included butchered game, homegrown or foraged food items, hard-to-find car or tractor parts, or handmade goods like the quilts and soap Thistle had made. In return for housing and managing the Exchange, everyone delivered to Rug and Abby a barter value of 10 percent, on the honor system. It worked to everyone's benefit, and the couple always had whatever help they needed on their farm.

There was no roadside sign for the Escanaba Exchange. It was never advertised. There was just the Trimble's large mailbox at the end of their long, dirt-and-gravel driveway. The large mailbox had a two-sided, enameled metal art piece affixed to the top: a bright green John Deere tractor with a spotted goat standing on the hood and a large dog with a long, curly tail at the wheel. It had been created as a 10-percent payment. If you knew, you knew. And if you didn't, you perhaps shouldn't.

Daniel stood in the Trimble barn and perused the three-by-five cards for game, aware of Ethan sneaking out to visit the goats. The dogs knew him by now and tolerated his visits. Daniel had seen Rug nearby, and Abby would likely give him a few carrots from her garden. Daniel plucked one card from its tack, took another from his own stack, and put both in the pocket of his Carhartt jacket. Emil always had wild boar—it was legal to hunt them year-round since they were so damaging to crops. Daniel would call him and offer a trade of venison. He'd gotten a large doe with his bow yesterday morning and had it hanging in the root cellar. He'd need more, but this one plus what he had already would be enough for his barters.

 He thumbed through the rest of his cards: apple brandy—that was a must—pheasant, duck, turkey. Wiley buggers, turkey. He would try to get one himself, but deer were easier, so if he could barter . . . He'd hunted for pheasant and duck before, but he knew there were traders at the Exchange who lived for bird hunting. He'd tried out a new recipe at the September Royal Trolls dinner using birds the men had shot. It had been a definite success, so he'd added the recipe to his October *terroir* competition menu. He also needed acorn flour. Ethan had collected a small basket of them, and they spent several evenings shelling. They then soaked them a few days, changing the water every half day to remove the tannins. Roasted and chopped, the acorns would provide texture for his first-course soup. But to make the bisque, he needed acorn flour, and he didn't have the time—nor the inclination, truth be told—to collect that many nuts and go through the arduous process of turning them into flour. But he knew of two people active in the Exchange who did. One of them was always looking for someone to help clean the leaves out of her gutters, and the other liked venison jerky but thought it was too much trouble to make. Daniel would scout the Exchange to see if either of them had posted a card yet.

 He looked at his last card. Wild mushrooms. Now, for that, he was counting on the Exchange. Knowing which mushrooms were edible and where and when they could be found was not his forte. He needed a variety and a lot of them. Cooked down to an intense stock, it was a key ingredient in his signature jaeger sauce and his acorn soup.

He'd also need cream but wasn't planning to get it in Escanaba. He'd been intrigued by his conversation with Eden Ross as she sat on the bench swing with a glass of wine at the Forager Chefs Club back in July. He didn't doubt her for a moment—the quality of everything humans consumed was largely the result of what something else consumed, whether plant or animal. Her comment that the best dairy didn't come from cows that ate only what they found in pastures or the hay delivered to their barns rang true. But was there a dairy where that wasn't the case? She obviously knew of one. She was from Idlewild. She'd mentioned forest ingredients when she came upon him and Ethan making currant jelly. Daniel had done some homework.

He'd used his most charming manner on the phone. He'd been truthful.

Mrs. Abrams had agreed: he could visit her.

She'd decide then.

# Eden

Eden put a hand to her forehead; the other held her cell phone to her ear.

"I'm sorry, Mrs. Abrams, *who* did you say is there?"

"He's a very nice young man, Eden, very polite. And his son is just adorable! He said they know you from the Forager Chefs Club. Did you know the boy's favorite animal is a baby goat? Although his father rolled his eyes at that. They do have a dog, and at first, I told them that under no circumstances would I allow a strange dog on my farm; it would have to stay in their truck, but then the little boy—I don't recall his name—Evan, Everett?"

"Ethan."

"Right! Ethan! Well, he looked at me with the most angelic, sincere eyes and said Biscuit would never, ever chase farm animals, only animals that tried to hurt someone. Eden, the dog's name is Biscuit! How cute is that? Well, the dog did sit there next to the boy just as calm as could be, so I said I thought maybe it would be okay, and sure enough, that dog has been just the picture of politeness the whole time they've been here, and so I asked how it got its name, and then the boy said that his mother named it when she and his dad rescued it along a highway, and it was scared, and all it would eat were biscuits his mother had made *from scratch*—isn't that nice?—that were left over from their picnic lunch, and I thought, oh! So, where is Mom? Because the man, you know, all of a sudden, he looks a little uncomfortable. Others, Eden, might not have noticed it, but as you know, I have a knack for picking up on these things. I thought to myself, Well! If this man thinks he's going to get into the good graces of my Eden simply by showing up at my farm to buy cream, but he's one of those who just uses and discards women, he has got another thing coming!"

"He wants to buy cream?"

"Yes, dear, that's what I said. But then, just when I'm ready to ask a few questions, the boy puts his hand on the dog's head and explains that his mama is *dead*. Dead! But that Biscuit is still here to protect him, and his dad too, and I have to tell you, it was all I could do not to draw that sweet boy into a hug because I could tell by his daddy's face that he would have *much* preferred that the boy hadn't said a word about his mama being gone. Which then made me think, how did she die? Oh, sweet Jesus. Could this man have had something to do with it, and the boy unaware?"

Eden took advantage of Mrs. Abrams pausing to take a breath. "No, Mrs. Abrams, I've met Daniel. And Ethan." *And his dog*, she thought. "Daniel has been vetted by the Forager Chefs Club." She thought of Randall and heartily hoped this was the case. "He certainly did not have anything to do with his wife's death." She tamped down a prurient interest. How *had* she died?

"Well, and I'm relieved to hear it." Mrs. Abrams paused. "So, I've been prattling on and on because you still haven't answered my question!"

Eden took a breath. Let it out. "I'm so sorry, Mrs. Abrams. Remind me of the question?"

"This man, this Daniel Metsja. He says he's in the competition at the Forager Chefs Club. That he met you, and you told him that the best dairy to be had was from my cows. He wants to buy cream from me." Her tone softened. "You are so good to me, Eden, talking up my girls—and the Lord knows that with the rising cost of everything, I need every customer I can get!" Her voice turned firm again. "But all that aside, I told him that I would have to check with you first. You say the word, Eden, and I'll send him, his son, and his dog away empty-handed. I wouldn't want you to think that I'm choosing anyone over you in the competition!"

The woman finally stopped talking.

Eden considered.

"Eden? Did I lose you?" Eden heard cows lowing in the background. Mrs. Abrams's voice got a bit distant, and Eden imagined her holding the phone at arm's length, examining it for connectivity bars. "Lord, I hate these cell phones."

"No, you didn't lose me," said Eden loudly so the woman would hear her, arm's length notwithstanding. Daniel had to have done some serious work to find Mrs. Abrams just based on the brief exchange they'd had back in July. This meant two things: he valued her opinion merely at face value since they'd just met, and he considered her a chef who knew her ingredients. But, as he'd said, it wasn't just ingredients that made a great meal, though they were, of course, critical. And it really wasn't right for her to deny Mrs. Abrams a customer.

"Go ahead and sell to him," Eden said.

# Christian

Now what? Christian took a long pull from his beer and pushed his foot against the ground to set the bench swing again into motion. He remembered seeing Eden on this swing. It had been early July, and he'd taken a few days to scout out resources for his dinner. He'd met Daniel and his son. Randall had said at the February meeting that a fifth competitor was a possibility. He'd drawn October. The two had carried fishing rods on their way to catch dinner, the boy had said. He'd nodded confidently, clearly not even entertaining that they might come back empty-handed.

The three of them had walked outside together, the boy—Ethan was his name—running ahead with his dog toward the tree line where a woman sat on a bench swing hung from a large beech tree. Eden. He hadn't seen her since February. She'd looked different, her face turned up to dappled sunlight spilling through verdant leaves, sipping from a glass of white wine, one bare foot reaching to the ground now and again to keep the swing moving back and forth. Gone was the watchfulness, the coiled energy cataloging and assessing. She'd been friendly in February, particularly with Celeste, the girl from Mackinac Island who'd seemed so out of her element. But Eden had been there to compete—Christian had recognized that. Sitting on the swing, her June dinner behind her, she'd been relaxed. She was really pretty, especially when she smiled as she had at Ethan and his dog.

That had been back in July. Before everything unraveled.

It was late October now.

He and Randall had talked the evening he came back to the Club after burying his mother's ashes; that was more than a month ago now. The talk hadn't been over the desk in the man's office, as he'd expected, but over glasses of whiskey sitting on Adirondack chairs outside, listening to tree frogs and cicadas and the wind moving leaves that were just beginning to take on their autumn hue. Randall had been somber, offered his condolences. Christian had thanked him for the flowers the Club sent. He didn't tell him that they'd sat at the church for several days before the church office called to tell him they were there, and Randall didn't tell him he was kicked out of the competition. Quid pro quo. Then again, Randall didn't have to. Christian's assigned dinner on the last Saturday of August had come and gone, and he hadn't cooked. In a way, it gave everyone an easy out. He and Randall had sat in mostly silence as the evening sky deepened to blue-black in the twilight, the life-changing fifty thousand dollars no longer a possibility.

On the bright side, he did still have cost-free room and board at the Club for the rest of the year. And a few months left to figure out what he wanted to do next.

He'd decided his immediate future the next morning after seeing Bradley come into the adjunct kitchen for coffee.

Now that he knew Blaise had a twin, he could tell them apart by what they wore and their mannerisms. Bradley's clothing style was much more relaxed than his asshole brother's; his interaction with people—other than Celeste—was much more stilted. They'd nodded at one another, Christian staying seated in his chair to not make Bradley feel ill at ease, though it was difficult to tell if he was successful. Remembering that August encounter and all the repercussions of once again losing his temper had given his coffee a bitter taste. That's when he decided what would occupy his time until the last Saturday in September.

In the days leading up to his dinner, he'd done what he could to rattle Blaise, but he hadn't resorted to anything as low as what the man had done to him. He didn't know if his wordless presence, turning up at unexpected times in unexpected places, had had any effect at all. But it had given him something to do, something to occupy his time.

Now it was late October. Blaise and Bradley had gone back to Grand Rapids.

Which brought Christian back to the question he'd put off.

Now what?

He could go to Flint. To their—his—house. He'd even packed his stuff one morning last week, intending to do just that. He sat in his car for fifteen minutes before getting out, grabbing his duffel bag from the passenger seat, and going back into the Club.

He drank a lot that night.

He could get a job, live lean—hell, maybe stay at the Club through the end of the year before finding an apartment—squirrel away money until he had enough to go back to the CIA in New York and pick up where he left off. Randall could make a call or get one of the Club members to do it so they'd let him back in. The man seemed to be connected. Christian took another long pull from his beer. He wondered where Rachel was now, then put that thought away.

Then again, he could just get in his car and point it in a direction that wasn't Flint or upstate New York, drive until he just didn't want to drive anymore, and find someplace new. Let the squatters and the scrappers have the house in Flint, let the bank fill the mailbox with foreclosure notices. Maybe the herb garden would run wild, take over the yard, and share it with the tomato and squash that would send up volunteer plants every spring from the previous year's dropped fruit. Become like the yard with the blackberry canes and the skeleton of a children's swing set and its two lichen-covered sentinel plum trees. Someone might come there one day to forage. Would they wonder who had lived there? Who had planned, planted, and tended the garden? Wonder why they'd left?

The point was, he had options. He was only twenty-seven. Plenty of time to choose a direction, find a path—or make one.

Christian set his now-empty beer bottle aside and picked up another from the small ice bucket he'd brought out to the swing. Removing the cap with an opener emblazoned with the logo of a Frankenmuth brewery, he noticed someone coming across the lawn toward him. It was Daniel. He thought again about July, but now it was him pushing his foot against the ground to keep the swing in motion instead of Eden, the leaves were mostly gone, and Daniel was alone.

He came to a stop a couple of yards in front of Christian, hands in the pockets of his jeans. He nodded at the ice bucket.

"Two down, how many to go?"

Christian looked at the ice bucket.

"Two more, I guess. That's all that would fit. Want one?"

"Sure."

Christian pulled a beer out of the bucket. Condensation running down the side of the bottle made the label slide as he handed it and the opener to Daniel. He moved over on the swing and motioned to the spot beside him.

"Have a seat."

Daniel sat down, opened the bottle, tossed the cap and opener next to the ice bucket, and drank.

They sat there, not saying anything, for a few minutes. It was a companionable silence, Christian decided. Daniel seemed to be the kind of guy who was comfortable in his own skin, who didn't need to fill empty space with idle chatter. Christian liked that. He never liked talk for the sake of talk and wasn't in the mood for it now.

Christian's second bottle was mostly gone when Daniel finally spoke.

"I heard you missed your dinner in August. I'm sorry about your mom."

"Thanks."

They were silent again for a while. Christian didn't push the swing into motion, and neither did Daniel. It was one thing to sit side by side on a swing, but there was no need to make it weird.

After a time, Daniel took a final long pull, finishing his beer. He got up and placed the empty bottle upside down in the ice bucket.

"Christian, you look like a man who needs a job. I've got some furniture I need to move tomorrow morning. I could use a hand. Wanna help?"

# Daniel

Daniel saw Randall striding toward him across the back lawn. He looked annoyed.

"So," he said. "Here it is."

"It" was the long trestle table that, until recently, had been the focal point of the Forager Chefs Club's dining room. The dining room was now mostly empty, its table and five of its eight chairs now set up a half-dozen yards away from the outdoor cooking area Daniel had created.

The space mimicked what he did for the Royal Trolls. He had three separate fires going, forming a rough triangle. He wanted the area to have an established feel by the time of his dinner tomorrow, not look like a few new campfires on the lawn, so earlier in the week, he'd turned the sod between the three and had been distributing ash as the fires burned down. He'd clean up and reseed the grass next week. Along one side of the cooking area were his folding prep tables and his water stations: two large tubs for washing and rinsing and three five-gallon containers with spigots for cooking water. It had taken him a good deal of effort and a lot of trips to get his equipment and all the water out here, but he hadn't wanted to crush the grass with his truck tires, leaving visible marks to show how this outdoor kitchen had come into being.

With Christian's help, they'd separated the trestle tabletop from its base and brought it out here. His makeshift dining room was roughly a dozen yards away from the cooking area, far enough to avoid campfire smoke should the wind change direction but close enough to enjoy the ambiance and mood Daniel would create. Strategically set tiki torches should keep any late-season bugs at bay.

Randall stopped between the table and cooking area.

"Daniel. What the hell?"

Daniel picked up a long-handled ladle and the iron tool he used to lift the lids of his Dutch ovens.

"I'll put it back after the dinner."

"No, you'll put it back now."

Daniel lifted the lid on his mushroom stock, ladled out a portion, poured it into a small glass prep dish, and held it up to examine it. It was clear, the color of deer antler velvet. He bent his head close and inhaled the fragrance. It was nearly there. Another hour, and he'd leave the lid off and let the stock reduce until it became the rich liquid that was the secret ingredient for his signature jaeger sauce.

Putting the lid back, he shook his head.

"Randall, you said you have a file on me. And you knew about the Royal Trolls back when we talked at the Escanaba diner. I'm sure that file has details about the dinners I cook for them. So you know they pay me very well. Part of the reason is because I provide an experience they can't get walking into a restaurant. Why would I want to do any less for a dinner with fifty thousand dollars on the line?"

"Because you don't get to have an advantage over your competitors."

Daniel gestured at the cooking area with the ladle. "Do you know how much work it is to put something like this together? How much harder this is than just walking into a fully decked-out kitchen and turning on a burner? An oven? Pulling on a lever and out comes fresh, potable water, both hot and cold? If this gives me an advantage, it's one I've damn well worked to get."

"You can have your outdoor kitchen. What you can't have is the judges dining where you can see and hear them."

Daniel straightened from poking at the fire. "What?"

"There is to be no interaction between the judges and the competitor chef. You'll have two servers who will take your dishes from your kitchen—wherever you decide that is—to the table. At the end of each course, dishes are removed to the adjunct kitchen so you don't see if they barely touched what you prepared or licked the plates clean. Your servers are employed by the Club and have been instructed not to share anything they might hear or see of the judges' reactions." He indicated the table. "So, having your diners a few yards away gives you an advantage. The table has to go back."

Daniel's eyes went from Randall to the table to his outdoor kitchen. Then from his outdoor kitchen to the Club building and back again to the table.

"Well, hell," Daniel finally said. He set down the iron lid-lifter and ladle. "Any idea where Christian is?"

"Y'know, if I'd had my competition dinner back in August, I wouldn't be helping you with this." Christian grunted as they got to the top of the short flight of stairs that led from the back lawn to the main level of the Club with the last section of the table base. "Hold up a sec. I gotta breathe."

They set down the heavy wood.

"I know," said Daniel. "I owe you. What do you like to drink?"

Christian waved his hand. "No need," he said. "But what would you have done if I had competed? Or just wasn't around?" He indicated the base. "I don't think Ethan could have helped you with this. Where is he, by the way? Back in Escanaba?"

"I'd have figured out something. And, no, Ethan is upstairs with a tutor Elena found for me. I didn't want him to miss a lot of school." He dipped his chin at the large piece of wood. "Ready?"

It took another forty minutes to put the table back together, and then they brought in the chairs. Setting the last one in place, Daniel walked over to the large windows. The view was a different area of the Club grounds than from the common room. There were more trees, with little to no grass or vegetation between them. He couldn't see his kitchen. He leaned on the windowsill, noting a clearing around a wide tree stump about a foot high.

Christian came to stand beside him.

"They sure do have a nice piece of property here."

"They do."

"Ready for a beer? Or I guess you've got more cooking to do to prep for tomorrow."

"Definitely more cooking to do, but something else to do first." He looked at Christian with a speculative gleam in his eye.

Christian noted it and sighed.

"Sure, what the hell," he said. "What are we moving now?"

# HUNTER & FORAGERS' REPAST

APERITIF:
Michigan Sunset cocktail

FIRST COURSE:
Acorn bisque with apple brandy
Wild boar lonzino

SECOND COURSE:
Venison loin with signature jaeger sauce and wild mushroom medley
Wild wing pie
Grilled sunchokes with wild boar lardons
Dutch oven campfire rolls

THIRD COURSE:
Coals-baked cherry clafoutis with brandy sauce


Exceptions: Cointreau liqueur, Domaine de Canton ginger liqueur, lemon juice

# Daniel

For the second time in two days, Daniel saw Randall striding toward him from the Forager Chefs Club building. He looked annoyed. Again.

On the far side of the fire, Biscuit lifted his head from the beef bone he was gnawing. Ethan, sitting cross-legged on the ground next to him, put a hand on his back and told him in a soft voice that it was okay. Biscuit didn't get up, but he didn't go back to gnawing his bone either. Anytime they went camping, the dog put people he associated with indoor environments through a new layer of perusal. Cooking outdoors was camping, so far as Biscuit was concerned.

"Don't worry. I'll fix up the old spot, good as new. Grass seed and everything," Daniel called out, stirring what would be his acorn bisque. "I just can't do it today."

"Do you think I enjoy hunting you down? Repeatedly? I told you the *table* had to go back. You didn't have to move your kitchen. That could have stayed."

"I like this spot better," said Daniel.

He did. When he selected the first location, he'd been focused on one that would accommodate not only his cooking area but a nearby outdoor "dining room" that would require no more than a short walk from the Club's main entrance for the judges. But since he was now setting up only a kitchen, this spot was better. With no grass, his grouping of cookfires already had a "been here a while" look. Plus, the stump he'd seen from the windows of the dining room was, as he'd hoped, mostly hollow. He'd dug out some additional rotted wood, and now it was filled with glowing coals—perfect for baking his bread and clafoutis dessert. And the metal cloches he and Ethan found in one of the kitchen cupboards would help ensure his dishes arrived to the judges at the correct temperature despite the distance they had to be carried.

"Why?" asked Randall, just a hint of exasperation in his voice.

Daniel pointed to the large windows of the Club's dining room.

"You said I wasn't allowed to see or hear the judges. You didn't say they weren't allowed to see me."

Daniel tasted his acorn soup, watching Randall out of the corner of his eye as the man turned to look at the windows. He added a few more dried green alder catkins. With their spicy taste, albeit with a hint of resin, they took the place of black pepper. He'd add cream shortly before serving. Eden had been right. Mrs. Abrams's cows did produce the best dairy products he'd ever tasted. It had been well worth the time to find and visit her.

"Fine," said Randall. "I'm here for the review," he added.

"The review?"

"Yes, the review."

Daniel looked over to Ethan, who looked back and shrugged. Daniel echoed the shrug and looked back at Randall.

"The review of the ingredients you're using in your dinner tonight. To compare them to your submitted menu and note any exceptions," Randall said.

"That's really a thing?"

"Yes, Daniel, that's a thing."

Daniel gestured to the camp tables set up along the periphery of the cooking area. "Review away."

Randall stepped through the cooking area, avoiding the smoke as it rose and drifted east in the slight breeze, noting with interest the multi-campfire setup, particularly the one in the tree stump. He picked up one of the iron tools strategically placed to be accessible, hefted it like a fencer gauging the worthiness of a new blade, then put it back. He reached the camp table that held the dinner ingredients grouped by course and picked up a jar of homemade jelly. As he held it up to the sunlight, the contents shone the deep red of a maple leaf at peak autumn color.

"Currants?" he guessed.

Daniel nodded. "Nothing better with venison than currants—and juniper berries," he added, pointing to a small jar about half-full.

"I helped pick them!" said Ethan. "And I helped with squishing the currants through the sieve to get rid of the skins and seeds, but I'm not allowed to do the canning until I'm older."

"You made the jelly?" Randall asked Daniel.

Daniel leaned to poke at the fire he had dedicated to producing hot coals for baking. He needed to get his rolls in the stump soon. To maintain a 350-degree "oven," he'd need eight coals under the cast-iron Dutch oven and seventeen arranged on the lipped lid. He'd have to swap out the coals twice, maybe even three times. And he'd need more coals to bake his cherry clafoutis, but he wanted to do that when he was sure the judges had arrived and could see him and what he was doing if they cared to look out the dining room windows. Sunset would be about a half-hour before his dinner was scheduled to start. In the deepening twilight, he expected the glow from his cooking fires, along with the torches and lanterns he'd strategically positioned, would draw their eyes.

"Yes, I made the jelly. Please don't start about antiquated household roles, Randall."

"No, of course not. It just so happens, I make cherry preserves every year. Stay on my good side, and you might even get a jar at Christmas." Randall hesitated when he saw the shallow wicker basket of mushrooms. "Did you collect these?"

"No, someone I know—and trust—did, back in Escanaba."

"How many different kinds?"

"As many as she could find, plus others she collected and dried earlier in the year."

"Don't poison the judges."

"Wouldn't dream of it. This isn't my first rodeo."

Randall turned his attention to a nearby bowl. He smiled as he picked up a knobby tuber. "I see you found our sunchoke patch."

"*I* did!" Ethan jumped up, startling the dog, who had finally settled down to his bone. It stood up and eyed Randall.

Daniel pointed his wooden spoon at the dog. "Biscuit, stand down," he commanded. Ethan patted the dog's head and softly repeated the command. The dog sat, albeit a bit reluctantly. He watched Randall.

"I found them when we were here in the summer," the boy continued. "And I showed Dad. We harvested them a few days ago. But we didn't take all of them, and we didn't take them from all in one spot," Ethan assured Randall.

"That's good," said Randall. He kept his voice even and his eye on the dog. "Good foraging technique. Your dad has taught you well."

"And my mom. I was really little when she was alive, but Dad says I learned a lot from her and just don't remember when she taught me."

Daniel continued to swap out coals in the oven he'd created in the maple tree stump. He liked having Ethan here, watching him work, perhaps even learning, though he wasn't actively taking part today. And this *was* exactly the kind of thing he and Thistle had planned to do with their children—create memorable meals in outdoor spaces—maybe even make a business out of it.

Randall picked up the dense ham Daniel had made from the boar loin he bartered with Emil and sniffed it.

"You cure this yourself?"

Daniel nodded but didn't stop moving between his fires, lifting lids, stirring, tasting, adjusting coals, and adding new ones where needed.

Randall pulled a rolled-up piece of paper from the back pocket of his jeans.

"So this must be the lonzino," he said, referring to the menu Daniel had provided to Elena yesterday.

"Yup."

"Mind if I shave off a piece?"

Daniel waved the long lid-lifting tool. "Shave away."

Randall sliced off a piece of the meat and put it in his mouth. His face didn't give anything away, but Daniel smiled. He knew it was good.

"Try it with a bit of the apple brandy. And then, if you're about done, can you get the hell out of my kitchen? You make my dog nervous."

Randall picked up the bottle of brandy—the scrawl on the handwritten label identified it as homemade—but didn't open it as he finished chewing and swallowed. He looked over at the dog, who hadn't moved since Daniel's command but was still watching him intently. He set the bottle down and looked at the other bottles, labels showing whether or not they came from Michigan distilleries.

The Royal Trolls always wanted to begin their dinners with a cocktail, and Daniel was starting his competition dinner with one as well. His "Michigan Sunset" used a bourbon from a Traverse City distillery that he then smoked himself. The aromatic bitters were from a different distillery not far north of where he stood. The other three ingredients—Cointreau, Domaine de Canton ginger liqueur, and lemon juice—couldn't be sourced in Michigan, but since he hadn't used any of his three exceptions for the meal, he had them for his cocktail. Daniel saw Randall cast his eyes between the collection of bottles and the menu in his hand.

"Your two servers should be here in a couple of hours," Randall said as he tucked the paper back into his jeans pocket and turned to leave. "I warned them to wear comfortable shoes and be ready for quite a bit of speed walking." After a half-dozen steps, he called over his shoulder, "Be glad I came out here. You might think it a pain, all these checks and balances, and Biscuit clearly resents it, but if I hadn't come, it's unlikely your servers would have found you at all."

"We're always glad to see you, Randall," Daniel called after him as the man continued his trek back to the Club building.

Despite the distance, Daniel heard Randall's amused harrumph. Daniel waited until he was sure Randall was out of earshot.

"Give the guy a break," he said to Biscuit. "He's just doing his job. I think he's one of the good ones."

Daniel poured himself a finger of the apple brandy and drank. He was on edge but shouldn't be. He was in his element. He had prepared. He had everything he needed to deliver a dining experience that would be talked about for years to come.

Years to come.

Well, and that was the gist of it, wasn't it? He looked toward the Club building, though the balcony that ran the length of their rooms wasn't visible from here. Elena had taken Ethan and Biscuit back for some dinner before Julia, the tutor—the babysitter for tonight—arrived. Prior to leaving Escanaba, he'd made an appointment with the pediatric burn surgeon. It had taken a call from their pediatrician to get a new-patient appointment, and even so, they would have to wait until December. Daniel had no idea how he was going to pay for successive graft surgeries if he didn't win this competition.

Which meant he had to win this competition.

He set the brandy glass aside, picked up one of his many long-handled tasting spoons, and went to check on the filling for his wild wing pie. He lifted the lid, and steam rose, releasing a tantalizing fragrance of rich meats and vegetables. He stirred, scraping the bottom of the pot as he'd done every fifteen minutes for the last hour to make sure it didn't scorch. He dipped the spoon, blew on it, then tasted. He rolled the meat and vegetable filling around in his mouth, tasting and testing the texture. Careful, slow cooking ensured the pheasant, duck, and turkey didn't have a gamey taste. Cutting them up into small chunks for his wild wing pie was also some insurance against breaking a tooth on bird shot. He put the lid back on, moved the iron pot off the direct heat, and prepped the pastry in the individual stoneware ramekins for baking.

Daniel's mind eased as he finished his signature jaeger sauce. It always did. Bringing together the individual ingredients brought back memories of smell, taste, and mood. The rich, deep-colored stock was the warmth and comfort of their cabin last winter. The whole house had been scented with the roasting of meaty bones from his hunting and barter endeavors and vegetables from the root cellar. These had been added to fresh water and handfuls of dried herbs to bubble in their largest stock pot for hours. It was cooled, strained multiple times, and then gently simmered and skimmed for hours again to create liquid the gleaming color of burnished leather. The sauce included the currant jelly of a warm summer afternoon of canning after a morning of plucking clusters of small, tart berries that stained his and Ethan's hands red while insects hummed and Biscuit watched for errant rabbits. Tasting, he reached for the small jar of juniper berries, remembering the day late last fall when he'd been on a friend's property, ostensibly deer hunting, and had come across an abundance of laden bushes. He'd filled his pockets and judged the hunt successful, even though he left the next day never having fired his rifle.

He glanced at the Club and saw lights in the dining room that echoed the light of the setting sun filtering through the trees behind him. It was time. He added the reserved mushrooms, roughly chopped, to the sauce that already had its portion of his carefully prepared mushroom stock, gauged with a practiced eye how much cream from Mrs. Abrams's "girls" to add, and stirred it all together. He tucked a footed grate under the pan and added a lid. He'd already let the coals burn down on this fire; the pan would stay warm without scorching the sauce, and the lid would ensure a film didn't form. He straightened, satisfied. It was almost time to sear the venison loin that had been soaking in buttermilk—another gift from Mrs. Abrams's girls.

He turned. Remembered he had an audience.

"This. Is. So. Cool." The young man in somewhat oversized black dress pants and a white button-down shirt, sporting a shock of strawberry-red hair and freckles, had a look of awe on his face. Joe, Daniel recalled.

His two servers had found him, thanks to Randall. They'd arrived about fifteen minutes ago. Or maybe it was a half-hour. He looked toward the trees through which he could see the angle of the setting sun. Yeah, closer to a half-hour. Joe and Josephine. Who wanted to be called Jo.

Sure. Your name, you get to choose, he'd told her.

"Very cool," Jo agreed, looking around, taking it all in.

Daniel liked that they seemed to really appreciate the setup, what it involved, and what he was doing. They weren't standing around with their arms folded and scowling, knowing that serving was going to be more intense than prior dinners of just walking dishes down a short hallway. He didn't know what the Club was paying them, but he had a couple of twenties in his pocket to give them at the end of the night.

"Thanks," he said. "It's how I like to cook." He looked toward the liquor bottles. "Either of you ever professionally bartend?"

Joe and Jo exchanged a glance. Neither nodded.

"Either of you want to learn how to make an exceptional cocktail?"

Jo's hand shot up.

Daniel rinsed out the martini shaker. It was fully dark now, and his cookfires had burned down to glowing embers. By the light of a camping lantern, Daniel measured out the smoked bourbon and other ingredients. There wasn't much ice left, but he fished out enough for his purposes, tapped the metal lid onto the shaker, and mixed his drink, the rhythm matching the cadence of the insects that hadn't yet succumbed to the advancing autumn season.

He'd set out two camp chairs and positioned them to see both the edge of the forest and the dining room windows of the Club. The room no longer glowed with light. Likely, the judges were all in the common room now, enjoying a dram or two from the replenished sideboard, chatting about—what?—the dinner he'd served? Or would that come only later, when they gathered next month to dissect all five—no, four—competition dinners and come to a decision? He poured his Michigan Sunset into two glasses he'd reserved for the end of the evening, added the juice of a lemon wedge to one, then walked past his prep tables with their depleted ingredients and the embers of his cooking fires and settled himself into a camp chair. He took in a long breath, held it a moment, then let it out. A smile crept across his face. He took a drink from his glass. Savored it.

His glass was about half-full when he heard the steps on fallen autumn leaves that he'd been expecting.

"I'd almost decided you weren't going to make it," he said. "I have beer in that tub over there, but I did save you half of what I made in the cocktail shaker if you want to start with that."

Christian came into the light spilled from the lanterns and torches, hands in the pockets of a flannel-lined jean jacket. He walked to the table Daniel indicated. He picked up the glass and sniffed the contents.

"What is it?"

"Michigan Sunset. Or it will be once you squeeze a lemon wedge into it."

"What the hell is a Michigan Sunset?"

"You unsophisticated troll, a Michigan Sunset is an unparalleled cocktail of smoked bourbon with hints of orange, ginger, bitters, and lemon." He took another drink.

"Never heard of it." Christian squeezed the lemon wedge Daniel had left on the table.

"You have now."

Daniel watched Christian take a careful sip.

"You know what I think?" said Christian, sitting down in the chair next to Daniel.

"You think it was good I brought out an extra chair?"

"I think most people have never heard of this. But that's their loss." He took another drink. "You made this up and put it on your menu, didn't you?"

"Aperitif."

They drank for a few minutes, listening to the night. Christian broke the silence.

"I didn't hear or see anything from the judges. I felt like I was in elementary school again—sent to my room and told to stay there so the grownups could talk."

"Randall?"

"Elena."

"Yeah, well, there you go. If it had been Randall, I'd have expected you to find a way to sneak out. But since it was Elena . . ."

"Exactly."

"And thanks, but I didn't expect you to find out anything. I cooked, they ate, they'll decide."

Christian looked around the outdoor kitchen. "Are you happy with what you cooked?"

Daniel tipped his glass to his mouth, draining the liquid. He got up and walked to a small tub that held a dozen beers in an icy bath. He set his glass on a nearby camp table.

"Beer?"

Christian drained his glass.

"Sure," he said, setting the glass on the ground beside his chair.

Daniel picked up a bottle opener and threaded four beers between his fingers. Coming back to the chairs, he handed two to Christian. He popped the cap off one, then handed the opener to Christian.

"Yeah," he said, settling back into his camp chair. "Yeah, I am." He took a long pull from his bottle.

"So, what now?"

"Now?" Daniel considered. "I'll start off tomorrow by making waffles for Ethan. I promised. And apparently, in a weak moment, I also promised that I'd make one for Biscuit. Then, I gotta clean up this area, plus where I had the original kitchen. I can afford to take a few days to do it, but by the end of the week, I need to head back north." He took another drink and looked at Christian. "How about you? What's next for you?"

# Christian

"What's next for you?"

*Well, hell,* thought Christian, *that is the burning question, isn't it?*

He'd really enjoyed helping Daniel. The man clearly knew what he was doing. Well, in the kitchen, anyway. It had been a pain in the ass to move that table twice. Though they had to do that anyway, right? And it had been an education to help Daniel move his outdoor kitchen. He talked to himself as Christian helped him set up the new area.

"Yeah, this is good. Sweep away the loose leaves. The composted ones underneath are fine where the tables and water stations go, but we need to rake down to bare earth around and between the campfires. Set up one fire here, another there, and clean out the rotted debris from that stump. It'll be great as an oven . . ."

Christian had never heard the man talk to himself before. Then he realized that Ethan was never more than ten steps behind or to one side of his dad, and Biscuit was never more than five away from Ethan. *He's teaching him,* Christian thought and had been glad to be included in the lesson. It felt good to move, to do something constructive. And since he wasn't in the running to beat out Blaise, he was more than willing to help anyone who was.

But now Daniel's dinner was done. All the competition dinners were. The judges would meet in a couple of weeks, and then Celeste, Eden, Daniel, and Blaise would gather here at the Club in December to learn who had impressed them the most. Who would walk away with fifty thousand dollars.

It wouldn't be him.

What was next for him, Daniel had asked.

He realized Daniel was looking at him, waiting for an answer.

"I haven't decided yet," Christian said, finishing off his beer. He set the empty bottle down and picked up the other.

"You could come to Escanaba for a while," Daniel said. "I've got an extra room in my cabin. You're welcome to it. All this time downstate has me behind on splitting firewood, and it's practically winter already up there. I could use the help."

"What the hell would I do in Escanaba? Other than split firewood?"

Daniel shrugged. "You'd have to figure that out. Winter is good for taking time to figure things out. Start fresh in the spring." He finished his first beer and, like Christian, reached for the other and popped off the cap. "That's what I plan to do with the winter," he said. "Depending on what happens in December."

*December*, thought Christian. *Winter, a good time to figure things out.* Even if he stayed here, he'd need to leave the Club at the end of the year. He could go back to the Flint house. To do what? Be the neighborhood vigilante? Tend vegetables by day and by night shoot holes in abandoned houses to discourage druggies and scrappers? Then there was his plan to just get in his car and point it somewhere, anywhere. Why not north? He'd never been to the Upper Peninsula.

"When do I need to let you know?"

# NOVEMBER

# Randall

Randall strolled to what had been Daniel's outdoor kitchen—the second setup and the one from which he'd cooked. Randall hadn't been sure it would work, given the distance between the rustic kitchen and the Club dining room, but Daniel had clearly captured the imagination of Joe and Jo, and the two of them had been instrumental in the dinner's success. Each had been slightly out of breath and Joe's freckled face more flushed than usual as they served each course, but the dishes had arrived at the correct temperature and with aplomb.

And the judges had been intrigued, the view from the windows the source of more conversation than Celeste's eclectic candle and flower decorations back in April.

Chase was at the now-abandoned kitchen site, poking with a stick at the ashes left in the hollow maple stump. In his other hand, he held a cocktail.

"Thought I'd find you here," said Randall.

"Well, you wouldn't let me come out here during the dinner, nor the next morning before I had to catch my flight to Toronto." He looked up and raised his glass to Randall, a smile belying the grumpiness of his words. "It's a good idea," he said, gesturing at the stump with the stick. "I'll bet he used this one for the rolls and the clafoutis." He indicated the rest of the area. "He cleaned everything up," Chase said approvingly, "so it's hard to tell, but I think I saw three other cookfires going that night." He looked past Randall and toward the windows of the Club's dining room, his eyes gauging the distance, likely doing the same math Randall had.

Randall didn't provide any further information. The competition wasn't done. It was why he and the judges were gathering today at the Club, with Thanksgiving only a few days away. The contestants hadn't been told they *couldn't* be here this weekend, but, as expected, they had other places to be this close to the holiday.

"Thaddeus just arrived. He took the ferry over from Wisconsin."

"Cool. I'll have to make time to take that ferry one of these days. I think I saw Adam going up the stairs as I was making my cocktail. Is Gabi here yet?"

"Arrived just before Thaddeus. The gang's all here."

Chase nodded and downed the rest of his drink.

"Let's get to it, then," he said.

"I think the April dinner was the most 'foraged,'" said Gabi, "although the menu was somewhat simple." She took a sip of the cocktail Chase had made for her and looked at the notes she'd jotted on her copy of the menu. "Not that simple is, in and of itself, bad."

"I'm not a fan of 'themed' menus," said Thaddeus. "I can't see a restaurant basing one on a Greek myth."

"Can't you? I can," said Adam. "I think it's creative. Particularly since the Persephone myth coincided with the time of year. I really thought the chef did a good job of fulfilling the expectations of that theme. The start is a cold soup with nettles and root veggies, and the finish is a light dessert that includes bee pollen and cloudberries. I agree with Gabi, great foraging on this one. Nettles, ramps, fiddleheads, wood sorrel, redbud blossoms, cloudberries—you don't pick those up at the local market. And I really like how the salt came to the flatbread dish through the dandelion petals. Between those and the sugared violets and redbud blossoms, this chef gave the dehydrator a workout." He looked around at the group seated in the common room before the crackling fire. "It's creative," he said again, leaning back in his chair and crossing one leg over his knee.

"But did the ginger overpower the trout?" asked Chase. "And ginger with hazelnut? Was that the right combination?"

"I thought the trout was a little overdone, and I would have liked to have had some creaminess to the fish sauce," said Gabi, "but I did really like the subtle tang of the wood sorrel."

"Too subtle," said Thaddeus. "It could have used a lot more."

Adam rolled his eyes. "Hell, Thaddeus, choppy ride on the ferry? I thought you'd love this menu because of how much was foraged. This wasn't just a trip to the farmers' market. Chase, make him another drink, would you? And maybe a bit stronger. Our friend here needs to wind down."

Thaddeus obligingly held out his empty glass to Chase, who stood up to take it.

"Sorry, I didn't mean to come across so negative. I agree—strong foraging is commendable. April in Michigan isn't the easiest month for it, but this chef clearly knows what grows when and where to find it."

*High praise*, Randall thought, *given Thaddeus's background*. Now in his early fifties, he'd grown his reputation over decades and was one of the country's leading experts on foraging, the author of multiple books on the subject. His in-field, hands-on classes on his extensive property in the wilds of Wisconsin attracted students from across the country and beyond.

Randall watched and listened but didn't take part in the conversation. His role here was arbiter. And he was the fifth judge, though none of the contestants knew it. Should there be a tie, he would decide the winner based on his observations of each contestant's adherence to the spirit of the competition.

"I thought the June menu had some good foraging," said Gabi, sorting through the papers she held. "Starting out with dandelion wine was an interesting choice."

"Did you get the reference?" Thaddeus accepted the drink Chase offered him and looked from one to the other of his fellow judges, a gleam in his eye.

"I noticed the quote marks around 'this fine fair month' but didn't know where it was from," admitted Chase. "Shakespeare?"

Adam shook his head in mock sorrow. "What do they teach you in the Canadian school system? No, not Shakespeare. Ray Bradbury. He wrote a novel called *Dandelion Wine* that references June as 'this fine fair month.'"

Gabi leaned toward Chase. "Don't feel bad," she stage-whispered. "I didn't know either."

"I really liked the dandelion wine. Have been thinking about sourcing it. Using it in a new cocktail," said Chase.

"You know you're a chef, right? Not a mixologist?"

"I can't be both? How unimaginative." Chase gestured toward the glasses in each person's hand. "You seem to be enjoying my liquid creations."

Randall said nothing but lifted his glass in acknowledgment. Chase was a renowned chef with a successful restaurant in Toronto that specialized in regional, seasonal, and wild foods. It also had an extensive menu of creative cocktails that included ingredients such as juniper syrup, rhubarb shrub, and black walnut bitters.

"I think my favorite thing on the June menu was the crayfish mousse on the watermelon radish disks," said Gabi. "And I liked the use of cattail in the Duchess potatoes. I thought this menu was a good balance of foraged and locally sourced ingredients."

"But was enough of it foraged? Or was it just shopped?" asked Thaddeus. "We are, after all, the Forager Chefs Club."

"Oh, Thaddeus, I love you, but don't be pretentious," said Gabi. "There are a *lot* of ways to forage, not just hiking through the fields and forests with a bag on your hip."

"I agree," said Adam. "That mascarpone cheese was delicious. That definitely didn't come from a chain grocery store." He turned to Randall. "Are you allowed to tell us if the chef made that in-house or sourced it?"

Randall inclined his head. "I am. The chef made it in-house from locally sourced cream."

Adam nodded, pleased. "And the meadow greens puree it was paired with," he continued. "Thaddeus, you have to admit, that's a great example of locally sourced ingredients, whether they were found in the wild or at a local farm."

Thaddeus tilted his head from side to side as though weighing the proposition. "Yes, you're right," he said finally. "Not a whole lot of cheese waiting to be collected in field and forest. And I could taste in the puree that it included foraged greens, not just gardened." After a pause, he added, "I thought the elderflower meringues were a nice touch. I've made elderflower fritters, but they can be a bit heavy. The meringues paired very nicely with the lemon verbena sorbet."

"I would have liked to see some wild game instead of beef," said Chase. "Rabbit, maybe?"

"Rabbit doesn't exactly lend itself to a surf-and-turf theme," said Adam.

"Okay, moving on to September," said Gabi, shifting the menu printouts in front of her. "Though, before we do . . ." She craned her neck to address Randall, seated on the periphery. "Can you tell us what happened with August? There were supposed to be five dinners?"

Randall hesitated. "The chef had a family emergency," he said finally. "And so had to withdraw."

The judges were quiet for a moment.

"Must have been one hell of an emergency," Adam said finally.

"It was," said Randall, his mind jumping to the last time he'd seen Katherine, opening her front door to his knock on a cold January afternoon when he'd gone to Flint to deliver a thick envelope of opportunity to her son. She hadn't recognized him.

"Well, it's a shame," said Gabi. "So, as I said, moving on to September."

Randall took a drink of his cocktail and thought about Blaise and wine bottles and a phone call from a friend in town but kept his thoughts to himself.

"The chef used all three of his exceptions," said Adam, consulting his copy of the menu and then looking to Randall for affirmation.

"The chef did," Randall said. He'd been careful throughout the competition not to reveal anything about the chefs, including their gender.

"It was a very delicious meal," said Gabi. "The duck breast was cooked perfectly, and the cherry reduction sauce complemented it very well."

"Clearly a trained chef," said Chase. "Sauce bretonne. Sauce Anglaise. The fig glaze. A perfect caramel with a gorgeous French apple tart."

"A delicious meal," agreed Adam. "And one I could have likely gotten at a top-notch restaurant in any of a dozen cities around the country."

"Except for the whitefish quenelles," said Thaddeus. "Not a whole lot of whitefish on the menus of big-city restaurants."

"The quenelles were perfect to the eye and to the taste," said Gabi, "and, no, you likely wouldn't find whitefish on the menu in a big-city restaurant." She turned to Adam. "But I get what you're saying, and I agree. A very delicious meal prepared by a chef who clearly knows how to cook. But is it a meal you'd expect to have at the Forager Chefs Club?" The gaze she cast around the room ended on Randall.

Randall kept his face blank. This was theirs to judge, theirs to decide. He didn't have a role—yet. He may not have one at all. He was always on the periphery of important decisions, it seemed. He pushed the thought down.

Gabi was the only judge who lived in Michigan. She and her husband ran a farm-to-fork restaurant on the eastern side of the state, much of what was on the menu coming from their own farm. It was quite a challenge, Randall knew, managing both a restaurant and a farm, but she had a passion for it. There were forest-to-fork items on their menu as well, which is why she'd been a good choice for this panel, balancing out Thaddeus's strong leaning toward foraging and Chase's equally strong penchant for hunting and game. Chase couldn't serve what he hunted in his restaurant, but his private dinner parties were legendary.

Randall took a drink from his glass. It was very good, with hints of blackberry and tobacco. "Excellent cocktail, Chase," he said. "You should put it on your menu."

"I will," said Chase. "You've been my test subject." He shifted through the papers in front of him. "Speaking of cocktails . . ." He cast his gaze around the table. "Shall we talk about October?"

Adam snorted. "You've got a man crush, don't you?"

"Are you going to say you don't? I saw you watching out the windows just as much as I was."

"No one was watching out the windows as much as you were," said Adam.

Randall laughed with the rest of them. Adam hid his smile in his drink. He was a bit more retrospective than the other judges, Randall knew. He'd been professionally trained and had worked in some of the best kitchens in the country until a series of medical issues had made it impossible to work the grueling hours demanded of a restaurant's executive chef. But he'd healed. And had found purpose in learning to forage and bring what he harvested from meadows, streams, and forests to the table. Now in his late forties, he'd traveled from Minnesota to be a judge for this competition, and Randall was grateful for it.

"I didn't care for the acorn bisque," said Gabi, bringing the conversation back to food.

"Do you have any idea how much work it is to prepare acorns to make a bisque?" asked Adam.

"I do. I get it. I can't imagine going to all that trouble. It was well done and tasted exactly as I expect acorn bisque to taste." She shrugged. "I'm just saying that it's not a taste I care for." She held up both index fingers, nails short and a bit ragged, a testament to frequent work in the soil. "Now the wild boar lonzino? That I liked—a lot. I'd love to know if he made it himself or sourced it somewhere. And if he sourced it, I want to know from where." She looked again to Randall. "You told us about the mascarpone—what about the lonzino?"

"He made it himself," Randall said. No need to hide gender— they'd all watched Daniel silhouetted by the cooking fires.

Adam let out a low whistle of appreciation.

"Hands down, the best thing on that menu was the venison loin with that jaeger sauce," said Chase. He shook his head. "I'd really like to taste that again. I got the currant, and I think green alder—it had just the slightest hint of resin and a pepperiness that wasn't black pepper—but there was something else that gave a great depth of flavor. I thought it was the mushrooms, but it was deeper than what you'd get just from adding that wild mushroom medley."

"I agree," said Adam. "The sauce for the venison was really good. So was the wild wing pie."

"But did it all fit together?" asked Thaddeus. "Was it three complimentary courses or throwing everything from the larder into the mix?"

"I think it worked," said Chase. "And I saw you mopping up sauce from both the venison and the pie with those rolls, Thaddeus."

Thaddeus took a drink from his glass. "I admire someone who can bake with coals."

"Sunchokes were an interesting choice," said Gabi. "Not really a vegetable, in my view. Was there one on this menu?"

"Did there have to be?" asked Chase. "An October dinner, cooked outdoors over open fires. You could just imagine people gathering at the end of a hunt. Starting with a cocktail is brilliant. I don't know many hunters who would bemoan a lack of vegetables when there's all that good protein to be had. And I do think that sunchokes, as a tuber, are technically a vegetable—but I get your point." He leaned back in his chair again. "The only thing that would have made that dinner even better would have been to eat it outdoors."

"There's the man crush," said Adam. "Expect Chase to offer campfire-side dining next season."

"Not sure that will work in downtown Toronto. But it would be fun, right?"

Sensing a break in the discussion, Randall rose.

"Okay, then, it's the moment of truth." He handed out four small sheets of paper and four pens. "Here's how the judging will be done. On your paper, please score the dinners, one through four, with four points for your favorite and one point for your least favorite. I'll tally them up, and the chef with the most points wins the fifty-thousand-dollar prize."

"And you're our tiebreaker, should there be one?" asked Thaddeus.

Randall inclined his head.

"I feel this should be like horse racing," muttered Gabi, looking at her paper, pen poised. "Or golf tournaments. Multiple prizes. Not just one winner takes all."

"It's how the sponsor funded it, and the Founders Circle agreed. One winner takes it all."

"I'd love to meet the sponsor," said Adam, picking up his pen. "There's got to be a really good back story to this whole thing." He bent to his paper but looked up at Randall under strong, thick eyebrows. "Think we could get it if Chase plied you with a few more cocktails?"

"Not a chance." Randall didn't tell him he didn't know the back story—if anyone did, it was within the close-knit Founders Circle. "Finish your work, and then you can have dinner."

"Who's cooking?" asked Gabi.

"A guest chef," said Randall.

# Christian

Sure. Why the hell not?

That had been Christian's thought when he took Daniel up on his offer. He'd never been to the UP, let alone Escanaba. It was as good a place as any to spend a few months and get his bearings. He wondered how much snow they got up there. A lot, he knew, but how much at one time? He needed to swing by the Flint house to grab his winter gear. He had a good pair of boots—two, actually—as well as a warm jacket, a couple of winter hats, thick wool socks, and clothing suited to layering. He'd invested some of his earnings the first winter he drove a salt truck in making sure he was dressed for being outdoors in cold, wet weather. It wasn't really cold yet, so chances were, even if looters had come by the house during the six weeks he'd been gone, no one would have sought out winter clothes.

He helped Daniel clear, reseed, and lay straw over the original outdoor kitchen site and then clear the second one too. As they had a couple of beers when it was all done, he told him he'd like to take him up on his offer. Daniel had clapped him on the back and seemed genuinely pleased. Ethan, who had helped spread the grass seed and straw, let out an enthusiastic whoop, then asked him if he knew how to whittle and if he was any good at chess. Even the dog had wagged its tail.

It felt good to have a plan.

Then, Randall had approached him the morning he was leaving

for Flint with another offer.

Sure. Why the hell not?

Christian drove to the house in Flint and loaded up his car with what he thought he'd need to winter in Escanaba and take up Randall's offer.

He visited each room.

He stood in the living room, the kitchen, his bedroom, his mother's. His reputation had done its work—like a sci-fi force field or fantasy magic spell—no squatter or looter or scrapper had crossed his threshold. Each room looked as it had when he'd left, but the air tasted stale, and dust motes danced in the thin sunlight. Her room no longer smelled of lemon verbena and medicine, the kitchen of sauces and stews and soups simmering on the stove. The rooms didn't smell of urine and feces and decay like so many of the empty houses did, but it was different from when he'd left. The house smelled of absence—or maybe resignation. As though it had known that he'd left without a firm intention of coming back. He wandered, picking up this and that, setting a few select items on the kitchen table near a sturdy cardboard box. He descended the steps into the basement and walked past the colicky furnace—still running, thank God—to peruse the nearly depleted shelves. It smelled musty—but then it always had, a bit. He took the last jar of bread-and-butter pickles he'd made with his mother the year before and another of pears and went back up the stairs and out the back door. He let the screen door slam noisily behind him—another announcement of *yep, neighborhood, I'm here!*—to stand and survey the garden and take deep breaths of November air. The garden looked as it typically did after multiple frosts and hard freezes, reduced to brittle stalks, wilted greens, and a few stalwart herbs. He found a handful of hazelnuts on the bushes along the back fence that the squirrels had missed. He put them in the pocket of his jacket. He'd have to find a source for more, but he liked that he'd have a few from home for his upcoming dinner at the Club. He stood silent for a few minutes over the section of recently dug soil before going into the house.

He made sure the back door was locked, shut the front door firmly, and made a show of locking it as he left. He hoped it was noticed that he'd been here overnight. That he'd taken care to lock up the house, as he'd always done when going to work or on errands, even when his mother was home. That it wasn't noticed that he'd loaded his car with winter clothes and boots, three handmade quilts, his shotgun, and two cardboard boxes.

Back in September, before heading to the Club, he'd paid enough to the electric, gas, and water companies plus the bank to keep the house going through November. He'd gone to the post office yesterday to mail four more checks. That would carry things through February. Lamps would turn on in various rooms via timed switches, and the pipes wouldn't freeze if the furnace continued to cooperate. Mailing those checks had left him with not much in his bank account beyond beer and gas money. *Sorry, House,* he thought as he loaded the car, *after February, all bets are off.* There wasn't going to be any income from driving a salt truck in Flint this winter. He wasn't even sure why he'd sent those checks—good money after bad, probably—but it grated to just give up on the house he'd fought to keep for so long. Hell, he had an arrest record because of defending this house.

He set one cardboard box in the back seat. He needed two hands to carry it. That was a good thing. It would be depressing if everything he cared about, everything that represented anything to him, was made up of three quilts made by a long-dead grandmother who'd emigrated from Germany and items that fit into a box he could carry under one arm.

The framed photo he'd found in his mother's nightstand was at the top of the box, wrapped so the glass wouldn't break. That she'd kept it close to hand meant it had been important to her, and he liked that it showed her younger self, beautiful and smiling.

He set the second cardboard box on the front passenger seat. It held the glass jars from the basement and a few other ingredients he'd foraged, dried, and preserved, including just over a pound of hazelnut flour. He was glad he hadn't thrown the Manoomin and demi-glace in the stream that ran through the Club's acreage back in September after his encounter with Blaise. It had been a near thing. Turns out, he was going to use them, after all.

He looked back at the house, wondered if he'd ever see it again, what it might look like if he ever did, and how long his reputation might keep it safe. That reputation was the only good thing his anger had ever produced.

He shifted his car into gear and drove away.

Back to the Forager Chefs Club.

He was provided with two servers who would deliver his courses and clear away dishes, and he was free to drop by the dining room to chat as he chose and time allowed. He was cooking for the four competition judges and Randall. This wasn't part of the competition; Randall had made that clear when he invited him to cook.

"Why?"

"Why am I inviting you to cook, or why should you do it?"

"Both."

"You spent time and effort devising your menu. I believe you to be talented. This is an opportunity to show four well-respected forager chefs what you can do. Nothing may come of it, but you never know."

"That answers the second question."

"Because I was in love with your mother."

Randall had paused before saying it, Christian remembered, as if weighing whether he should say it at all. Christian now knew who had taken the photo he found in his mother's nightstand. The photo she'd kept within arm's reach in those last days, for maybe many, many days before. A photo of friends—all in their early twenties, smiling, optimistic, their lives ahead of them—lounging around a campfire in friendship following a good meal they'd prepared with and for each other. He remembered wondering when he'd first found it why his father wasn't in the photo and whether it had been because he was the man behind the camera. Now he knew: it had been Randall.

It was the greatest regret of his life, Randall had told him as they sat in Adirondack chairs sipping bourbon and watching the twilight deepen into night, that he'd never told Katherine how he felt. He'd always been the most introspective of their group, included but always on the periphery, sometimes questioning how he fit in at all. And Katherine had been vibrant, a force of nature. So he'd waited, been her friend, always seeking to summon up the courage to tell her how he felt, to see if perhaps she could feel the same way about him. And then she'd met the man who would spirit her away from all of them. Over time, communication had dwindled . . . until it was nonexistent. It hadn't been until the Club was approached about this competition that Katherine's name had come up again among the Club's Founders Circle, several of whom were in that photo. Randall had been tasked with seeking her out. And had learned that the dark-haired man who won her heart had left her, and she was dying. And she had a son who just may have inherited her creativity in the kitchen.

Because he wasn't competing, Christian also didn't need to limit where he got his ingredients. Still, this was the Forager Chefs Club, and he wanted to adhere as closely as possible to the menu he had devised to take advantage of August's late-summer bounty.

It was November, so most of the local farmers' markets were closed for the season, and his own foraging resources were past their harvest, but at Randall's suggestion, he'd driven the short distance from the Club to the curiously named Gourmet Bait Shop. There, he met Annie Tate, the gatekeeper to a treasure trove of top-quality, local ingredients, both in her shop and beyond.

Christian eyed the plating of his first course before nodding to allow Jo and Joe to carry it down the short hallway to the dining room. The two were curious about him, but he didn't feel talkative and hadn't offered details about his role here tonight.

The first course for his August menu had been individual charcuterie boards that included herbal butters, whitefish spread, and pesto, along with a selection of breads, cheeses, and fresh berries. But he didn't want to use greenhouse basil to make his pesto, and fresh berries in November could only come from southern climates this time of year. So, instead, he'd made a rich onion soup, sautéing yellow onions and shallots in butter, then simmering them in a beef stock he'd taken two days to prepare from meaty bones and roasted vegetables, adding a liberal douse of sherry near the end. Accompanying the soup were slices of crisped bread he'd baked with locally grown and milled flour from the Gourmet Bait Shop and caraway seed harvested from his garden in Flint, served with a small crock of whitefish spread he'd smoked in the maple stump in what had been Daniel's outdoor kitchen.

Leonard had been understandably annoyed—"pissed" with an accompanying expletive was more to the point—when his brother had been left waiting in Bear Lake back in August with six uncollected squabs. But he got quiet and refused the payment offered when Christian explained why he hadn't been there to collect the poultry as arranged. Christian paid him extra for the squab for this November dinner, saying it was harder to get so late in the season. Leonard knew it was a pretense but accepted the money.

The plums from the trees in the abandoned backyard in Flint were long gone, but Annie had come through with some home-canned ones that would do. She'd also been able to provide beets and dried cherries. So his main course would be the same as he'd planned in August: roasted squab stuffed with plums and served with the demi-glace and the Manoomin he hadn't thrown into the Club's stream in a fit of anger, accompanied by glazed beets with cherries.

Remembering a conversation with Daniel while sitting outside in the hours following the October dinner, Christian had made the drive to a dairy farm near Idlewild, where he'd met a very talkative Black woman who was a close friend of Eden's. She warmed up to him considerably when he told her he knew both Eden and Daniel. Her face beamed when he confirmed he'd also spent time with Ethan and Biscuit. She'd taken him by the arm, and he'd spent a good portion of an afternoon helping her round up her cows from the state forest that bordered her property. Apparently, the cows had found a break in her fence and wandered through to graze. They would come home on their own in the evening for milking, she explained, but a neighbor had called just a while ago to let her know that the forestry service was conducting land inspections, so it was best she got her cows home sooner. Christian had offered to help mend the fence, but Mrs. Abrams had demurred, saying she had someone who would take care of that for her. His reward had been two pounds of butter and a quart of cream to which he'd added a touch of Frangelico and then whipped to decorate his hazelnut tart.

Christian thanked Jo and Joe as they returned from the dining room after serving dessert. He offered them dinner—he'd made extra of each course as insurance, a thank-you to them if he didn't need it. He didn't join them as they ate but did pour himself a glass of wine from a bottle he'd set aside. Accepted their compliments and thanked them again. He leaned against the counter and took a few sips. Watched the clock on the wall. When it had been ten minutes since dessert had been served, he said goodnight to Jo and Joe, topped off his glass, and pushed through the swinging door that opened to the short hallway that led to the dining room.

As Randall had said, nothing may come of it.

*But you never know.*

# Randall

Randall parked his car in front of the inn in Bear Lake. It was late, but he'd promised. The night was quiet, the songs of the frogs and crickets gone for the season. The season was leaning into winter.

He loved this time of year, though it wasn't a popular opinion. Late November. The leaves were gone, the harvest in, so it wasn't a favorite of those who enjoyed autumn color tours, corn mazes, and pumpkin spice concoctions. No measurable snow yet—though that varied year to year. Icy crusts on ponds, but nothing thick enough for skating, so not a favorite of those who looked forward to the sports of the winter season. These were weeks when it was typically chilly, on the brink of truly cold. Often wet—but not the summer dance-in-the-rain kind of wet—it was the damp, bone-chilling kind of wet. Past the point of autumn's lavish display but too early for social media-worthy images of cross-country skiing or horse-drawn sleigh rides. Late November, Randall contemplated, was on the periphery. He often walked the Club's property at this time of year, confident of solitude (though always wearing an orange vest). He loved late November because of the solitude. And maybe because no one else did. No one, it seemed, ever longed for late November.

To him, late November was candlelight. A candle lit between the bonfires of the autumn harvest and the hearth fires of the winter season.

A single candle could provide all the light needed, hold back the darkness.

On his walks, his footsteps making little sound on sodden leaves still colorful, if not as bright as when they'd drifted down from branches now bare above him, he sometimes wondered what that said about him.

He'd done what he could while maintaining the integrity that defined him. Her son had cooked for the judges, even if it hadn't been as a part of the competition. What may come of that, if anything, wasn't his to decide.

Getting out of his car in front of the inn, he adjusted his fedora against the cold, misty rain that had started to drop from the sky.

She would be waiting.

Randall had met her only once before. He nodded to the inn's night clerk, walked down the carpeted hallway, and knocked on the door with the room number Elena had given him and said was hers. Recognized her when she answered. She recognized him as well and invited him in. He thanked her and took off his hat as he crossed the threshold.

He'd thought her cold, impersonal, when they met the year before. She wanted to remain anonymous, she'd told the Club. Money transfers and expense account transactions had been conducted via a law firm in Detroit. *"You may call me Mrs. Rose,"* she'd told him then. She was an elegant woman who looked to be in her midsixties and accustomed to getting her way without having to raise her voice. Like that first time a year ago, tonight she wore a knee-length wool skirt, sweater twin set, and low-heeled shoes. A string of pearls was around her neck, and a small, bejeweled watch was around her wrist. She wore several rings, but not a wedding band. She was widowed, he knew, but didn't know how long ago her husband had died.

She didn't appear cold or impersonal this time when she invited him to sit on the couch in the small seating area of her suite. She perched herself on the edge of one of the two cushioned chairs facing it and crossed her ankles. The curtains in the room were pulled shut against the night, and the heat was turned up. It was overly warm, and Randall considered taking off his coat. He decided against it; he wouldn't be here long. He sat and looked at the woman across from him. She was pensive, wound tight, her hands clasped in her lap and her eyes on him as though waiting to hear the results of a medical test that could change her life. She clearly wasn't interested in small talk.

"The judges have made their decision," he said, without preamble. He told her.

"Oh, thank God," she said with an expulsion of breath that Randall hadn't realized she'd been holding. She squeezed her eyes shut and put a hand to her mouth. She swayed a bit on her perch. A sound Randall couldn't quite identify escaped her mouth.

It was a little alarming.

"Can I get you anything?" he asked. He stood and looked around the room. *Bloody hell, not even a bottle of water?* He glanced at the closed door that likely led to the bedroom.

"No, no, I'm fine." She lowered her hand, opened her eyes, and gave Randall a tentative smile. "It's just—well—it's just such a relief. It's been months, you understand. Months of waiting and wondering and not knowing how anything might turn out."

He didn't understand, not really, but nodded anyway. This woman had spent well over one hundred thousand dollars to fund a competition over which she had virtually no control. Clearly, she'd hoped for a particular outcome—apparently, the one he'd just delivered. But why?

"When will you tell them? The competitors?"

"Early December."

"And they'll come to the Forager Chefs Club? To hear the news in person? All of them?"

"That is the expectation, yes."

"I'd like to be there," she said. "Not for the announcement. But later. After the winner accepts."

There was something in her eyes. She was still taut, still perched, but there was something else. Like someone who had just received the results of their medical test and now perceived a future of possibilities. Nothing definite, but possible.

"We'd be delighted to have you," Randall said.

The woman stood, and Randall took that as his cue. He picked up his fedora from where he'd set it on the coffee table and walked to the door.

"Mr. Randall, could you wait a moment?"

She remembered his name. She walked to a side table and took a checkbook out of her purse. Randall heard the scratch of a pen, then the sound of paper being torn along a perforation. She crossed the room and handed him a check.

"For the others—the ones who didn't win. I don't want them to leave empty-handed. Divide this as you see fit."

He folded it and put it in an inner pocket of his coat without looking at it. "I'll make sure Elena gets you the specifics on the December announcement gathering."

She closed the door quietly behind him, and he walked down the carpeted hallway of the inn, out the front door, and to his parked car.

As he started the engine, he took the check out of his coat pocket and turned on the car's interior light. Her name wasn't Mrs. Rose; it was Mariam Streng. Apparently, the need for anonymity—at least with him—was gone. He looked at the sum she'd written in elegant cursive. Forty thousand dollars. And she'd done it seemingly without a second thought.

Then he noticed something else.

The check was made out to him, not the Forager Chefs Club.

*Divide this as you see fit*, she'd said.

Who *was* this woman?

# DECEMBER

# The Competitors

Elena stood at the entrance to the common room, a tray of champagne flutes on a small table next to her, bubbles rising in energetic lines. She handed one to Eden.

"Welcome," she said.

"Thank you," said Eden, accepting a glass. She took a few steps into the room and then turned. She didn't usually give in to impulses but decided to indulge this one. She picked up another glass from the tray and held it out to Elena. "I suspect there will be more toasts this evening, but I'd like to offer one now."

"Don't tell Randall I'm drinking on the job," Elena said in a mock whisper as she took the glass.

"Please. We all know by now that you do pretty much whatever you want in this place." Eden paused. "In fact, if it weren't that you're too young, it wouldn't surprise me to find out you're one of the Club's elusive Founders Circle with knowledge of the secret handshake and everything."

Eden thought she saw a flash of surprise and wariness in Elena's eyes, but then it was gone, and the twinkle of mischief was back. The Club's manager raised her glass.

"So, what are we toasting?"

"You," said Eden, clinking her glass against the other woman's. "I don't know who will be announced the winner tonight, but this has been a year and an experience I will never forget. Thank you for your generosity of spirit and efficiency and for always providing a welcome." *And for proving not to fit the stereotype I'd painted for you,* Eden thought to add but didn't. That would be taking her impulse too far. She tipped the glass against her lips and drank.

"You are always welcome as a guest of the Forager Chefs Club, Eden," Elena said. "And always through the front door."

*So she hasn't forgotten that barbed exchange back in June,* Eden thought as Elena set her glass down to reach for a full one to present to Daniel.

He was wearing his usual jeans, but over a button-down shirt with a textured weave, he wore a tan suede sport coat. His boots were polished to a dull gleam.

"Thank you," Daniel said. "Hello, Eden."

"Damn, you clean up good, Yooper," Eden said in amusement.

He laughed self-consciously, put one hand in a pocket of his jeans, and took a sip from his glass. "You're looking very nice tonight as well," he said with a dip of his head. "I'm glad to see you. I was hoping we'd get a minute to chat before the announcement."

"Oh?"

"I wanted to thank you for the good word you put in for me with Mrs. Abrams. It was definitely touch-and-go there for a bit."

"Well, she's very protective. But I think Ethan and Biscuit helped win her over too." Eden lifted her glass to Daniel. "And kudos to you for finding her just from our conversation back in July. That took some detective work."

"Well, I can't fault your logic about sourcing great ingredients. And you were right. I've never tasted better dairy than from Mrs. Abrams's—what did she call her cows?— girls."

"Yeah, well, if you beat me out in this thing, I may regret letting you know about those girls, unintended as it was."

"I can't deny that's exactly what I hope will happen. But Eden, I may not have ever tasted your cooking, but I did hear about what you do at your father's mission in Detroit, and I think it's amazing. I'd like to come cook with you sometime . . . if you'll let a Yooper into your kitchen."

Eden drained her glass. "How about I let you come cook the celebration dinner when I announce to the mission that I've just won the funding that's going to change lives?"

*Likely prosecco or some other sparkling wine, not true champagne, but not bad*, Blaise thought as he stood by the windows of the common room and looked out. There wasn't much to see beyond his reflection in the glass, what with the light cast from the leaping flames in the fireplace on one side of the room and the glow of lamplight throughout. The days were yet to get shorter, but it was nearing dark already. Standing, ostensibly looking out the window, kept up appearances. He took another sip from his glass. He knew who was in the room. He and Daniel had nothing to say to one another. He didn't think Eden was in the mood for small talk with him, though she did seem engrossed in whatever conversation she and Daniel were having. Celeste hadn't arrived yet. Elena had been polite, as always, but unless he won this competition, he didn't think she'd give him the time of day. He didn't think she was a lesbian, but he did see her exchange a toast with Eden, so who knew?

He wondered if Bradley would come down later. Randall had said he was invited, and Bradley knew Celeste was here. But when the announcement of the winner was made—and he was moderately confident it would be in his favor—Blaise didn't want any appearance of that win being anything but his own. This time, it was truth. Bradley hadn't helped him with the recipes for this competition, had withdrawn from the kitchen and cooking when Blaise had needed his foraging creativity most. So if—*when*, he corrected himself—he won this competition, he would do it solo.

Solo.

Alone.

It was a weird feeling, he thought, looking at the pane of window glass, pretending to see a view beyond and not just his own reflection. They'd always been two people but one person, he and Bradley. Even more so after that surreal conversation after their high school graduation when they'd learned—well, he'd learned; he had to explain it to Bradley repeatedly and over time—that their parents didn't want them anymore, were moving on to new marriages and new families that didn't include them, but their father would provide a monthly stipend, at least for a while.

The lesson he'd learned there was that money could fix just about anything. Or maybe at least atone for it.

He wasn't sure that money was going to fix this, however. Bradley didn't care about money—*well, lucky for him, he hadn't had to think about it, had he?* Since high school, he'd always had Blaise, his twin brother, to manage the finances and make sure they had a place to live, food on the table, and clothes on their backs. But now Bradley had the girl. The girl—this young, weird girl who somehow had connected with his brother in a way that no one else, other than he, ever had. And she was going to replace him, Blaise suspected. Replace him and be more than him.

*And where does that leave me*, he wondered, looking at the image of his brother in the windowpane in front of him.

Celly paused in the doorway of the common room. By his stance and the way he held his shoulders, she knew the man staring at a window that only threw back his own reflection was Blaise, not Bradley. She glanced around the room. She saw Eden and Daniel. She hadn't really expected Christian, though she would have liked to express her condolences—she'd heard about his mother from Elena. Randall wasn't here. Bradley wasn't either. Someone touched her shoulder.

"Sorry, what?" she said.

It was Elena, her brow smooth and her smile perfect, as always. "Celeste, would you like a glass of champagne?"

Celly took a glass from the tray Elena offered. Inhaled as she took a sip. The bubbles tickled her nose, and she almost sneezed. She remembered the promise she'd made to herself in the contemplative days before boarding Icarus's plane for one more flight to the Forager Chefs Club.

"Elena?"

"Yes?"

"Could I ask you a favor?"

"Of course. I'll do what I can."

"Could you call me Celly?"

She'd always been a little intimidated by Elena. The woman was beautiful and elegant, always in control. Even after that horrible fight in August—amid broken glass, shouting, anger, violence, and blood—Elena had been calm. She was always friendly but with boundaries Celly couldn't imagine anyone daring to cross. But now, at her request, Elena looked at her in a way she hadn't before. It reminded her of late nights with Aunt Tilda and her mom, sharing tales and reminiscences and observations beside the campfire on summer nights.

"I would love that, Celly."

"Celly? I remember that name. I haven't heard it in a while." A masculine hand reached over and plucked a glass from Elena's tray.

Celly turned her head and saw Randall. Remembered their first meeting nearly a year before in the St. Ignace air terminal. She blushed but lifted her chin.

"I've decided it's time people did. And not just people on the island."

He clinked his glass against hers. "You look lovely, Celly," Randall said. He looked around the room. "Seems we're almost all gathered."

"Almost," agreed Elena. "Are you sure he was planning to attend?"

Randall handed his glass to Elena.

"I'll be right back," he said.

Celly watched him leave.

"Who?"

"Christian."

He'd decided to take Daniel up on his offer to spend the winter in Escanaba. And since Daniel and Ethan would be coming back to the Club for the announcement of the competition winner, it just made sense to stick around after cooking for the judges and go north when Daniel did. Plus, it gave him time to think, to consider.

Christian had enjoyed his conversations with all the judges, but the one with Chase had been particularly interesting. He agreed he could learn a lot in the chef's renowned kitchen while maybe bringing some fresh perspectives of his own. A season working in Chase's restaurant in Toronto might open all sorts of possibilities if they could work out the visa situation. He could use the time in Escanaba to help Daniel with firewood and whatever else he needed doing and then begin the spring with a fresh start, a fresh outlook.

There was a knock on the door. Three firm raps.

He'd thought someone might come. He had his answers prepared for whoever was on the other side. Different answers—different reasons—but the same outcome. He wasn't going downstairs for the announcement.

He crossed the room and opened the door.

"You're late," said Randall. "Is that what you're wearing?"

"C'mon in," said Christian, stepping aside in invitation. "Pour yourself a drink."

Randall entered the room but shook his head when Christian indicated a tray set with three glasses and an open bottle of bourbon. "I've got champagne waiting for me downstairs. As do you."

"Randall, we both know there's absolutely no reason for me to be there when you announce the winner. Unless you think I need a further reminder of what an idiot I was?"

"You being an idiot isn't what kept you from cooking in August. We both know that. Everyone downstairs knows that."

"My mother dying gave you an out. You seriously would have let me continue in the competition after breaking up the furniture? If I had shown up that Saturday to cook, what would you have done?"

"There was blame on both sides for that incident. And the judges were here that Saturday, expecting a competitor's dinner. I never told them not to come. They ended up dining in Manistee. You can ask Elena; she hosted them that evening."

That shook him a bit. He'd assumed . . . but still . . .

"I couldn't have cooked that day."

"I know." Randall opened his mouth to say something, then closed it, letting out a breath through his nose. "I think I'll take that drink after all. I have something I want to say to you."

Christian poured a liberal portion into a glass. He added a bit more into his own before taking a seat opposite Randall.

"The others are waiting, and I've got a beef roast in the oven that'll need checking in just a little while, so I'll get to the point," Randall said. "I've spent some time in introspection the past few weeks and have come to realize a couple of things about myself. And since I've never been one for regrets, I'm just going to call it 'learning.'"

"And now you're going to pass this 'learning' on to me?"

"I am." Randall took a drink. "Christian, don't live on the periphery of your own life."

"I don't think avoiding humiliation is living on the periphery of my life. Sounds more like self-preservation to me."

"Why would you be humiliated? There are three other people in that room downstairs who aren't going to win this competition either."

"They competed."

"So did you." Randall held up his hand to forestall Christian's denial. "You didn't cook in the competition, but you were part of it, participated in it, right up until you got that phone call about your mother. And you've done something that none of them have. You've met the judges, talked with them. Whether they win or lose tonight, don't you think Eden, Daniel, and Celly would be interested to know about them, hear your perspectives, what you learned about them?"

"Celly?"

"Celeste. It's her nickname at home. It's how we were introduced when I first met her. Apparently, someone else has been practicing a little introspection. She asked Elena tonight to call her Celly. Has probably asked the same of the others by now."

"You didn't mention Blaise in that list."

"Oh, I'm confident Blaise would also like to learn about the judges."

"I'm not interested in talking to Blaise."

"So then come down and talk with the others."

Christian pointed his glass at Randall. "I see what you did there." He took a sip. It would be nice to see them. He could tell Daniel he was taking him up on his offer to spend winter in Escanaba. See Celly's reaction when he called her by her nickname. And he'd been wanting to talk to Eden again, maybe get to know her a little better. Although where that could possibly lead, he had no idea. "So this introspection, this 'learning' of yours," he said. "Do you think you've been living on the periphery of your own life?"

"Not always," Randall said after a moment, "but too often. I did it in the years that I didn't tell your mother how I felt about her. In some ways, I've done it here at the Club. Even though I was there, part of the group—or I thought I was—when the idea of forming this Club first came up, I'm the director of it, not one of the Founders Circle. I'm typically there when the big decisions are made, but my voice doesn't really count for much, doesn't sway anything."

"You've been on the periphery."

"I've been on the periphery."

"And here I thought you just drew the short straw when you were the one to show up in Flint last January."

"That's what I'm telling you, Christian. I've come to realize that too often in my life I've stood by and waited for someone to hand me the short straw." He took a last drink and stood up. He set the glass down and crossed to the door. "But going to Flint wasn't a short straw. Kathrine didn't recognize me, but I recognized her. And I'm grateful to have had the opportunity to see her, talk to her, one more time." He opened the door. "See you downstairs, Christian."

Christian looked at the shut door after Randall left.

He got up to find a fresh shirt.

Randall withdrew the instant-read thermometer from the roast. Twenty more minutes, he judged; then he'd take it out of the oven to rest. He'd decided on a simple menu. He wanted to spend time with the people in the common room, not just be in the kitchen. So he was making an herb-crusted beef roast, his favorite recipe for Florentine potatoes, and maple-glazed acorn squash. Nothing fancy, but it would satisfy.

Tonight, he wanted time and space to chat and interact with these people he'd come to know, not just observe them and their interactions with one another.

And he had four envelopes that he would give out over the course of the evening. Mariam Streng's check had been made out to him. He'd informed the Founders Circle, of course. There had been pushback from one of them—the guy had been a bit of a jerk even when they were in college—but he had been firm. Mariam Streng had made her check out to Dane Randall with instructions for him to distribute it to the nonwinning competitors as he saw fit. He'd deposited the check and then, after careful deliberation, made his decisions. The four checks he'd written out were in thick, creamy envelopes bearing the Club's insignia. Gabi would be pleased, he knew, that this was no longer a winner-take-all. He'd tell her the next time he saw her.

He wasn't on the periphery—not for this.

Elena waited for Dane, knowing he was checking on the dinner they would share after the announcement. She rarely called him Randall. It sounded too much like a butler's designation. Going by just his last name had started back before the Club was formed, he told her once, and the name had just stuck. He'd gotten used to it.

She didn't like it. Once she'd started college and worked summers at the Club, he'd told her she didn't need to call him Mr. Randall. Since then, she'd always thought of him as Dane.

She replenished all the glasses in anticipation of Dane returning to announce the competition winner and now stood near the back of the room, watching. Daniel, Eden, and Celly stood in one group. Christian stood near but a step apart, as though acknowledging that the pending announcement didn't include him. She didn't know what Dane had said to get him down from his room, but she was glad he was here.

Christian was sorrowful, she decided soon after they met—sorrow guarded by a shield of anger. She tended to categorize people that way, by what she perceived to be their essence, their truth, rather than physical traits. Daniel had seen the sorrow too, she knew; he recognized it. He was one with sorrows of his own. But while it was a part of him, it wasn't his core. Daniel's core was resilience. And love. Jo was upstairs with Ethan. Elena wished she could have met Daniel's wife. He hadn't yet let go of her, she was certain.

Blaise was on the other side of the group, a few steps away from Celly. Between the two of them was Bradley, who had also come down late.

The anticipation was palpable when Dane entered, glass in hand,

and went to stand in front of the fireplace. He smiled as all eyes turned to him. Eden saw Celly's free hand graze Bradley's, as though on the verge of grasping it, but then she instead gripped her glass in both hands. Bradley turned his head to look at her and didn't look away as Dane spoke.

"It's been quite a year," said Dane. "Elena and I feel that we've gotten to know each of you. Some of you have gotten to know one another. And now, because I'm sure you don't want me to ramble on, and because in just a few minutes, I need to take a roast out of the oven to rest before we have dinner, please raise your glasses."

Elena raised hers, along with everyone else in the room.

"The winner of the Forager Chefs Club Competition and the fifty thousand dollars"—he paused, and Elena sensed an invisible pendulum in the room—"is Daniel Metsja."

Randall lifted a bottle of French red wine and nodded toward Blaise's glass.

"A favorite of yours, as I recall," he said as he filled the glass.

Blaise's eyes went from the bottle to Randall's.

"I see," he said.

Randall met Blaise's look as he finished pouring.

"The rules, and the spirit of the rules," Randall said. "You'll recall I stressed that back at the initial meeting in February." He didn't elaborate, and Blaise didn't ask.

It was Annie Tate who'd been with a friend and her child in the park at Bear Lake back in September when she'd watched the "snooty competitor" transfer wine from one bottle to another. She'd fished the empty bottle out of the recycling bin after he drove away and sent Randall a photo, thinking he might be interested. He was. Blaise had listed three exceptions on his September menu. French wine wasn't one of them. He'd had a bottle of Michigan wine on the counter when

Randall reviewed his ingredients.

"Is that why?" Blaise asked, indicating Daniel with his glass.

"No, I didn't tell the judges about your . . . indiscretion. I would have, had it been a tie."

"I see. No tie. Was it at least close?"

"It was." Randall kept his eyes on Blaise for a moment, then let the man see him shift his gaze to where Eden chatted with Christian at the long dinner table. "A single point, actually."

# Daniel

Daniel's head was spinning, and not because of all he had to drink the night before. It had been the outcome he'd hoped for, worked for—but what he hadn't expected was the reaction of his fellow competitors. Sure, there was disappointment—how could there not be?—but Eden and Celly seemed genuine in their congratulations once the initial shock passed. Christian had whooped and pounded him on the back until Eden mock-punched him in the arm. Christian had spent a good part of the rest of the evening telling everyone who would listen about helping him with his outdoor kitchen not once, but twice, and lugging the trestle table outdoors only to have to bring it back in again a few hours later. Eden told Daniel that she only mildly regretted endorsing him at Mrs. Abrams's dairy farm and that he still owed her cooking at the Detroit mission. Celly had seemed almost relieved that someone other than she had won, which was a bit odd. But he may have read that wrong—her primary focus all evening had been Bradley, who seemed uncomfortable with all the hubbub and wouldn't meet anyone's eyes but hers. The two of them had left the dinner early, Blaise watching them leave the room. Blaise hadn't congratulated him. He seemed more shocked than anything else. He sat next to Randall and drank a lot of red wine.

Jo had met him at the door when he came up to his room, a finger to her lips. Ethan hadn't wanted to go to bed before finding out if his dad had won, but he'd finally given in after three books and Jo's firsthand description of watching Daniel cook his competition dinner and how she and Joe had run all the courses to the Club's dining room. She hugged Daniel when he told her the news, and he thanked her again for her help. Jo asked about Celly. The two of them were her favorites, Jo confided. She was glad the prize had gone to one of them.

Splashing water on his face, Daniel made a mental note to work with Elena to provide an additional tip for Jo and Joe. He couldn't possibly have won this competition without them going above and beyond to get the courses from his outdoor kitchen to the judges in the dining room.

"Dad?"

Ethan wandered into the bathroom, rubbing his eyes, Biscuit at his heels.

Daniel set aside the towel he'd been rubbing on his face. His son wore long-sleeved pajamas that hid the ropey burn scars. No one else would notice how the boy's right shoulder dipped.

Daniel noticed.

They had an appointment with the pediatric burn surgeon next week. *We'll get this fixed*, he told Thistle in his mind. *I promise.* He'd have figured out a way regardless, but this fifty-thousand-dollar prize meant they could begin graft surgeries right away, along with whatever else the doctor recommended.

"We won, buddy. We won."

Ethan's whoop rivaled the one Christian had let out the evening before.

It had snowed overnight. Ethan wanted to go out immediately to build a snowman but settled for a quick snowball fight on the balcony outside their room and a promise of more extensive play after breakfast. Biscuit peed in the snow near the railing, and Daniel made a mental note to clean it up later.

"Let's leave Biscuit in the room for now," he told Ethan after feeding the dog. "There may be a lot of people in the kitchen. We'll fetch him afterward when we go outside."

It was only Randall in the adjunct kitchen when they arrived, a cup of coffee in his hand. He smiled when he saw them, the smile reaching his eyes when he saw Ethan carrying his boots, bits of snow from the balcony clinging to them.

"I see you've already been enjoying our early snowfall," he said. He got up and poured another cup of coffee. He handed it to Daniel. "You take it black, as I recall?"

"You recall correctly. Thank you."

"We already have snow at home. I built a snowman before we came here. And I'm working on a snow fort, but then we had to come here, so I'll finish it when we go home." Ethan looked up at his dad. "That's next week, right?"

"Right. Probably."

The appointment with the doctor was in four days. They'd flown down this trip, courtesy of the Club. He'd have to rent a car to get them to Ann Arbor. Their exact itinerary would depend on what the doctor said.

"Dad said we could play in the snow after breakfast."

"Care to join us?"

"I may take you up on that offer," Randall said. He paused. "There's someone who would like to meet you, first, if you're amenable."

"Who?"

"The sponsor of the competition you just won."

Daniel blinked. He hadn't thought about there being a single sponsor other than the Club at large. But of course, someone had put up the prize money, paid for all the travel, and the generous ingredients allowance he and the others had been given. He remembered going through the competition agreement. There hadn't been any reference to the winner being bound to represent or endorse any corporation or other entity. The money was simply given to the winner, no strings attached, no further involvement required. Had he missed something? Or was he being unnecessarily wary? Again, it was a lot of money. It would make sense that whoever provided the funding would like to meet the winner. Should he offer to cook them dinner?

"Sure," Daniel said. "I'd love the opportunity to thank them."

Randall nodded toward the range top. "I've got some hot chocolate there for Ethan. Why don't you pour, and I'll go get her?"

*Her*, thought Daniel as he selected a cup from the cupboard and settled Ethan at the kitchen table.

She must have been waiting in Randall's office, which was nearby. Daniel looked up as they entered the kitchen.

"Daniel, may I introduce you to—"

"Mariam." Daniel's tone was flat.

"Mariam Streng." Randall's voice trailed away.

"Hello, Daniel."

Ethan looked up from his hot chocolate.

"And you must be Ethan," said Mariam.

# Randall

Mariam's tone was light, but Randall could hear it in her voice, see it in the way she held herself. She was taut, pensive, just like she'd been back at the inn in Bear Lake when he'd come to bring her the news of the judges' decision. What happened here in the next few minutes mattered to her very, very much. He cast his mind back to Daniel's file. He looked between the three of them. The woman in her sixties, the widower, and his young son. He thought he now knew who this was. Mrs. Rose, she'd called herself the first time they met.

"Did you know?" Daniel's question was directed at Randall.

"Not then. Not until just now."

Ethan gave a small wave to the woman who remained in the doorway, not presuming to step into the room.

*On the periphery*, Randall thought.

"Hello," Ethan said. "I'm having hot chocolate. And after breakfast, we're going to build a snowman."

Daniel took a half-step forward, somewhat blocking Ethan from Mariam's view.

"Is this the next gambit? Is Marcus waiting in the other room, lawyers and God knows who else with him? Lure me down here, and then try to physically take my son from me?" He didn't raise his voice, kept his tone even.

*He doesn't want to scare Ethan*, Randall thought.

"Marcus passed away eighteen months ago. There's no one waiting in the other room, Daniel. I came alone."

"Why?"

*That one word encompasses myriad questions*, Randall thought.

"Because I'm trying to make right, if I can, something done that was very, very wrong."

"You chose an interesting way to do it." Daniel turned to Randall. "So it was all an elaborate setup? The contest a foregone conclusion? I didn't win anything, did I? This is just a payoff."

Randall felt a wash of anger. He opened his mouth to reply. Mariam beat him to it.

"No. You ask if this is the latest gambit. In a way, it is. I admit when I came up with the idea, I thought I could ensure you would win. That it would be a way for me to offer amends. To help provide for Ethan. I know one of the founding members. His first wife was my sorority sister. But it was made abundantly clear to me that if the Club were to accept my proposal and host this competition, it would be on their terms, not mine. And those terms did not include stacking the odds in anyone's favor. The most they would do is commit that you would be invited to compete. Beyond that, I had no control. If you hadn't won, it would have all been a waste. I'd have lost another year, and I'd be no closer to having this conversation with you." She paused. "You'd never have agreed to meet with me, listen to me—not after everything that happened. I had to think of something."

"It was a lot of money to gamble," Randall said. It was clear Daniel was still weighing, deciding.

"It sounds very cliché, but I've come to the realization a lot of people eventually do about money," said Mariam. "I don't have limitless resources, but I can help, Daniel. Please, for Thistle, let me help." Her voice caught as she spoke her daughter's name.

Randall knew it wasn't the name she'd been born with. He suddenly remembered a line from a children's book: *Where you tend a rose, my lad, a thistle cannot grow.* He wondered if she'd chosen her *nom de plume* as a penance.

"You broke her heart. She just wanted you to accept who she was. And who she loved." Daniel's voice was no longer flat. He spoke quietly.

Randall went to the range top and topped off Ethan's cup. *He shouldn't be hearing this. The child shouldn't be hearing this. Maybe more cocoa will distract him.*

"I know. She wrote to me."

"You never wrote back."

"That was Marcus." Mariam pulled back her shoulders. "I should have been stronger. Stood my ground. I know that now. But he had such plans for her, and his plans were my plans, too, for so long. I thought they were *our* plans. But then she went away. She stood up to him in a way that I never had. And I was angry about that, I admit. And then, after a while, I wasn't angry anymore. I was just sad. I wanted to go to Escanaba. See for myself what she'd written about. The life the two of you were building. Especially after the baby was born." Mariam looked past Daniel to Ethan. "Marcus wouldn't allow it. So I subscribed to the Escanaba online newspaper and any other community news I could find, thinking maybe her name would come up. Maybe she'd win a baking contest or chair some cause that would make news." Mariam took a deep breath. She stopped looking at Ethan and raised her chin to look at her son-in-law. "That's how I learned about the fire."

"And you decided the best thing to do then was to try to take Ethan from me?"

Mariam shook her head. "Again, that was Marcus. You have to understand, Daniel, I was distraught. I was grieving. No parent should ever outlive their child. And I hadn't seen her since that last blowup. Marcus went out of his head. She was our only child. Ethan, the only grandchild we'd ever have. Carrying on the family bloodline and all that. Marcus said Ethan needed access to opportunities he couldn't get where you live. How you live."

Daniel crossed his arms. "And you?"

"I admit, at first, I thought it was a good idea to have him with us, make sure he received good schooling, all the opportunities we could provide. I thought maybe you would see the benefit of having us involved in his life, that you might decide to move downstate. And I didn't know what his injuries were. The newspaper didn't elaborate."

"He's fine." Daniel took a few steps closer to Mariam and lowered his voice even further. "And there's a big difference between being involved in his life and repeated attempts to declare me an unfit father and legally take him from me."

Mariam took a deep breath. "I know. I asked him to stop."

"When does this stop being Marcus's fault?"

"I'm not sure it ever does, honestly. But that's for me to work out, Daniel. After he died—a stroke during a board meeting—I came to realize how little I knew about my own life. How much I'd allowed Marcus to lead and direct everything. I'd never so much as balanced a checkbook."

"How very 1950s of you."

"That's accurate, actually. But it was how I was raised. And I guess maybe it was just easier to have Marcus take care of everything. But after Sarah—Thistle—left, and Marcus refused to even let me correspond with her . . ." Mariam shook her head. "Again, that's for me to work out, why I let it go on. I should have left him," she added in a whisper. "I should have left him and come to Escanaba to see if there was a chance I could be part of your lives."

"And now he's gone."

"Yes. Eighteen months now. And it's been a learning curve, believe me." Mariam reached out and put a hand on Daniel's arm. "I knew that after everything that happened, I couldn't just appear on your doorstep and expect a welcome. I'd pretty much resigned myself to the fact that I'd never be part of Ethan's life. Not after I'd been part of trying to take him from you. But I wanted to help, to do something. Thistle had written about the dinners you cook for that hunting group. I knew you wouldn't accept financial help directly, so I came up with the idea of the cooking competition. It's been a year of waiting and hoping and not knowing if the money would go to you and Ethan or not. I had planned to stay anonymous. But then when Randall came and gave me the news . . ." She took a deep breath. "I decided to be something that I haven't been my whole life, Daniel. To be brave. To step out and make my opinion known. Mine, not one I was told was mine. I asked Randall if I could meet the winner, and he agreed." She took her hand away and clasped both at her waist. "I wanted to see you to tell you this: I am deeply sorry for all the wrongs committed by Marcus and me against you, my daughter, and your son. I know you loved her very much. She was so very happy as your wife. I will never try to take Ethan from you. I would like to be part of your lives, but I understand if you don't want me to be. I can't change anything but who I am moving forward."

"That was quite a speech," Daniel said after a moment. "Did you practice?"

"Repeatedly. I wanted to make sure I didn't leave anything out."

Daniel stood a moment longer, then turned his back on Mariam to walk over to Ethan. Randall's heart sank as he saw Mariam's shoulders do the same. Daniel stroked his son's head for a moment. He seemed to be listening for something. Ethan looked up from his nearly empty cup. The boy was quiet, picking up on the mood of the room. Randall watched. Maybe he should escort Mariam back to his office? She seemed lost, standing there in the doorway.

Daniel put his hand on the boy's shoulder. He turned to the woman. "Ethan, I'd like you to meet your grandmother."

A small smile that didn't quite reach his eyes played around his mouth. *He's not sure*, thought Randall. *But for some reason, he wants to try.*

"Mariam, I was about to make a celebration breakfast. Would you like to join us?"

# Elena

Elena poured red wine into her glass, then walked across her bedroom, through narrow, double glass doors, and out onto the shallow balcony that overlooked the west side of the property leased by the Forager Chefs Club. She was met by a December wind that whipped around the shingled gables and embraced her, whisking her robe and nightgown against the curves of her body, beckoning and then abandoning her to dance in the nearby bare limbs of oak, maple, and beech.

This had been her favorite place since she was ten years old and discovered the abandoned room at the top of a set of erratic staircases while her father and uncles laughed, sawed, and hammered below, restoring walls and floors long left to neglect. She'd been tired of hauling pieces of rotted wood to the large bin. She'd snuck away, leaving the cleanup work to her older brothers and cousins, and gone exploring.

She climbed her way to the highest point of the west wing of the building, worming her way through one of the attics, ignoring the skittering of what she hoped were only squirrels or mice. There was a door at the far end of the attic. With a firm grip on an ancient knob, a firmer shoulder against swollen wood, and multiple heaves, the door had given way, its hinges screaking.

Only later did she tell anyone of her discovery.

She'd invited her grandfather to have hot chocolate with her.

It was his kitchen—what would later become the Club's adjunct kitchen—and very late, but she'd bought the milk from a local farmer, riding her bike and helping with the milking to pay for the quart she brought back. The cocoa and sugar had been in the cupboard.

She explained to her grandfather as he sipped the hot chocolate she made. She served it in a mug she found in one of the attics and scrubbed clean.

There was a lot of renovation going on, she said. He had big plans. She understood. It was a lot of work. She was helping as best she could. Okay, maybe not as best she could. She did drift away to explore. Which led to what she wanted to talk about.

She described what she'd found. The attic space on the western wing with rotted floor-length doors that opened to a narrow balcony with a rickety rail and a view like nothing she'd ever seen.

*I'd like it to be my place. Reserved for me. Please don't make it something else or for someone else. I'll work. Tell me what I need to do to earn it.*

Her grandfather had sipped the cocoa made with milk earned by her own labor and nodded solemnly as she made her request. He asked her to take him to the attic space she wanted to claim.

They brought a camp lantern, and he'd had to duck his head under the rafters. But he stood in the spot that was the reason she loved this place, looked out on the view, and nodded.

*We'll need to do something about the rafters. A dormer, maybe. You'll be taller soon. And these balcony doors, they're rotted. Window doors, I think—for light.*

Her breath had caught at his words, and she thought she might swell up and float against the too-close rafters.

*You asked. It's yours.*

She had burst into tears and hugged him.

Elena had no idea of the extent of his words—his promise—until years later.

This attic space—updated as a bedroom with a small seating

area and a bathroom—was where she lived. The swollen, stuck doors leading outdoors—wooden shutters—had been replaced with four-season glass doors. It was more of an exaggerated window ledge than a balcony—it didn't even fit a chair—but it allowed her to be outdoors in her private space. It had a sturdy, decorative wrought iron railing. She was slim enough to close the glass doors behind her if she chose. And just as she had since she was a girl, she came out here most evenings, if just for a few moments.

She leaned on the railing, balancing the wineglass between her long fingers, and looked out on the December landscape. The sky was clear with a bright moon casting shadows on the snow. There was a line of deer tracks from the woods into the clearing and then back again. The breeze was sharp and from the west. She lifted her chin, relishing the feel of it. She lifted her glass in a silent toast to the moon, the wind, the bare trees swaying in the moonlight, the shadows, and the trek of hoof prints in the snow.

Today was the winter solstice.

It was her birthday.

It was also an anniversary.

Her grandfather had waited until she turned twenty-five. Until she spent time here as an adult, not just as a child, enamored of all the nooks and crannies with their window seats and cozy chairs for reading away a rainy afternoon and the acreage with its endless possibilities for getting muddy and lost and found again and scratched up by blackberry canes. He waited until she had time to appreciate the essence of what he had created here and why, the history and proclivities of the people who were part of it, and the surrounding community ecosystem that allowed it to thrive.

She embraced it all. Had gone away to college to learn business and hospitality management and then come back. Had worked side by side with Dane Randall, he the director of the Club, she the manager of the space in which it existed. Along the way, her grandfather had included her in the negotiation discussions when he renewed the lease with the Forager Chefs Club Founders Circle.

On her twenty-fifth birthday, her grandfather gifted her the building and acreage. The property had been in the family for six generations, he'd reminded her, as she sat, stupefied, the documents in her lap. She was now legally its owner—*and never let the damn Founders Circle forget it*, he'd said—but she should always think of herself as its steward, focused on what was best for it and respectful of its history.

Six months later, her grandfather died.

The lease was coming up for another five-year renewal. And Elena had some ideas. There may be resistance, but she thought some of the Founders Circle may be open to her suggestions, particularly if Dane helped present them.

If they didn't like her ideas, she'd tell them they could find a property to lease elsewhere. Yes, she needed the income to keep this place maintained, but they also had a good deal here—and they knew it. It was in everyone's best interest to negotiate.

She was hopeful Dane would be her ally.

He was a bit different these days. He'd always been reserved but had been more contemplative since the call in August that Christian needed to come home immediately and then word that Katherine Koch Gallo had died. But the real difference, she thought, came with the check Mariam Streng gave him that evening in late November when he'd left the competition judges—chatting, reminiscing, exchanging viewpoints on foraging and cooking techniques, and Chase talking with Christian—to drive to the small inn in town to tell the secretive sponsor of the competition who would be declared the winner.

Dane had decided how that money would be divided, had written out the checks himself. When he asked her for envelopes, he showed her the checks. She was glad about all of it. First, that he hadn't let the Founders Circle bully him into delegating the decision of how the money should be divided. He shouldn't be anyone's butler. Second, that he shared his decision with her.

Of the forty thousand, Dane had given twenty thousand dollars to Eden. She'd been in second place, losing the competition by only one point. *Daniel's outdoor kitchen weighed in his favor and swung the vote*, Elena thought. He'd given both Celly and Blaise five thousand dollars each. She thought that was generous for Blaise but suspected Celly had been awestruck by the five thousand.

The last ten thousand dollars went to Christian.

She wondered what Christian would do with it. If it would be something that would rid him of his sorrow. Let him set the anger aside.

As for her, she wanted to have an annual cooking competition at the Forager Chefs Club. Elena liked the energy of it: bringing in new people, new ideas. Not just the same people and their same guests month after month. It wouldn't have the extravagant prize money that Mariam Streng was able to offer, but she and Dane could position it in a way to make it desirable, memorable. Maybe the prize wouldn't be money but mentorship—they had strong relationships with some very well-known chefs, including the judges of this most-recent competition. There were details—a lot of them—to be worked out. She was good at details but wasn't sure she could do this alone. Didn't want to do it alone. Which was why she had asked Dane to be her partner. He had relationships—albeit with baggage—with the Founders Circle that went back to their beginnings, as well as with many of the members.

She heard a knock on her door.

She set her glass down as she came back inside and crossed the room. She tightened the belt of her robe and opened the door.

Dane looked startled to see her standing in her nightgown and robe.

"Oh, sorry. I didn't realize it was so late."

"It's not. I'm just indulging this evening."

"I can come back tomorrow."

"Not at all. Do come in."

"No need. I just wanted to give you an answer. To the question you asked me earlier."

Elena waited. She would do this by herself if she had to. She'd rather not.

"Let's do it," said Dane. "They'll push back; they're pretty set in their ways, as you know. But it's a good idea. I'm confident I can swing some opinions in our favor."

"And if they won't agree?"

"We'll do it anyway."

She wanted to hug him but knew that would make him uncomfortable. He'd always had his boundaries.

Instead, she smiled.

# EPILOGUE
# Blaise

Blaise looked around the apartment. He and Bradley had always kept the place pristine—well, that was Bradley, more than him, truth be told—but now it looked sterile. The cupboards were empty, and most of the furniture was gone. He'd sold a lot of it. He rented a small storage unit for a few boxes: the really good cookware, the cookbooks that mattered to him, and some of Bradley's things he thought his brother would want to keep. What was left would be picked up by a truck from Goodwill, arriving any time now. After that, he'd turn in the keys.

Tomorrow evening, he'd board a plane in Chicago.

After the New Year's ball had dropped, the toasts made, the kisses exchanged, and her guests found their ways either home or to one of her guest rooms, Lyra Markham had invited Blaise to join her for a glass of champagne. She'd been wearing a low-cut dress of midnight blue with subtle sparkles woven into the fabric. The dress was floor-length, with a slit up the side that stopped short of exposing too much. Her high heels had come off long ago, so the dress trailed on the floor a bit. She'd reapplied lipstick. She was a little tipsy, but not too much. Lyra Markham never overindulged at parties. In this age of smartphones, she learned long ago that the media were always watching.

He'd left his toque in the kitchen, and they sat together at one of the draped tables she rented for the party, the detritus of streamers and confetti around them. She complimented him on the New Year's Eve buffet he created. She made some observations about her guests and several predictions for the new year: a likely business merger, a likely divorce, a likely affair in the works. Then she made Blaise her offer.

*You need a change of scenery. A fresh perspective. Of course, you must promise that when you come back, I'll be the first to experience all your newfound creativity.*

He was pretty sure she'd been talking only about cooking.

She hadn't mentioned the competition, though he was certain she knew about it and its outcome. For him, it had started here in her home, after all. It had been January then too. Another dinner, Randall seated at Lyra's right, a conversation, and then an envelope.

*Why?* he'd asked her.

*Why not? A woman doesn't need a reason for everything she does. And if she has one, she definitely is under no compulsion to share what it is.*

She said that last with an arched brow, and he left it at that. Maybe he would find out later about strings attached to this offer. Maybe she saw him as akin to the group of homeless men she'd hosted with shaves, haircuts, new clothing, and a good meal. He remembered how she sparkled listening to their stories, their histories as they shared them, men revived, over dinner. He decided he didn't care. He had some money saved, the monthly stipend from his father for about another year and the unexpected check from Randall. It wasn't the fifty thousand dollars he anticipated, but five thousand was enough for him to take some time. To take Lyra up on her offer.

Now, a month later, it was all arranged. In his backpack, he had his laptop, passport, copies of the emails Lyra had sent ahead, some cash in euros, and a key to her Paris apartment in the sixth arrondissement. It wasn't anything lavish, she had warned him, but it was his for six weeks, along with introductions to some influential friends and colleagues. After that, he'd head to Gordes in the Provence region. She had assured him her friends' villa had plenty of room and that he'd be welcome. They'd been guests at one of her dinner parties that he'd cooked, and although he didn't remember them, apparently he'd made an impression. He could stay there a while and explore the region. After that? Well, he'd have to see what possibilities opened. Maybe he'd come back to Grand Rapids. Maybe not.

Maybe he'd drop by Mackinac Island.

He suspected Bradley would still be there.

# Christian

*The daffodils are in full bloom here. How are things there?*
Christian snorted at Eden's text message.
*No daffodils yet in Toronto. But I did cook elk last week over an open fire at a hunting lodge north of here. Chase made the kitchen staff we brought with us clear away the snow.*
*Name dropper.*
She knew who Chase was, of course. And it had been a good decision to take the renowned chef up on his offer. In the two months he'd been working with him, he'd learned a lot. Christian liked to think he'd contributed as well. Much of the design of the open-air kitchen they'd set up at the hunting lodge had come from him, gleaned from helping Daniel set up at the Forager Chefs Club. He also learned a lot during his time in Escanaba. Christian would now not only pit his outdoor cooking skills against anyone's but also his wood-splitting skills.
He took another sip of coffee. Picked up his phone again.
*I'm heading back south at the end of next week.*
Technically, he could stay in Canada for almost another month. But he felt he'd done what he came to do. It was time to decide what was next. Not just wait around for something or someone to make the decision for him. Randall would approve.
*Destination?*

*Flint. Gotta check on the house.*

*And after that?*

He knew what she was asking. Well, he thought maybe he knew what she was asking. You could never really be sure with Eden. She had big plans. Randall had given her a check as well.

The check had been unexpected. And the amount had been shocking. There was a lot he could do with ten thousand dollars. He'd been thinking about a small café he'd visited here in Toronto. It was run by a church with a pay-what-you-can model that leveraged volunteers and donations. Yes, a lot of the patrons were homeless or on their last dollar, but just as many were bighearted people who paid full fare and more. And the food was good too. He could maybe open something like that in Flint. And then there was the conversation he'd had with Eden before heading to Escanaba.

*Not sure,* he typed into his phone. *If the daffodils are blooming, they likely don't need salt truck drivers anymore this season.*

He waited for a response. After a few minutes, he put his phone in his pocket. After puttering around the small studio apartment Chase had found for him, he decided to check out that café again. Maybe he could talk to one of the managers, get some more insight into their model. He looked at his phone. No further texts.

He took the bus to the stop nearest the café, then walked the rest of the way.

He never thought of Eden as a politician but had no doubt she'd make a positive impact right away if she won a city council seat. Finding time to fully own the Thursday night dinners would be a challenge, she shared with him, though she'd always want to be involved. She needed someone she trusted.

He'd resigned himself back in the fall to the fact that he may never return to the house in Flint. But that had been before Randall gave him a check for ten thousand dollars. Flint to Detroit was one hell of a commute. Of course, Eden went between Idlewild and Detroit all the time, and that was three times as far.

Christian came to the door of the café. He pulled out his phone again. Still nothing. He put his phone back in his pocket, went in, sat down, and ordered coffee. He looked at the menu. The soup was steak and potato. That sounded good for a cold day like today. There were no daffodils yet in Toronto.

The coffee arrived, and he ordered the soup. There was coconut cream pie too. He'd have a slice for dessert.

After a few minutes, the soup arrived. The server topped off his coffee.

Christian pulled out his phone. Still nothing more from Eden.

*I thought I might stop by Detroit after checking on the house. Maybe on a Thursday,* he typed.

Then, he set his phone on the table so he could see the screen and picked up his spoon.

# Eden

It was Thursday night, she was at the mission, but Eden wasn't the one leading the cooking in the kitchen. It was an odd feeling. The hall was nearly full, and between the chatter and music, it was louder than she was used to. She was usually in the kitchen at this time, engrossed in last-minute preparations. She saw her father greet a few latecomers, the pastors who would support her at his side. Her grandparents were here too, sitting with a group near the front of the room. She glanced at the large clock on the wall. It would be time to start the meal in just a few minutes. Just like every Thursday, her father would give the blessing before the servers came out of the kitchen with trays of hot plates.

But this time, Eden would speak first, before the blessing and the food. She would formally announce her candidacy for a seat on the Detroit city council. She was doing it for this community and to stretch beyond this community, so it was only right that they hear about it first, her grandfather had told her.

*You're choosing where to jump off your pendulum. And I know you're going to land solidly on two feet.*

*Hopefully, I can stay on two feet, Grandpa. There are so many things that could go sideways.*

*There always are, darlin'. But you have a lot of people who love you and a bunch more who respect you, who will be there to help. You won't be doin' this alone.*

She'd feel more confident if she had the fifty thousand dollars. But she'd make twenty thousand work. And she was grateful to Randall and Mariam Streng for it.

She walked toward the kitchen, the place that always settled her. She'd promised herself she wouldn't—she had a different role tonight—but found her feet taking her there anyway. Stacy came out the swinging kitchen door a few steps before Eden reached it.

"How's it going in there?"

"Good. Fine. He's a little bossy. But the kid is cute as a button. I'll warn you—he's making a list."

"A list?"

"A list of things the kitchen doesn't have that he thinks it needs."

"Is he being an asshole about it?"

"Nope. He just looks for something, and when he can't find it, he asks. And then we either show him where it is or tell him we don't have one. If we tell him we don't have one, he pulls this little notepad and pencil out of his back pocket and writes it down. Then, he just carries on like he never needed it anyway."

"Like what?"

"Well, he wanted a chinois. Whatever the hell that is."

"We're cooking for sixty people. What's he making that he needs a chinois?"

"Some sort of sauce. He ended up using a sieve. So what is a chinois, anyway?"

"A fancy sieve. What's Ethan doing?"

"Stirring. And talking. A lot. He insisted he needed an apron. So I folded one up so he wouldn't trip on it and tied it around him. He likes it. He's having surgery next week?"

"He is. You think dinner is going to be okay?"

"It's going to be more than okay. You set a very high bar, but Daniel seems determined to live up to your expectations. Where did you find him again?" Stacy looked over Eden's shoulder. "Never mind. Tell me later. Your dad's motioning for you." She put her hands on

Eden's shoulders and turned her around to face the room and not the kitchen door. "You're always doing amazing things. Now go tell everyone what you're going to do next."

# Daniel

Daniel stroked back the blond hair from Ethan's forehead. The boy didn't stir. The nights were getting better, but they'd be better yet when Ethan was discharged. Hospitals weren't conducive to getting a good night's sleep. Daniel straightened and bent backward slightly, feeling muscles protest. He and his back were looking forward to a real bed. The reclining chair wasn't conducive to a good night's sleep either. But being anywhere else these past two weeks had been out of the question.

He heard the door latch and turned. Mariam entered quietly, balancing two lidded coffee cups in one hand. Daniel crossed the room and took the top one from her.

"Thanks," he said quietly.

She looked toward the bed. "How did he do last night?"

"Pretty good. He woke up when the nurse came in to check his vitals but went right back to sleep."

"I saw the doctor with his trailing entourage. They're a few doors down."

Sipping his coffee, Daniel went to the chair, set the cup down, and folded the sheet and blanket. He put them on the windowsill and his pillow on top. "I'm hoping the doc tells us I won't need those again."

"Here's hoping. He said yesterday he was really pleased with everything."

Mariam had offered to trade off the nights with him, but the fragile trust he was building with his mother-in-law didn't go that far yet. Accepting her invitation to stay in her St. Clair Shores home for a month once Ethan was released had been a big step. This hospital stay was to control pain and monitor for any sign of infection. There would be follow-up visits, and Escanaba was nearly a day's travel from Detroit's Children's Hospital. A month would have been a long time to spend in a hotel, not to mention the expense and finding one that would let them bring Biscuit.

He watched Mariam set her own coffee cup on the nightstand. She reached out a hand and stroked the hair back from Ethan's forehead just as he had done, her expression tender. Daniel was used to it by now, though he'd tensed up every time she touched her grandson in those first days following the cooking competition. He'd taken her at her word, knowing Thistle would want him to—the apology, the explanation, and the promise to not renew any efforts to take his son away from him—but trust took longer.

If the doctor discharged Ethan today, they would pack up and drive to Mariam's house. He'd given Eden the address. She had visited the hospital a couple of times, and Christian had come with her the second time.

Daniel watched Mariam carefully perch herself on the edge of Ethan's bed. The boy stirred and opened his eyes.

"Hi, Grandma."

"Good morning, love."

"How is Biscuit?"

"He's doing great. Ate all his breakfast this morning. He really likes the backyard. Was chasing squirrels again but hasn't caught one yet."

*Children trust so much more easily*, Daniel thought. He'd see how the month in St. Clair Shores went. He hadn't mentioned anything to Ethan or Mariam yet, but he was thinking about inviting her to Escanaba for an extended visit once they headed home.

Mariam had said she liked to garden. And that kind of

exercise—reaching and stretching—would be good for Ethan once he was fully healed. Maybe she and Ethan could get the vegetables planted and spruce up the herb bed.

Thistle would like that.

# Celly

"So, what do you think?"

Celly had only ever brought her mother or Aunt Tilda here. Never a boy.

Or a man.

She watched Bradley as he stepped to the rocky edge—a view of the straits and wooded shore of the Upper Peninsula west of the bridge and St. Ignace. Although the list of places she loved on Mackinac Island was long, this glade was at the top. It was her private sanctuary. No one ever came here. Certainly not the Fudgies. Rarely the locals.

She'd found it while foraging—a spit of rock among the trees, high up in the middle of the island with a view worthy of a postcard. She never brought a camera. Would never. You either experienced it in person, she decided, or not at all. When she brought her mother and Aunt Tilda, they had a picnic, the hand-dyed cloth spread on the rock, a feast of cheese, bread, berries, and a sausage so dried, they laughed as they tried to cut it with Aunt Tilda's camping knife. They'd toasted with wine her mother noted was none the worse for the jostling it endured getting up here. They enjoyed the day and watched it dim, pointing out the acrobatics of the bats silhouetted against the deep blue twilight. And then the mosquitos joined, and they packed up and made the trek back to the sheltered screened porch with its fragrance of drying herbs and sealed pots of dyes.

Celly smiled at the memory and the man she'd brought here. He was looking out over the straits where she'd indicated, his legs solidly braced on the rock outcropping. She didn't repeat her question. Instead, she waited. She knew he'd heard her and knew she wasn't just asking his opinion of the view. Bradley would answer when he was ready.

He'd arrived on the island with Blaise after the new year. They'd stayed at the Bicycle Street Inn, one of the few places open all year. After a few days, Blaise had left. After another week, Bradley had moved in with Aunt Tilda. That was three months ago. It was nearly spring now, and following a lot of conversations with her mother, Aunt Tilda, and Bradley—in different combinations—Celly had decided what she wanted to do next. The unexpected five thousand dollars from Randall would make it possible. Aunt Tilda's legal eye and negotiating skills would help ensure they got off on the right foot.

They. She and Bradley. But only if he wanted it too.

It would be a small café with limited days and hours so it wouldn't be overwhelming for either of them. The menu would change as the seasons did. Bradley would stay in the kitchen where he felt most comfortable. She would move between the kitchen and the front of the house. Front of the house. It seemed a very professional term for what would be no more than five tables. Her mother had offered to help too.

Bradley turned from the view. Celly saw him look around, take it all in, and breathe in deeply.

"I like it," he said. "It smells like you."

"And the other question?"

Aunt Tilda had found a building with a one-bedroom apartment above the space that would be the café. They could sign the lease this week.

"I like that too."

He walked to her and took her hands.

"Now I have a question for you," Bradley said.

# ACKNOWLEDGMENTS

I first came up with writing *The Forager Chefs Club* at dinner with my husband, Tim, at the wonderful restaurant Légende in Quebec City. That restaurant focuses on the culinary history and *terroir* of the area, and when we dined there the first time, we were told that all ingredients in the kitchen could be sourced within a fifty-mile radius. Tim and I love to watch cooking competition shows, and much of our dinner conversation was around how interesting it would be to have a competition that focused on what could be sourced from a specific region. I grew up in Michigan—that state that is largely isolated from its neighbors by the Great Lakes and is, in many ways, a region unto itself. And so the idea for my second novel was born over a fabulous meal at Légende. I heartily endorse a visit to Quebec City and that singular restaurant and am grateful for its inspiration.

I've grown and cooked food all my life. But writing this novel meant learning more about foraging than I'd previously known growing up in Michigan, picking wild blackberries in June and pears in August from a rogue tree grown when someone had discarded their snack along a country road. There are amazing resources available, and I'm grateful to the Horn Farm Center for Agricultural Education in Pennsylvania, The Wilderness School at Rolling Ridge in West Virginia, and foraging experts Samuel Thayer, Leda Meredith, and

Hank Shaw. Through workshops, their amazing books, podcasts, and other sources, I've learned about the bounty that is all around us.

I want to thank my husband, Tim, for his patience as I experimented with salted dandelion petals and sugared violets and created spaces on our homestead in Virginia for nettles, fiddlehead ferns, and ramps. It took three years, but he built for me the most incredible greenhouse out of old windows we found on our travels. (It's now dubbed the She Chalet.) It was watching Tim plan and then create incredible meals for the "Old Goats" of Boy Scout Troop 961 that inspired much of Daniel's outdoor kitchen. Tim's venison loin cooked over an open fire and pineapple upside down cake baked in a Dutch oven with campfire coals is the stuff of legend.

I want to thank Tori Wymer Bratcher for her creative mixologist skills. Over the course of several of our Thursday "date night" outings at the West End Pub in Purcellville, Virginia, she and Tim concocted what became this novel's signature cocktail, the Michigan Sunset.

Thank you, also, to my sister Linda Dart. While I roamed over the decades, moving from state to state with a couple of stints in Europe, she never strayed far from our home state of Michigan. Thank you, Sistorial, for your love and for always welcoming me when I need some time in "the Mitten."

In my efforts to authentically represent Bradley, my sincere thanks go to my daughter-in-law, Melissa Walston. She is an incredible woman with expertise working with children and young adults with autism. Thank you, Melissa, for your resources and consultation to bring Bradley to life.

I am indebted to Köehler Books for embracing me as part of the family when my first publisher succumbed to the incredible pressures put on businesses by the pandemic. Thank you, John Köehler, for your expertise and encouragement. And heartfelt thanks to my editor, Miranda Dillon, for providing the patience, direction, and suggestions to transform The Forager Chefs Club from a manuscript to an actual "have-you-read-it-yet?" novel. Thank you also to Suzanne Bradshaw and her marvelous design skills. You took the picture that I painted with words and made it come to life.

There are so many places in Michigan that inspired aspects of The Forager Chefs Club, but I want to note in particular the Old Mission General Store in Traverse City, which inspired the Gourmet Bait Shop; Chateau Grand Traverse Winery for a delightful white wine called "Ship of Fools" that I simply had to give to Celly and Bradley; the unique island of Mackinac; and the lovely village of Bear Lake near Lake Michigan. The Forager Chefs Club is a fictional place, but I know exactly where it "lives" a short drive beyond that village's border.

# RESOURCES

Please take care to never eat any foraged food unless you are one-hundred-percent sure you've identified it correctly. There are a lot of "look-alikes" in fields and forests.

Only forage where you are sure neither pesticides nor herbicides have been used.

MANOOMIN

The Michigan Wild Rice Initiative (MWRI) is a collaboration of Michigan and twelve federally recognized Native American tribes within Michigan. Michigan Sea Grant is a member of the MWRI outreach and education subcommittee. You can find a wealth of information about Manoomin and this program by going to MichiganSeaGrant.org and searching on "manoomin." Manoomin can be purchased online from Native Harvest Ojibwe Products at NativeHarvest.com.

EXCELLENT RESOURCES for foragers of all levels and those who want to learn how:

» Falconi, Dina. *Foraging & Feasting: A Field Guide and Wild Food Cookbook*. New York: Botanical Arts Press, 2013.

- Meredith, Leda. *The Skillful Forager: Essential Techniques for Responsible Foraging and Making the Most of Your Wild Edibles.* Colorado: Roost Books, 2019.
- Shaw, Hank. *Hunt, Gather, Cook: Finding the Forgotten Feast.* New York: Rodale, Inc., 2011.
- Video classes and recipes available at Honest-Food.net
- Anything by Samuel Thayer, including:
  - Thayer, Samuel. *Incredible Wild Edibles: 36 Plants That Can Change Your Life.* Wisconsin: Forager's Harvest, 2017.
  - Thayer, Samuel. *Sam Thayer's Field Guide to Edible Wild Plants of Eastern & Central North America.* Wisconsin: Forager's Harvest, 2023.
  - Class information and blog posts by Sam Thayer available at ForagersHarvest.com

CLASSES AND WORKSHOPS I've personally attended and recommend:
- Horn Farm Center for Agricultural Education, York, PA HornFarmCenter.org
- The Wilderness School at Rolling Ridge, Harpers Ferry, WV RollingRidge.net/workshops

## MICHIGAN SUNSET COCKTAIL

*2 oz. bourbon (Traverse City Distillery)*
*.5 oz. ginger liqueur (Domaine de Canton)*
*.5 oz. Cointreau*
*4-6 dashes of aromatic bitters (Iron Fish Distillery)*
*Ice*
*Juice of one lemon wedge*

Smoke the bourbon either in a shallow tray in a food smoker or with a cocktail smoker. Add all ingredients except the lemon juice to a cocktail shaker. Shake well. Pour into a glass, add the lemon juice, and serve.

## SALTED DANDELION PETALS

*1/4 c. fine sea salt*
*1/4 c. water*
*1 egg white*
*20 or so dandelion flowers*

Stir water and salt together in a small saucepan and heat over medium-low heat until salt is dissolved (or nearly so). Let mixture cool. Whisk egg white until frothy. Whisk in salt water. Dip the dandelion flowers into the salt mixture. Dehydrate in a dehydrator at 100 degrees F for 2 hours or until dried. (Alternatively, place on a baking sheet lined with parchment paper in the oven set at 100 degrees F.) Once dried, pull the petals loose into a small prep dish. The main petal will be yellow, while the base that is attached to the flower's receptacle will appear as a bit of white fluff. Sprinkle on flatbreads or anywhere you want color with a hint of salt.

## SUGARED WILD VIOLETS

*1/4 c. granulated sugar plus additional for sprinkling*
*1/4 c. water*
*1 egg white*
*20 or so wild violets*

Stir water and sugar together in a small saucepan and heat over medium-low heat until the sugar is dissolved. Let mixture cool. Whisk egg white until frothy. Whisk in sugar water. Dip the violet flowers into the sugar mixture. Dehydrate in a dehydrator set at 100 degrees F for 1 hour and 45 minutes or until dried. (Alternatively, place on a baking sheet lined with parchment paper in the oven set at 100 degrees F.) Once dried, these can be used on desserts for a pretty presentation and a hint of sweetness. Wild violets are small and smaller yet when dried. Don't expect them to look like flowers; they'll be pretty "dots" of sweet color.

www.ingramcontent.com/pod-product-compliance
Lightning Source LLC
LaVergne TN
LVHW091708070526
838199LV00050B/2308